"Then the fire of the LORD fell and burned up the sacrifice, the wood,
the stones, and the soil, and also licked up the water in the trench.
When all the people saw this, they fell prostrate and cried,
'The LORD—he is God! The LORD—he is God!"

—1 KINGS 18:38–39 (NIV)

MYSTERIES & WONDERS *of the* BIBLE

Unveiled: Tamar's Story
A Life Renewed: Shoshan's Story
Garden of Secrets: Adah's Story
Among the Giants: Achsah's Story
Seeking Leviathan: Milkah's Story
A Flame of Hope: Abital's Story

MYSTERIES & WONDERS *of the* BIBLE

A FLAME
OF HOPE
ABITAL'S STORY

Beth Adams

A Gift from Guideposts

Thank you for your purchase! We want to express our gratitude for your support with a special gift just for you.

Dive into **Spirit Lifters**, a complimentary e-book that will fortify your faith, offering solace during challenging moments. Its 31 carefully selected scripture verses will soothe and uplift your soul.

Please use the QR code or go to **guideposts.org/ spiritlifters** to download.

Mysteries & Wonders of the Bible is a trademark of Guideposts.

Published by Guideposts
100 Reserve Road, Suite E200, Danbury, CT 06810
Guideposts.org

This is a work of fiction. While the characters and settings are drawn from scripture references and historical accounts, apart from the actual people, events, and locales that figure into the fiction narrative, all other names, characters, places, and events are the creation of the author's imagination or are used fictitiously. Every attempt has been made to credit the sources of copyrighted material used in this book. If any such acknowledgment has been inadvertently omitted or miscredited, receipt of such information would be appreciated.

Scripture references are from the following sources: *The Holy Bible, King James Version* (KJV). *The Holy Bible, New International Version* (NIV). Copyright © 1973, 1978, 1984, 2011 by Biblica, Inc. Used by permission of Zondervan. All rights reserved worldwide. www.zondervan.com.

Cover and interior design by Müllerhaus
Cover illustration by Brian Call represented by Illustration Online LLC.
Typeset by Aptara, Inc.

ISBN 978-1-961251-83-0 (hardcover)
ISBN 978-1-961251-84-7 (softcover)
ISBN 978-1-961251-85-4 (epub)

Printed and bound in the United States of America

A FLAME
OF HOPE
ABITAL'S STORY

CAST OF CHARACTERS

Aaliyah • the king's third wife, an Ammonite, from Rabbah

Abital • the queen's seamstress

Adinah • servant in the king's household

Anu • previously worked in kitchen and now sent to work for Aaliyah

Ayla • Keziah's daughter

Channah • kitchen helper, and later Keziah's maid

Elijah • Yahweh's prophet

Elkanah • servant at Abital's grandfather's home

Elon • a kind guard in the palace

Gershom • a man from Saba's village, has a son called Ezra

Gershon • benefactor who donated the gold and marble to build the altar to Baal

Golyat • one of the king's guards

Haran • one of the king's advisers

Hiram • a guard at the palace, always outside Jezebel's door

Ira • cloth merchant

Jezebel • the king's wife

Joram • the leader of Yahweh's prophets

Keziah • second wife to King Ahab

King Ahab • the king of Israel

Mara • the queen's handmaid

Michal • kitchen maid

Obadiah • Keziah's brother and administrator at the palace

Ofir • servant at Abital's grandfather's home

Saba • Abital's grandfather

Shifrah • an older servant who had served Ahab's mother

Soraya • a cook at the palace, married to Amir

Tamar • kitchen maid

Ushmuel • prophet of Baal

GLOSSARY OF TERMS

abba • father

Adar • Hebrew month, roughly February–March

imma • mother

Iyar • Hebrew month, roughly April–May

saba • grandfather

Shebat • Hebrew month, roughly January/February

Tishri • Hebrew month, roughly September-October

Tebet • Hebrew month, roughly December-January

.

CHAPTER ONE

The servants had been preparing for the banquet for many days. King Ahab had insisted that no cost be spared, and Soraya had been happy to oblige, turning out more roasted meats and platters of cheese and loaves of fresh bread than could be eaten in weeks. She had ordered honey and spices from the East, and the smells of the roasting birds and the sweets, layered with nuts and flaky pastry and dripping with sweetness, filled the whole lower level of the palace.

Far from the kitchens, Abital had been kept busy as well, for Queen Jezebel had declared that she must have the finest gown yet for the celebration of the new altar to Baal. Abital had ordered silk from Damascus, this time a deep royal purple shot through with golden threads that would catch the light as the queen moved. She had worked for many weeks, sewing golden trim to the edges and fitting the fabric tightly against the queen's smooth skin.

"Does it look all right?" Jezebel asked as Abital draped the gown softly around the queen's shoulders. They had finished the final fittings earlier, and now Abital was helping the queen dress for the banquet in her rooms. Even with the doors to the balcony thrown open, the rain outside and the walls hung with dark-colored tapestries made the rooms feel gloomy. The oil lamps set around the chambers did little to brighten the space. The month of Adar was often quite wet, and though the rain brought the flowers back to life, everyone in the palace had grown tired of the rainy season, which never seemed to end.

"It is the most exquisite gown I have ever seen," Abital said soothingly to Jezebel. "And you are the most beautiful queen Israel has ever known. When they see you in this, everyone will admire your good taste and your beauty."

Abital had learned over the years she had served in the household of Queen Jezebel that lavish compliments always pleased the queen, and they also usually made her task easier. Jezebel's moods could be unpredictable, but stroking her vanity nearly always made her more gracious to her seamstress. Jezebel turned as Abital tied the golden cord around the queen's waist.

"You have never been more stunning," added Mara, who stood to the side, by the open archway to the balcony that overlooked the city. Mara was Jezebel's handmaid and served her in her daily tasks. Mara also often bore the brunt of Jezebel's temper and was quick to offer kind words to soothe her queen's fragile ego.

Jezebel studied her image in the polished bronze mirror. She turned, first one way then the other. Jezebel truly was a strikingly beautiful woman, a fact that she knew full well and used often to her advantage. Her smooth olive skin, glossy black hair, fine features, and large, wide-set eyes made her hard to look away from, even when she wasn't wearing a gown that cost more than most Israelites would earn in a lifetime. The birth of her daughter Athalia last year had not ruined her figure, and she was as young and fresh as the day Abital had arrived at the palace. Jezebel smiled, obviously pleased by her reflection, and turned back to Abital.

"This gown *is* exquisite," Jezebel finally said, nodding. "They will be talking about it for years to come."

"Yes, my queen." Abital ducked her head. "It was your design. I only made it happen."

Jezebel came from Phoenicia, a kingdom north of Israel, where it seemed the fashions were more elaborate than was customary in Israel. Abital had learned how to create gowns according to her queen's taste, creating styles that she desired, and that looked nothing like what everyone else in Israel wore.

"Let us put on the necklace the king gave you as well," Abital said.

Jezebel pulled her hair up as Abital fastened the thick gold band, adorned with rubies and sapphires, around her neck. Once the necklace was secure, Jezebel reached for a bottle of sweet perfume, scented with myrrh and balsam, and dabbed the fragrance behind her ears before she let down her hair and gazed at her reflection once more. She nodded. "It is time to go."

"Yes, my queen." Abital understood the cue to step aside.

"You will stay outside the doors, with the others, in case I need you." Jezebel did not wait for Abital to respond. Abital knew her role. She would not attend the banquet but stay close to the great hall, hovering just outside with the guards and guests' attendants, in case the queen needed an adjustment to her gown. Abital would smell all the delicious food but could only watch and wait in case she was needed. Mara stepped forward to open the door, and Jezebel walked out, her head high, her shoulders back, humming softly under her breath.

"I will be waiting outside the rear doors." Abital would wait a few moments before she left, so Jezebel would not be seen walking with a servant. Once the queen disappeared down the hallway and was headed toward the banquet hall, the guard Hiram following a few steps behind, Abital turned and smiled at Mara. "I am so glad she was pleased."

"Yes. Well." Mara began straightening her own robes, trying to arrange them neatly. "With fabric as fine as that, it would be hard to mess it up, would it not?"

Abital tried not to let the words sting. She should have known better than to think Mara might commiserate about the difficulty of pleasing the queen. She knew well how Jezebel liked to keep her servants on edge, playing them against one another to jockey for position. Whoever was in Jezebel's good graces had a much easier time of it, and Mara, who spent the most time with the queen, was anxious to be seen as her closest and most trusted servant.

"I know you bear the most responsibility to our queen," Abital said, hoping she sounded placating. She did not wish to get into a power struggle with the maid. "You do a wonderful job."

Mara held her chin up and said nothing as Abital slipped out of the room. Abital had just enough time to return to her own shared quarters to refresh herself before rushing to stand outside the door of the banquet hall. She took off the long, dusty garment she was wearing and replaced it with a newer tunic made of finer linen. Jezebel liked her maids to look presentable, and as the seamstress to the queen, Abital was sometimes given discarded odds and ends that she stitched together to make simple tunics for herself, though she was careful to not make her clothing so fine as to make the other servants jealous. She had once returned to her room to find a new garment ripped in two at the foot of her sleeping mat. None of the maids had ever confessed to the crime, but Abital knew better than to complain, and she had been careful ever since to keep her clothing simple and unadorned.

She smoothed down her fresh tunic, pulled a simple cloak over it, and twisted her hair up, fastening it with a bronze clip. Then she walked through the maze of narrow hallways that threaded through the lower level of the palace. She hurried to the kitchen area, where servants were scurrying, carrying platters loaded with meats and cheeses toward the stairs.

"Can I help?" Abital asked Soraya, the head cook, who was directing servants to take up platters and jugs of wine.

"Can you give Channah a hand?" Soraya smiled gratefully for a moment before turning back to the platters around her.

Abital came up behind Channah, a small girl who was trying to balance a tray loaded down with bowls of dipping oils. Abital reached out to steady the tray, taking one side so they each carried half, and Channah gave her a grateful smile. They emerged onto the main floor of the palace, with its wide hallways and ivory-colored floors. They gave the tray to Adinah, one of the servants clothed in fine linen and silk who would be distributing the food amongst the guests, before Channah turned and scurried back to the kitchen.

"Thank you," Adinah mouthed to Abital, before hoisting the tray and sweeping his way into the great hall.

Abital smiled and then found a spot to stand where she would be out of the way of the servants bringing food up from the kitchen. A few of the king's guards stood nearby as well, wearing the armor emblazoned with the royal crest, ready if the king needed them.

The noise coming from the banquet hall was raucous, and it was not hard to see that the wine had already been flowing for some time.

Through the door which continually swung open, Abital could see that King Ahab was seated at the center of the long wooden table, wearing a richly embroidered vest and a deep purple cloak. Jezebel sat to his right, smiling and laughing as she spoke with the wealthy merchant on her other side who had donated the money for the new altar. Members of the king's family, his closest advisers, dozens of the prophets of Baal, and most of the wealthiest men in Jezreel joined him at the long table, which nearly groaned with the weight of the roasts and pheasants and loaves of freshly baked bread. Decanters of ruby-red wine dotted the table, and goblets were refilled with abandon as the most highly placed men and women in the Northern Kingdom celebrated. The enormous hall, with its soaring ceiling and marble walls and floors, echoed with laughter and conversation and the song of the lute, played by a young boy on the far side of the room.

It seemed as though every person of consequence in Israel had been invited tonight. King Ahab, urged on by Jezebel, had just completed the building of the grandest altar in all of the land, dedicated to the Phoenician god Baal, which Jezebel had worshiped back in her homeland. Dozens of men had died in the construction of the temple, but though the foremen claimed the king was requiring them to work too quickly, leading to accidents, the king had only shortened the deadline for the temple's completion. The lives of the workers, he declared, were nothing compared to the glory that was due to the god Baal. The altar had been unveiled to all of the most important guests earlier that day, and the feast tonight was a celebration in honor of the deity.

Golyat, one of the king's guards, spent much of the evening trying to get Abital to leave her post to go to his rooms with him.

"Baal is the god of fertility, after all," Golyat said, leaning in toward her.

"No thank you," Abital said firmly.

"I can think of no better way to honor the sacrifices of our king." He placed his hand on her arm.

Under Hebrew law, being this close to a man would be forbidden, but it had been many years since King Ahab had governed the nation with a strict adherence to the Hebrew laws.

"No thank you." She removed his hand.

"Leave her alone," said Elon, one of the older and kindlier guards. Elon had always been considerate to Abital and had known her *imma* when she served at the palace. Golyat listened to the older guard and stepped away, but he kept casting glances her way.

Abital decided that Jezebel seemed content enough, and the kitchen staff needed the help as they cleared dirty plates and brought up more jugs of wine, so she stepped away from the guards by the door and took a tray of used dishes from the slight Channah and carried them down to the kitchen once again.

"Bless you," Soraya said as she reached the kitchen. The cook handed Abital two jugs of wine to take up the stairs with her again.

Abital made several trips back and forth to the kitchen before Elon stopped her. "The king is about to speak," he said. "You should probably stay. If the queen has need, it will be now."

Abital thanked Elon, and she returned to her place, waiting, watching as the door swung open repeatedly. Jezebel was still seated at the head table, a placid smile on her face. A few moments later, the king rose, and a hush fell over the room. Once he had the crowd's attention, he began to speak. Elon propped the door open so they could hear.

"I would like to welcome all of our esteemed guests to the palace tonight," King Ahab said. His beard was neatly trimmed and oiled, and the jewels on his fingers and his robe shimmered in the light of the lamps. "It is an honor to celebrate with all of you. This is a great occasion. Today, the largest and finest altar to Baal in the land now stands right here in Jezreel."

A cheer went up from the crowd. "I have no doubt Baal will bless Israel richly for her sacrifice and for this amazing honor." King Ahab's voice boomed through the crowded room. "There are many people to thank for this incredible feat. Among them, of course, is Gershon, whose generous gift made it possible for the marble and gold to be imported and the altar fashioned. Thank you, Gershon, for this generous gift."

Gershon, a round man with a bulbous nose, stood to receive the accolades and cheers from the crowd. A merchant who traded in spices and oils, he was known for his shrewd deals, and Abital had no doubt the recognition he was receiving now made it worth every coin he donated for the statue to be carved.

"But of course, none of this could have been possible without the devotion and urging of my beautiful wife, Jezebel, whose dedication to the god who controls the rain and thunder and fills our land with life is the primary reason we in Israel have the honor of this new altar." The king took Jezebel's arm and gently guided her to her feet, then wrapped an arm around her waist and pulled her close to him. Her gown shimmered and sparkled. She looked stunning.

"Your queen," he said to the crowd, which roared with thunderous applause. King Ahab leaned in and kissed Jezebel, and even when he pulled back, he did not remove his hand from her. Jezebel gazed up at the king with what most probably assumed was devotion. Only those who knew her well, who had spent much time in her presence as Abital had, could see it for what it truly was: triumph. The king desired her, and everyone could see it. He had built the altar for her, and in that moment, Abital understood who the most powerful person in Israel truly was.

"May our sacrifices appease Baal," King Ahab said, and he raised his goblet in a toast. "May our people and our land be fruitful, and may he bless Israel richly."

"May Baal bless Israel," the hundreds in the room repeated, but Ahab had already leaned in to kiss Jezebel again, and the way he positioned his body against hers said he was no longer listening to the crowd of supporters.

Another round of whoops and cheers went up, and just as Abital was beginning to feel uncomfortable, believing the king had truly forgotten hundreds were watching him, a thunderous bang at the end of the room startled them out of their embrace.

Abital saw that the tall golden doors at the far end of the hall had been thrown open, and a man in a ragged cloak and dusty sandals was storming down the aisle between rows of tables, directly toward the king. His gray-and-white hair, its wild curls untamed, flew back behind him as he made his way to the king.

Elon and Golyat rushed into the room, and guards rushed in through the hall's other doors as well. The guards all raced after him, but the man did not falter or change his course. "King Ahab," the man cried, his hand raised, his finger pointed at the ruler. "The Lord God of Israel has sent me to give you a message."

Somehow—Abital did not see how it could be possible, but it was—the wiry man had eluded the guards and was still storming his way to the head table. From here, Abital could see that his cloak was torn and his feet were caked with dirt. How had he gotten in?

"Is that right?" Instead of anger, Ahab seemed more amused than anything. "And who, may I ask, are you?" He signaled to the guards to hold off, to leave the man be for now. They stopped, one guard on either side of him, Elon directly behind the man.

If the king had thought his attention might put fear into the man, he was wrong, and the man's voice grew louder as he neared the table.

"I am Elijah, the Tishbite, from Tishbe in Gilead, and I come with a message from the Lord." His voice boomed in the hall, which had fallen silent as the crowd waited to watch whatever would unfold.

The king crossed his arms over his chest, apparently unimpressed by this opening.

"Yahweh will not be mocked," the strange man cried. "As the Lord, the God of Israel who I serve, lives, there will be neither dew nor rain in the next few years except at my word."

King Ahab seemed to be waiting for this peculiar man—this man Elijah, from some place called Tishbe—to say more, but he didn't. Instead, Elijah whirled around, nearly knocking into the guards behind him. The guards grabbed him, pulling his arms behind his back and dragging him away, down the aisle that he had stormed up just a moment before.

"Lock him away," King Ahab said.

Abital watched as the oddball man let the guards drag him away. He didn't fight, just went limp as he was pulled toward the door.

Who was he, to burst in here this way, in the middle of a celebration, and to challenge the king? She didn't know what would happen to the man now, but she was sure it wouldn't go well for him.

After the guards had hauled the strange man off, they slammed the doors behind them. And then, after a long moment of uncomfortable silence, King Ahab clapped his hands.

"Let us put that strangeness behind us," he said, taking his wife's hand once again. "Let us remember that this is a celebration." With his other hand, he lifted his chalice. "To Israel, and to Baal."

"To Baal!" echoed the hundreds in the room.

CHAPTER TWO

The day after the celebration, many in the palace slept late, but Abital was up with the sun. She had always been an early riser, and she enjoyed the quiet morning hours before the rest of the palace was awake. Abital crept out of the room she shared with three other servants. Mara snored quietly and rolled over, but none of the others stirred. Abital made her way to the kitchen. She had helped the queen undress after the feast and had gotten to bed late. Her head was cloudy, and Soraya had a tea that would help wake her up and clear her mind.

"Up already?" Soraya was kneading dough on the wooden table, worn smooth over the years. Even after the elaborate meal she and her team had put together last night, Soraya would have the morning meal ready whenever the palace residents wanted it. Most mornings, though, she had a full team of helpers, keeping the coals spread evenly or kneading balls of dough.

"I could not sleep," Abital said. "I was hoping for some of that tea that wakes you."

"I have a feeling I will be serving a lot of that this morning," Soraya said. "Hot water is there. The leaves are in that jar."

Soraya did not allow most people to come in and make tea in her kitchen, which she controlled tightly. But Abital had spent enough early mornings in here to have earned Soraya's trust and know her way around.

"You are all alone today?" Abital asked.

"I decided to let them sleep," Soraya said. "It could be hours before the staff are needed, and they worked hard yesterday."

Soraya used her forearms to press the soft dough against the hard wooden table. The pop and hiss of the flames beneath the pot of water made the kitchen warm and cozy this quiet morning.

"What did you think of the party?" Soraya said.

Abital shrugged. "The king seemed happy, and the queen appeared to be pleased. That is what matters."

"I heard there was a surprise visitor."

"That was the strangest thing. I do not understand how he got past the guards." Abital scooped tea leaves out of the jar and placed them at the bottom of an earthen cup. "He threatened the king."

Soraya lifted an eyebrow but said nothing, turning the dough over in her hands and pressing it against the table.

"What?" Why was Soraya looking at her that way?

"Was it a threat?" Soraya asked. "Or was he simply making an announcement?"

It was too early, and her head too cloudy for these sorts of riddles. "What do you mean?"

"He was a prophet, was he not?"

"Not any kind of prophet I have seen." There were plenty of prophets around, men who devoted themselves to the gods, who lived in colonies together and spent their days working themselves into ecstasies as they worshiped their gods. Those men were respectable, well-dressed, shown deference in the streets, and given a high place in the courts. "What kind of prophet speaks like a madman and dresses like a shepherd?"

"Did he not claim to speak for Yahweh?"

Abital thought back. "I suppose he did." The prophets of Yahweh were less prominent now that Jezebel had brought the prophets of the other gods to the kingdom, but even they did not act wild like this man had. "None of the king's prophets would have behaved like this, though."

"Perhaps he does not serve the king, but Yahweh." Soraya shrugged as she turned the dough in her hands, shaping it into a ball.

"That is not possible." Abital had never heard of such a thing. Yahweh's prophets answered to the king of Israel, the ruler who had been appointed by God Himself.

"Maybe you are right," Soraya said. "Maybe I do not understand."

Soraya was from Persia, and though she had been in Israel since her marriage many years before, the ways of the people of Israel were still foreign to her.

"I think he was a madman," Abital said. "And I am sure who-ever was responsible for letting him in will be in trouble."

"I am sure you are right," Soraya said. "Now, your tea should be ready. Will you have some bread to go with it? And tell me what else happened upstairs last night."

Abital drank her tea and told Soraya how Haran, one of the king's advisers, had danced with many of the young women of the court and how well received the fresh apricots in sweet syrup had been. Eventually, the rest of the household began to stir, the kitchen filled with Soraya's helpers, and Abital moved along so as not to be underfoot. She took her tea out to the palace garden, where she liked to stroll among the fruit trees and rosebushes in the cool of the morning.

The garden was quiet this morning, like most everywhere else. The fruit trees were green and full, and the anemones and cyclamens and lilies were in full bloom. The rose garden gave off a sweet smell, and the vegetable beds were bursting with bright colors. Just beyond the palace walls sat a fine vineyard, managed by a neighboring landowner called Naboth, and Jezebel loved to gaze at its neat rows and full vines. Abital had tended the garden at her *saba*'s home outside Napoth Dor, and being out here in the lush garden reminded her in some ways of home. It was because of the land her saba had tended, and the sheep she helped care for, that Abital had been an early riser since her youth.

After a turn through the garden, she headed back toward the palace and to her workroom. Last night's gown had been a triumph, but she was already at work on another garment for the queen. Jezebel had requested a gown of scarlet wool, and for the past few weeks, when she was not working on the gown for last night, Abital had been weaving the wool into a fine piece of cloth.

Abital sat down at her loom and began work.

⁂

The next few weeks were full of glorious, brilliantly sunny days. The cold months had been wet and gloomy, and the mood in the palace was lifted by the appearance of the sun. Sunshine seemed to lift the spirits of the queen as well, and she sent for Abital a few days after the feast. Abital knocked on the door of her rooms and was admitted by Mara, who averted her eyes and refused to acknowledge Abital.

"There you are, Abital," the queen said, as though Abital had tarried. "Now, I need you to make me the most gorgeous gown you have ever made."

Queen Jezebel was reclining on cushions in a linen robe, her long hair loose around her shoulders. A plate of almonds dipped in honey sat before her, and as she lifted one to her mouth, the ruby on her finger glinted in the sunlight. The doors to the balcony were open, and a triangle of sunlight pooled on the ground, glinting off the polished marble, just beyond where she sat. The air smelled of lemons and juniper, tinged with a musky scent let off the by incense burning by the altar in the corner of the room. Statues and images of the gods crowded every surface.

"Of course. What is the occasion?" Abital stood awkwardly before the queen, who did not invite her to sit.

"The king is receiving visitors from Samaria," the queen said. "Very wealthy visitors, who have given much to our nation."

Samaria was Israel's capital, and though the king had built his palace in Jezreel, much of the day-to-day running of the nation took place in that city.

"I must impress the visitors," Jezebel said. "I am hoping to convince them to donate the money to build an altar to Asherah, even grander than the altar to Baal. I need you to sew me a gown that will make them forget where they have come from and want to invest their money here in the king's city."

"Of course," Abital said. She was quite used to such speeches. Every occasion demanded an outfit better than the one before it. Abital dreaded the day she could no longer top her last creation, but so far she had managed to keep Jezebel pleased. "What are you thinking? I have that scarlet wool I have been working on, or—"

"No, no, not wool," the queen said, shaking her head. "This needs to be much finer than that. We need more silk. There will be traders coming from Damascus soon, will there not? Have them bring back the finest they can find. I have heard that the women in Sidon are wearing a new kind of silk made from the threads spun by creatures who live in the sea. Let us see if we can get some of that."

Abital had heard of this silk; it was incredibly difficult to harvest and prohibitively expensive. It came only from the cities on the coast and would be nearly impossible to procure.

"I will see what can be done," Abital said. "It will be quite costly, but—"

Jezebel waved her hand dismissively. "You know the cost is not important. Just make me something that will impress."

Abital knew she could do that. "I will."

The queen lifted another honeyed almond to her lips. "The men are coming in two weeks. You will have it ready by then."

Two weeks was not nearly enough time to acquire the costly silk. It would take weeks to bring it here, even if the cloth had already been woven and dyed. Never mind the time it would take to purchase it and craft it into a gown that would impress the palace's visitors. But she ducked her head, thanked the queen, and said she would have it done.

Abital turned to go, but Jezebel spoke again. "Silk made from the sea. Is that not wonderful?" she said, stretching out on her cushion. "Imagine it, Abital. The visitors will be so impressed. And it will make me feel like I am home again. Our palace in Sidon had an incredible view of the sea." Jezebel was the daughter of the king of Sidon, a wealthy Phoenician city on the coast.

"It sounds lovely."

"I used to love swimming in the sea on hot, sunny days," Jezebel said. "Have you ever seen the sea, Abital?"

"No, my queen. I hope to see it someday."

But Jezebel didn't answer. She had closed her eyes and seemed to be lost in her own memories. It was as though she had forgotten Abital was there at all.

CHAPTER THREE

The days that followed were warm, and the sun shone brightly, lavishing its glow on Jezreel and the surrounding valley.

A week after the banquet, there was great excitement as the king gathered men from all around Israel in tents outside the city walls. He spent three days outfitting and training them before sending them to the border with Syria to fight against the Moabites, who were constantly encroaching on the land given to Israel. Those in the palace were called upon to cook and ferry food and drink to the soldiers in their camp, and some of the younger servant girls giggled and talked amongst themselves about which soldiers were the handsomest.

All were grateful for the fine weather. Spring was usually so cold and gloomy, which normally made the flat plains outside the city wall a pit of mud this time of year. Instead, those entering and leaving the palace could come and go without having mud caked onto their clothes and sandals. In the mornings and evenings, Abital walked in the garden and enjoyed the sunshine.

Word spread that the madman who had interrupted the banquet had been released from prison and told never to return, and that the king had summoned some of the prophets of Yahweh to find out if he was one of them. Yahweh's prophets denied knowing the man though. None of them had heard of Elijah the Tishbite, and said he was unlikely to speak for Yahweh if they did not know him. The king declared Elijah was not worth wasting more time worrying about. The nuisance had been banished from Jezreel, never to return.

Once the soldiers were gone, marching off in long lines toward the southern border, the palace returned to relative peace.

Abital wrote a letter to *Saba*, telling her late mother's *abba* about the strange encounter and sharing news from the palace. She used the parchment and ink she had brought from home, and was careful to keep the letter hidden in her things at the palace. Few here at the palace were aware she could read and write, and she knew it was best to keep it that way. No one trusted a woman who could read, Saba had warned her, even as he had quietly encouraged her to learn the skill.

Abital brought the letter with her when she went into town to see Ira, the trader who imported silks and other fabrics from the East, in his little shop inside the oldest part of the walled town. Abital did not leave the palace often, and when she did, she was often surprised anew at the smell in the streets and the throngs of people that crowded Jezreel's narrow alleyways. Abital had spent most of her childhood in the countryside, helping her saba with the sheep, and the close press of the town was still difficult for her. But she was also delighted by the sights and the sounds—the men and women bartering and arguing in the market, the colorful piles of spices and oranges and lemons on the tables, the aroma of grilling meat wafting from the doorways. She saw the laundry strung on ropes from one building to the next across the narrow streets, and the sounds of singing and the smell of incense emanating from the temple.

From down here, the ivory palace of King Ahab, perched high on the hill, seemed almost to guard the city and oversee the comings and goings of the residents. As she wandered the streets, winding her way to the shop of the trader in silks, she thought about how all day the people of Jezreel looked up at the palace, while those in the palace hardly gave a thought to the lives that went on below them.

Abital found Ira inside his shop. The ceiling was low and the shop dark, and every surface was jumbled with cloth from all over the land. The tables were crowded with stacks of coarse linen and poorly woven wool, and the walls were filled with rolls of finer weaves, many of them dyed in shades of green and orange and light red. These colored fabrics would be used for gowns and cloaks and tunics by wealthier citizens in town. They would be bought mostly by merchants and traders and those who worked at the treasury. But none of these was what Abital needed.

"Good morning, Miss," Ira said, ducking his head. "It is good to see you again. How did our queen like the purple cloth?"

"She loved it," Abital said. "I had it made into a gown that impressed the king and everyone else, and, as you know, that is our queen's primary goal."

"Our queen could not help but dazzle. She is so beautiful that any rag looks like a gown on her."

Ira did not realize his flattery was lost on Abital, who would not pass it along to Jezebel herself. But she smiled and returned the compliment. "It was the beauty of the silk that made it possible. The care that was taken to include the shimmery gold threads was what truly delighted."

"Only the best for our queen." Ira smiled, revealing several missing teeth and one that was turning black in his mouth. "Now, what is our queen in the market for today? I have a new load of silks in from Damascus. Come see."

Ira indicated that she should follow him into the back room, where the costlier fabrics were kept. Very few people were ever invited into the rear—few could afford the price—but Abital knew the room well.

"Do you see how cleverly this one is woven, with the colored flowers worked into the fabric itself?" Ira lifted the corner of a swatch of very fine silk. It looked as smooth as glass and as soft as a kitten.

"It is very fine," Abital agreed. "But our queen will greet some wealthy visitors soon, and she wants something different. She has heard that silk made from sea creatures is in fashion in the palaces to the north, and she has asked me to find some fabric of this type."

Ira scratched at his beard. "The palaces to the north are behind the times, in that case. This is what all the most fashionable queens are wearing," he said, and held out the material for her to touch.

"You do not have any sea silk."

Ira sighed. "You really are too clever. Most would simply have believed my story."

"I am too clever to fall for your flattery as well. Can you have some sea silk sent?"

"I can have some sent, but it will be quite expensive, and it will take some time. When does she need the robe?"

"In less than two weeks."

"In that case, we will have to convince her to try something different this time." He dropped the silk with the flowers woven into it. "I have a bit more of the purple—"

"She will not want purple again."

"It is the color of royalty. It will display her wealth to the finest advantage." Purple dye was made from the shells of sea snails, and it was very costly and difficult to produce. Only the very wealthy could afford such fabric.

"She will want something different this time. What is the next best thing you have to sea-creature silk?"

Ira showed her a bolt of deep red material that shimmered in the dim light. The pattern of raised flowers that was woven into the fabric—the hallmark of silk from Damascus—was beautiful to the eye and to the touch. Ira explained that this dye was made from the larvae of insects, not the cheaper madder, which could run and produced less-brilliant shades of red.

"Fabric from this same bolt was used to dress the daughter of the king of Nineveh for her wedding to the king of Moab," Ira said. "It is said that the king was so dazzled he gave back part of her dowry, because seeing his bride so beautifully clothed was already such a gift."

Abital knew he was spinning a story, as surely as the silkworms had spun this silk, bit by bit. But she also understood that he was giving her the story with which she could convince the queen that this was better than what she had requested. The truth was whatever got you what you needed in Jezebel's palace.

"If you sewed rubies and diamonds along the neck, the gown would make these rich men forget their own names," Ira said.

Abital was already envisioning a gown that would drape over the queen's shoulders and set off her long neck and fine features. The silk truly was beautiful, and Ira was a shrewd businessman. The fabric was costly, but she knew that would only increase its appeal in the queen's eyes. The more a thing cost, the more she valued it.

"She will have her heart set on sea silk," Abital said. "Can you try to find some for next time?"

"You will be able to convince her that this is better and more fashionable." Ira nodded. "But I will see if my connections can procure some sea silk."

"Thank you." Abital waited as Ira added the cost of the fabric to the total owed by the palace. He would come himself to retrieve payment from the king's bankers at the end of the month. "And would you please give this to your trader?" She held out the letter.

"Of course." Ira tucked the folded parchment into a pocket of his vest. He always gave her notes to a trader he knew who was headed toward the coast. Ira found it delightful that Abital could write, and had promised to keep her secret. "I will send word when he returns with a message from your grandfather."

He used sharp scissors to slice off the length of silk and wrapped the bundle in thick burlap with a promise to have it delivered to the palace that afternoon.

Abital took her time wandering back to the palace, enjoying, for now, the feeling of freedom she felt outside its walls. She knew she should feel guilty for enjoying the sensation of freedom. After all her imma had done and sacrificed to get Abital this appointment at the palace, she should be grateful every moment. But she could not help but enjoy being free of the palace politics and gossip for a few hours. She wandered through the market, gazing at the tables piled with animal skins and baskets and cooking pots and peaches and sweet greens. As she walked, she rehearsed in her head the story she would tell the queen about why she was returning without the sea silk she had requested.

By the time she returned to the palace, the fabric had been delivered, and Abital knocked on the door of Jezebel's rooms tentatively, carrying the costly silk in a woven bag. Many times when she arrived without being summoned, Abital was told the queen was busy, and to come back, usually by the sneering Mara, who delighted in giving such news. But today, Abital was told that the queen was in the palace garden, and Abital should meet her there. Abital hurried to the garden, where she found the queen resting in the shade of a tamarisk tree. Two of the palace guards stood nearby. The palace lute player, a young lithe man with long hair and golden skin, played softly.

They all turned to Abital as she approached.

"It is a beautiful day, is it not?" the queen said as Abital walked up. She gestured for the lute player to continue but spoke over him. "I cannot get enough of this sunshine."

"It is indeed, my queen." Abital moved the bag of silk from one arm to the other, trying to find a comfortable position to hold the heavy parcel. The sun shone down brightly, and its warmth seemed to bring everything to life. The sky was a soft blue, dotted with fluffy white clouds, and the warm air held the sweet scent of roses and honeysuckle.

"We are lucky to have so many nice days this early in the spring."

"Yes, it is nice to have the dry weather," Abital said. She searched her mind, trying to figure out if there was more the queen wanted her to say, but Jezebel just smiled. She was relaxed and seemed happier than Abital could remember seeing her.

"Have you brought the sea silk for me?" the queen finally said, gesturing at the bundle in Abital's arms.

"I have found something better," Abital said. "The dealer in silks had this special cloth, which is from the same bolt as the fabric that made the king of Moab give back his bride's dowry because she was so lovely in it." Abital set the bundle down on the ground. She reached inside and gently pulled out a corner of the brilliant red silk. "It the most fashionable color in all of the land, and it feels like sunshine on the skin."

Abital braced herself for a torrent of condemnation, as she had received on more than one occasion when she had failed to deliver on the queen's desires. However, today, the queen reached out and ran her fingers over the section Abital held out to her.

"It was very costly, but you deserve only the finest," Abital added.

"It is lovely," Jezebel said. "That color always flatters my skin tone."

"This color looks stunning on you," Abital added. "And I was thinking we could sew some rubies along the neckline to make it really shimmer."

Jezebel nodded. "That will work. You have done well, Abital. What would I do without you?"

Abital let out a breath. The sunshine must have had quite an effect on the queen indeed. Instead of falling into a rage, she seemed to be… Was she actually pleased? For a moment, Abital wondered if the queen had been to visit one of the opium dens in the city, but then Jezebel spoke, and Abital understood.

"You will need to make this gown a bit looser than normal," Jezebel said. "I am only a few weeks along, but I am already starting to see the changes in my body this time."

"Congratulations, my queen." Abital bowed her head. "This is wonderful news. You will give the king a son."

"I believe I will this time," Jezebel said. "So we must make sure the gown fits just right, so as not to restrain the king's son in my womb."

"Of course."

"You see how quickly Baal has blessed me?" Jezebel said. "You must offer a prayer of thanksgiving to the god who made this happen."

"Of course, my queen." Abital would offer the prayer this day to the idol Jezebel had given her when Abital arrived at the palace.

As Abital folded the silk again and gathered up her parcel, she understood the queen's good mood. If she gave the king a son, she would be valued and treasured, her place in the history of Israel secure. She hoisted the heavy bag and cast one last glance back at the queen, who had a serene smile on her face. Perhaps all would be peaceful in the palace.

Abital worked most waking hours over the next two weeks, stitching seams and sewing gems into the neckline of the gown. The whole palace was busy making preparations for the visitors from Samaria. Shifrah, an older woman who had served the former queen—Queen Ahab's mother, Dinah—and was now charged with keeping the servants in line, supervised as the whole palace was cleaned, each room aired out and given fresh linens.

The queen's good mood continued as the sunny days stretched on, and she even stood in the palace garden to watch as the visiting party marched through the streets of Jezreel and arrived at the palace. Abital heard later from those who also watched the group's approach that half a dozen men had come on horseback, and the horses also drew a covered cart. Only women or very important men rode in such luxury, and they wondered who the visitors might be. Abital wished she could have seen the visitors' approach, but she was busy in her workroom and could not pause to see them arrive. Still, she listened eagerly to the news, as did most in the palace. They knew not why this visit was so important to the palace, only that they were to prepare as though these visitors were kings and rulers.

Abital dressed Jezebel in her new scarlet gown that evening, and the queen was pleased by her reflection in the mirror. The style was bolder than what most women in Israel wore, with a neckline that draped low and a cut that showed off her curves, but this was how the most fashionable women dressed in the North, and Jezebel insisted that Israel would soon catch on.

"You have done it again," the queen said, touching the rubies sewn into the neckline. They danced and sparkled as she moved. Her belly was still flat, but her bust had swollen, and her figure showed the robe to its best advantage. "It is the most gorgeous gown anyone has ever seen. The visitors cannot fail to be impressed."

Soraya had spent many days preparing for the feast to greet the visitors, and the smell of roasted meat wafted through the halls of the palace. Abital sat with Jezebel in her rooms as the queen waited to be summoned to the meal, ready in case adjustments were needed to the gown. But as the moments passed, Jezebel grew more and more anxious.

"I am sure he will call for you shortly," Mara said, trying to soothe the queen's fraying nerves. She poured more wine into the cup the queen had drained and indicated that the queen should sit and relax, but though she took the cup, the queen paced up and down the long room. The doors to the balcony were open, but the room still felt stuffy and the air stagnant and close.

When the music of harps and lutes drifted up from below, Abital pretended not to notice, but Mara began to tap her foot in time with the beat. Jezebel shot her a glare, and Mara stopped. Jezebel continued to pace.

"This wine is not good. Why am I always sent the worst jugs from the king's cellars?"

Neither Mara nor Abital dared point out that it was the same wine she always had, and that she had liked it just fine an hour and a half before. The queen was agitated, and growing more so as the realization that she would not be attending the night's dinner settled over all of them.

Her quiet footsteps padded up and back along the marble floor. As she turned again, the fabric on one shoulder slipped down.

"Why is this gown so uncomfortable?" The queen yanked the shoulder back up. "Why can I not ever have just one thing that works the way it's supposed to? Is it truly so hard to make a gown that fits right?"

Abital knew better than to point out that she had made the robe, per the queen's instructions, larger than normal, or that she had fitted it to her form precisely in several fittings over the past few days. "Would you like help with it?" Abital asked instead.

"No. I want—I need to get this horrible thing off." Jezebel pulled at the neckline. "It is too hot, and it feels terrible." Once again, she yanked at the fabric over her chest.

"Wait, I will help you." Abital jumped up and started toward the queen, but not before she had yanked the fabric so hard that Abital heard a rip, and a handful of tiny jewels scattered onto the floor.

"Oh, Mistress, your jewels!" Mara exclaimed, jumping forward to pick up the tiny stones that glittered against the marble floor.

By the time she had helped the queen out of the garment, Abital knew it would take a huge effort to repair, and the damage might still be too great.

"I hate this thing. Why can you never make a gown that fits?" Jezebel screamed, just before she threw the cup of wine in her hand across the room, where it smashed against the wall. Broken shards shattered on the floor, and the red wine dripped down the wall. "I will find another seamstress, someone who can do it right the first time."

Mara glared at Abital once again, as if the gown truly was the reason for the queen's displeasure. Abital gathered up the remains of the garment and promised to make adjustments, but Jezebel did not seem to be listening, and Mara shooed her out. As soon as she was outside the queen's rooms, Abital took in a gulp of fresh air and placed her hand against the stone wall to steady herself. She had seen the queen's rage before, but it had never been directed at her. The problem was not the gown but the queen's anger at not being invited to the feast, and her fear and worry about why she had not been sent for. Abital knew that, but did the queen? Did she really mean it when she said she would get a new seamstress? If Abital was sent home—

She could not face that thought. Not tonight. For now, she took a deep breath, gathered the silk of the robe as neatly as she could, and headed back to her workroom. She would try to fix it as best she could, and she would pray to Yahweh and Baal and Asherah that she could keep her place at the palace. That the queen's rage would not be the end of everything.

CHAPTER FOUR

The days of unbroken sunshine continued, only now they did not seem to cheer the queen. Abital learned from Soraya that the queen had been eating alone in her rooms, but she sent most of the food back untouched. Meanwhile, the king had ordered lavish meals for his guests, and Soraya's staff was kept busy preparing roast quail and dove, cheeses wrapped in flaky layers of pastry, and apricots and plums soaked in wine and honey. Whoever they were, the king's guests were eating well.

When Ira sent word that the trader had brought back a reply to Abital's letter, she went to the cloth trader's shop to retrieve it.

> *Thank you for your note, child. I pray in the name of Yahweh that you are well and that the queen is treating you well. You are dearly missed here, but we know you are doing good work for the palace. Elkanah and Ofir send their love.*
>
> *This year's lambs are growing quickly, and we will sell some of them soon. Shearing season went well enough.*
>
> *We have heard word of this prophet Elijah. It is said he is a true servant of the Most High God, and he is hiding for fear of the king. You say he seemed like a madman, but I wonder*

if he has simply delivered the king a message he did not want to hear.

    Grace and peace to you.

    Saba

Three days after the visitors arrived, Abital was summoned from the workroom, where she was finishing repairs on the red silk gown.

"Bring your needle and thread," said Shifrah. Her hair and robe were neat, as always, and her tall frame made her somehow more intimidating. "One of the visitors needs your help."

Abital set down the scarlet silk. She was using tiny stitches to seal up the rip, and though she had had to turn a fold and raise the neckline some, she was hopeful the gown would be restored. She set her needle and thread aside, brushed her hands along her tunic to smooth it, and followed Shifrah.

"Who are the visitors?" Abital asked as they threaded through the narrow corridors of the palace servants' halls.

"They are from Samaria," was all Shifrah would say.

"Why are they here?"

"It is not for us to say."

Abital did not know whether Shifrah did not know or simply would not say. Shifrah had known and liked Abital's imma, so she had always been kind to Abital, but she also did not allow the servants to gossip. Abital was led upstairs to a part of the palace she had never seen before. Here, as in the queen's chambers, the halls were wide and the ceilings high, and many doors branched off. Shifrah knocked on one, and after someone called softly from inside, the door opened, and Abital was led into a chamber with big doors that led out to the balcony that ran along the back of the palace. A woman had been seated at a small table, bent over a scrap of parchment, but she stood when Shifrah led Abital inside. Abital was surprised to see that this woman could read.

"The queen's seamstress, my lady," Shifrah said, ushering Abital inside.

"Thank you so much for coming, Abital. I am Keziah, and I am sorry for the trouble." The woman was tall, with square shoulders and a long face. Her curly dark hair was pulled back under a scarf of the lightest blue, and she wore loose robes. "I am told I must wear a fine gown today, but the one I brought seems to have been damaged in the journey."

"Abital is extremely clever with a needle," Shifrah said. "She is the only one the queen trusts. She will be able to help."

"Show me what has happened," Abital said.

Keziah walked across the room and picked up a gown the color of the sky on a summer's day. Abital could see that it would fit looser and cover more than the garments preferred by the queen, but the fabric was very fine and no doubt incredibly costly. "There is a tear where it got snagged on the basket," Keziah said, holding out a spot where the silk had torn. "I do not believe it can be seen, but Obadiah insists I cannot appear before the king in a torn gown."

"He is quite right." Abital took the garment and looked over the spot. The fine threads had snagged, revealing a layer of tightly woven linen beneath. Abital wondered why Keziah would appear before the king, and who Obadiah was, but dared not ask. "I can repair this. It will not be perfect, but I can hide the rip."

"That would be wonderful. Thank you, Abital."

Shifrah nodded and stepped out of the chamber, leaving the two of them inside. Abital looked around the room, searching for the best spot to make the repair.

"May I use the table?"

"Of course." Keziah walked back to the table and removed the scrap of parchment, but not before Abital could see that it was a Psalm of David.

"You can read." As soon as the words were out, Abital regretted them. It was none of her business. But she had never met another woman who could read, and she wondered once again who this woman was and why she was here.

"My *abba* taught me, alongside my brother," Keziah said. "I was reading a song of David. 'I lift up my eyes to the hills—where does my help come from?' Do you know it?"

The words stirred something deep within Abital. Her saba often used to sing the song written by the former king of Israel, and hearing the words now, Abital was transported back to the hills where she had grown up, back to the table where Saba had prayed for Yahweh's blessing more times than she could count. In her memory, the fire blazed comfortably in the hearth, warming the small home, and the smell of wood smoke and roasting meat filled the rooms.

Abital looked down at the parchment and read the next line aloud. "'My help comes from the Lord, maker of heaven and earth.'"

There was a moment of silence as Abital realized what she had just done. She had always been careful to not reveal her skill at the palace. Many would not see her kindly if they knew. She had not intended to reveal her secret to this stranger, but somehow she had let it slip out.

"I know it from memory," Abital said quickly. "My saba used to recite it."

But Keziah was looking at her differently now and was shaking her head. "That wasn't from memory. You read that."

"I do not—"

"It is wonderful." Keziah's face broke out in a smile. "You can read."

"Not well," Abital said. "I have no formal training."

"So how...?" She let the words trail off.

"I learned from my saba," Abital explained. "He saw I was interested and encouraged it."

Abital could see that Keziah had questions but did not voice them.

"Most in the palace do not know. It would be better if they did not," Abital said.

"I will tell no one," Keziah said. "As long as you will not reveal my secret. I find that most men see a woman who can read as a dangerous thing."

Abital nodded, and she set the garment on the newly cleared table.

"I was reading the psalm because the words bring me comfort when I am faced with a challenging task," Keziah said.

Abital wanted to ask more about the task ahead for this strange woman, but she had already asked too much and did not want to be sent away for her rudeness. Instead, she sat down to work, pulling thread that had been dyed a light blue color and a needle out of her bag. Keziah lit a lamp and brought it closer to Abital, so she could see the fine stitchwork.

"Thank you," Abital said. No one in the palace had ever thought to help her in such a way. While Abital worked, Keziah gazed down at the parchment and murmured the words quietly to herself. Abital was filled with questions. Keziah was a Yahwist, that much was clear. Many in Israel still worshiped Yahweh, though it was often difficult to remember that, here at the palace. The queen had brought her own gods with her when she came to Jezreel, and even before that, King Ahab had largely abandoned the worship of Yahweh. There was not much mention of Him these days. Abital wondered again what this woman was doing here and why she must appear before the king.

A knock came at the door when Abital was nearly done with the repair. Keziah walked to the door and opened it, and Abital tried not to show her surprise when a man walked into the chamber. He was also tall, with the same smooth brown skin and curly hair as Keziah, and he had the same long face as Keziah, though on him it seemed to fit better. Abital could not help but notice he was a handsome man, and he wore a robe of silk the same sky-blue color as the one Abital was repairing.

"It is almost time. Is the robe ready?" He looked around the room and noticed Abital for the first time. He smiled, and she saw he had straight teeth and a kind face. "I see it is still under repair."

"It is almost done," Abital said. "Just a few more stitches, and it will be as good as new."

"Thank you for your help," the man said. "My sister will need to learn to be more careful with her fine things." The words could have been a chastisement, but the way he said them, with so much evident love and affection, Abital understood he was only teasing his sister.

"This is my brother Obadiah," Keziah said. "Obadiah, this is Abital, who I am told is the best seamstress in all of the land."

"Then she will be a very good friend to you indeed. You will need all the help you can get." Obadiah once again grinned at his sister and then turned and bowed his head toward Abital. "It is wonderful to meet you, Abital."

Abital ducked her head, and then she tied off the thread, snipped it, and held up the gown. "It is the best I can do right now."

Keziah came over and took the gown, and she examined the stitches. "You do good work, indeed. These are very fine stitches, and I can hardly even see the tear."

"That is good to hear," Obadiah said. "Now, you had better get it on quickly. It is nearly time."

"Thank you for your help, Abital," Keziah said. "May Yahweh bless you in your work."

Abital walked toward the door, where Obadiah still stood. He watched her and then gave a shy smile before he stepped aside so she could pass.

"Thank you, Abital," he said as she walked out. "We will not forget your kindness."

⸻

When Abital was summoned to the queen's chambers shortly after she returned to her workroom, she carried the scarlet silk gown with her. She had cleaned and repaired it as best she could, and the tiny jewels had been sewn back into place. She had had to adjust the way the fabric draped over the shoulder, but she hoped the queen would be pleased enough to let her keep her place at the palace. After all her imma had done to get her this position, Abital could not bear to be sent home. She hurried through the hallways, wondering why she was being called at this time of day. It was midday, many hours from when the queen would need to dress for dinner.

"There you are," Queen Jezebel said. Her movements were jerky, and her words clipped. She was agitated, that much was clear. Abital wondered once more what was happening. "I need to be dressed quickly. The king has called everyone to the great hall."

"What is going on?" Abital asked.

Jezebel did not answer the question. "He is expecting me shortly. It took you so long to get here that we must hurry. Get this thing on."

Abital bit her tongue. She could not tell the queen that she had come as soon as she had been summoned. Jezebel made no reference to the fact that the gown had had to be repaired, nor did she praise Abital's clever work in hiding the seams where the torn silk had been sewn together. She simply took one long gaze at her reflection in the mirror, nodded, and started to head to the great hall. The long silk dragged on the ground behind her, sweeping across the polished stone.

The queen turned back. She grasped at the neckline, where the tear had been repaired. "Will this hold? The seam is secure?"

"It is as secure as it can be," Abital said. She did not add *given the damage it suffered*, though she wanted to.

Jezebel started for the door again, but something made her stop. She adjusted the neckline again.

"This is not right. You have not fixed it right."

"It looks stunning on you, my queen."

The queen moved back to the mirror and gazed at her reflection once again. "It does not feel right."

"It is beautiful," Mara chimed in from the corner of the room.

Jezebel ignored her, continuing to look at her own reflection.

"You must hurry, my queen," Mara said. "Abital took so long to come. The king will be waiting."

"Come." She gestured for Abital. "Follow me, to make sure."

"Of course." Abital grabbed her bag and followed behind Jezebel as she stepped out into the hallway. Hiram, the guard who always waited outside the queen's door, turned and escorted her toward the great hall. Abital walked a few paces behind, her bag clutched under her arm, wondering what was happening. Around them, servants were scurrying around, and there was a loud hum coming from the direction of the great hall. Guards flanked the doors, spears and shields in hand, but Hiram led Jezebel to the far end of the room, to the rear doors where the servants always gathered. Golyat was already there and leered at Abital as she approached. The queen would not be making a grand entrance today, then. Hiram pulled open the heavy doors. Through the opening, Abital could see King Ahab's throne, currently empty, with guards and people gathered on each side.

Jezebel paused and took in a deep breath.

"Does it look all right?" Jezebel said, adjusting the neckline of her dress once more.

Abital was taken aback. She had never seen the queen this uncertain and insecure. "You look perfect," she said.

Jezebel took another long breath and then lifted her chin and walked into the great hall and toward the king's advisers.

Hiram waited until the queen had gone inside and then propped the door open by tucking his spear into the door frame. The three of them crowded around the opening and looked inside.

Abital gazed over the room, which was filled with people wearing richly embroidered robes and jewels. At the front of the crowd were the king's top advisers, his military commanders, and many of the wealthiest men in Samaria and Jezreel. She recognized many of them from the feast after the dedication of the temple to Baal.

To the right of the throne stood the delegation from Samaria. Keziah was there, in the sky-blue silk gown and matching robe. She had jewels in her ears and on her fingers, and she smiled serenely, taking in the scene before her. Next to her stood Obadiah, and Abital thought once again how handsome he was, how the angular planes of his sister's face were echoed in his features, though they seemed to settle more pleasingly on him. Next to him stood an older man, with white hair and a neatly trimmed beard, garbed in the same blue robes, but his were braided with gold. Their father, Abital guessed. Two other men stood around them, both younger than the old man and older than the siblings. Abital could not guess who they were and why so many in the palace had been summoned here.

To the left of the throne, the king's brothers and their families stood tall and proud. Jezebel walked up slowly to join them, her head held high. The members of the king's family bowed their heads as she approached. The members of the delegation from Samaria did the same. Jezebel lifted her chin and gazed out over the gathered crowd.

She looked stunning in her red gown, which showed off her fine figure to its best advantage. There was no denying her beauty, yet Abital could not help but compare her to the placid woman on the other side of the throne. Keziah's robes covered her form, and she had neither the natural beauty nor the grace the queen possessed, and yet there was something distinctly appealing in her calm demeanor. Abital watched the woman and her brother, hoping for some sign of what was to come. As she watched them, Obadiah looked over and caught her eye. He smiled, and Abital ducked her head quickly, her cheeks flaming. She should not be here at all, and she certainly should not have been caught gazing at the king's high-ranking visitor.

Luckily, just then, the guards to the sides of the king's throne banged the ends of their spears on the marble floor. The sound echoed through the hall and silenced the crowd. Once the room was quiet, the king entered the room from the other side and walked to the throne.

"Welcome all," the king said. He wore robes of deep purple, and many jewels sparkled on his hands. "I am pleased you have come today, for I have a very important announcement to make. I am glad to tell you that I will be taking a new wife. Keziah, daughter of Obed, will soon be joining the palace to help expand the reaches of our kingdom."

Abital's gaze flew to Keziah, who cast her eyes down toward the ground. A cheer arose from the crowd, along with murmurs and shouts of good wishes. The dignitaries and wealthy men clapped. Even the guards appeared to be smiling at this, evidence of their king's growing powers and command of the region.

Only Queen Jezebel did not seem pleased by this news. Her face betrayed nothing. She just stood there, not moving, as if she were not really in the room at all.

CHAPTER FIVE

That night, there was another feast, a celebration of the king's engagement, and Soraya kept dishes coming out from the kitchen until late in the night. Abital had accompanied the queen back to her room after the announcement, and stayed, at the queen's request, in case the king sent for her, insisting she attend the banquet after all, but he never did. The queen did not talk to anyone as she silently consumed one cup of wine after another, until she had to be helped out of her gown and into bed.

The next morning, Abital found Soraya in the quiet kitchen. Two maids were toasting pieces of flatbread over a hot flame, while Soraya chopped sweet-smelling herbs with a large knife.

"They say the feast was a triumph," Abital said, having heard it from kitchen maids Michal and Tamar, who came into their shared room whispering in the middle of the night.

"The king appeared pleased," Soraya said. "And the new wife sent her thanks directly, which was kind."

"She is kind," Abital said, and when Soraya's eyebrows shot up, Abital explained how she had been sent for and had met the new bride-to-be before the announcement was made. She also mentioned that the king's new wife worshiped Yahweh.

"A Yahwist?" Soraya said. "That should be interesting." The knife sliced through the herbs with quick strokes.

"What do you mean?"

"It will not please the queen, will it?" Soraya said. "She likes her own gods."

"I do not think being a Yahwist is the reason our queen will not care for the new bride," Abital said. "I get the sense she does not relish the idea of sharing her husband with another woman."

"No, nor would I," Soraya said. Soraya had been married to Amir for many years, and they had three grown children. Amir worked in the palace gardens, and the children all served in the palace as well. "But what did she think was going to happen? Did she honestly believe the king would only take one wife? How would he grow his kingdom that way?"

The fact that kings were not only allowed but expected to take many wives and concubines had at first seemed unfair to Abital. Hypocritical, even. But Saba had explained to her that it was the king's duty to marry the daughters of foreign kings and produce children to secure alliances with neighboring nations. It was a matter of Israel's security and survival.

"I do not know." Actually, Abital was pretty sure Jezebel truly had believed that. Abital had never heard the queen say so, but she carried herself as though she were the only thing the king should ever desire. "I believe she thought she would keep his attention longer than she has, at the very least."

"I imagine she was not pleased by the news, then."

"No." Abital remembered the sour smell on the queen's breath as she helped Mara lay her on her mat the night before. "She was not pleased."

"She has no need to feel threatened. Our queen is far prettier and more alluring, and she is already carrying the king's son."

"Perhaps the new wife will bear him a son as well."

"That would be a great blessing for the kingdom," Soraya said.

Abital nodded. The more sons a king had, the more powerful he was thought to be. That could only be a good thing for Israel in her wars against the Assyrians and the Moabites. But thinking about this made her realize something.

"The new wife is not the daughter of a foreign king. She is from Samaria. From the king's very own capital." Samaria was the city established by King Ahab's father.

Jezebel was Phoenician, the daughter of the king of Sidon, and her marriage to Ahab had created a strong alliance between the two nations. The marriage had secured the northern border. Why would he choose this Samarian woman instead of a bride who would help him build another alliance?

"Yes, this one must bring something else the king needs badly."

Abital had little experience with governing, nor with political strategy or warfare. But it still did not take long for her to see the connection. "Money."

"The loyalty of foreign kings is not the only way to win wars." Soraya used the edge of her knife to move the herbs into a neat pile at the edge of the table. "Wars cost money."

"And the new wife…"

"You saw her robe up close. It was silk, was it not?"

Abital nodded.

"And blue, at that. Do you know how costly that much blue dye is? Did that seem like the robe of a poor person to you?"

"The king is marrying Keziah for her money."

"For her father's money," Soraya said. "But yes, I have no doubt this marriage is quite advantageous for the king's coffers. The father will get the honor of becoming part of the family of the king, and the king will no doubt use the hefty dowry to fight his wars against the Moabites. It is a winning strategy for all involved."

"Except perhaps Keziah." Did her abba not know about the king's cruel reputation? Did he not care? Was the honor of being related to the king truly worth the difficult life his daughter would certainly have as Ahab's second wife? Did her life matter so little to him, compared to the honor that would bestow on him?

"She will be married to the king. She will be the mother of princes. Is that not a role to relish?"

"She will have to face the daily wrath of the queen," Abital said. "For that, I do not envy her."

Soraya laughed. "No, I suppose you are right about that. That might be the most challenging part of her life here at the palace."

After the engagement announcement, Keziah and her family returned to Samaria to prepare for the wedding. Abital expected to be called to the queen's rooms to discuss the outfit she would wear for the wedding. Jezebel's presence would be expected at the festivities, and Abital assumed Jezebel would demand the most ambitious gown yet. She hoped Ira had managed to get his hands on that sea silk, or something even more sensational, to impress the queen.

But the queen did not send for her, and Soraya confided that the queen was doing poorly and had been sent hot broth and dry bread to eat. She had not left her room in several days. Abital heard a couple of the maids whispering that the queen had lost her mind, but Shifrah had appeared from around a corner and sent them scurrying. Abital could not help but be grateful for the reprieve from the queen's demands, though she did worry about the queen's health.

The heat of summer had set in earlier than normal, and the string of unbroken sunny days meant there was no respite from the unusual temperature. The palace was hot, and on her morning walks, Abital noticed that the plants in the garden were beginning to look dried out.

Mara sent for Abital nearly a week after the announcement, and when Abital appeared at the door of the queen's chambers, Mara was waiting for her, holding a light-colored sleeping gown made of the finest linen. The whole bottom was stained with what looked like dried blood. A lot of dried blood.

"Can you get this stain out?" Mara shoved the fouled garment into Abital's hands.

At first Abital wanted to argue. She was not the laundry girl. Her job was to make the queen's clothes, not wash them. But as she gazed down at the rusty stain and inhaled the bitter, metallic scent of blood, Abital understood what had happened. She felt her legs go weak.

"I do not know," Abital said. Blood was nearly impossible to remove, and on fabric this light... But she had to, or the garment would be useless and thrown away. The cost of the thread alone would feed a family for many weeks. "I will try." Mara moved to close the door, but Abital blocked it with her hand. "How is she?"

For a moment, Abital wasn't sure if Mara would answer her. Knowledge, to Mara, was power, and withholding or doling out scraps was how she maintained her position as the queen's most trusted servant. But Mara gazed into the room and then turned back to Abital with a sigh.

"The physicians say she will recover," Mara said quietly. She leaned forward a bit, almost conspiratorially. "And have many fine babies."

"Let us pray it is so."

Abital took the silk garment back to her workroom, and she tried rubbing the stain with salt and with vinegar from the kitchen. She tried every trick she knew to remove the dark stain from the delicate silk, but nothing worked. The garment was ruined.

CHAPTER SIX

It was not until a week later that the queen summoned Abital to discuss a new set of gowns for the king's upcoming wedding. The air in the queen's room was stuffy and hot, and it smelled like sweat and dirty sheets. The queen was thin, her skin sallow and her hair lank, as though it needed to be washed. As expected, she ordered Abital to make the most stunning gown Israel had ever seen.

"All eyes must be on me," Jezebel said. "I want something that will make this new wife look like a pauper, and a plain one at that. You will spare no expense."

"I will make you a wonderful gown, but it will be your beauty that shines."

The words pleased the queen, as she knew they would. Abital promised to get to work and turned to go, but before she got to the door, the queen called out to her.

"We will go to the temple of Baal tomorrow, I and all members of my household. We will make sacrifices to Baal, asking him for a son for the king. Be ready to go after the noonday meal tomorrow."

"Yes, my queen." Though she prayed to all the gods, just as her imma had taught her, Abital had not been inside the new temple. She had heard rumors of what went on inside, of children sacrificed to the fertility god, and of acts performed in the temple before the altar that were said to lead to babies. She had never felt any desire to go, nor seen any need. She knew the gods were said to control all parts of their lives, but she had never seen any evidence of this herself. One god seemed just the same as any other. Saba worshiped Yahweh, claiming Him as the One True God and the defender of Israel. But if that was true, what to make of the other gods? Why would the king of Israel not only allow but encourage the worship of Baal and Asherah if Yahweh was Israel's One True God? It made little sense. And Abital did not relish the idea of witnessing or participating in what she was told happened inside the temple to Baal. But Abital had not been given a choice. The queen had commanded her to attend, and so she must.

Abital ducked her head and promised to be ready, and returned to her workroom before setting off to visit Ira in his little shop.

He smiled when Abital stepped inside, but there was something tight about the way he held his jaw.

"Good afternoon, Miss." He ducked his head.

"Hello, Ira. I have a new order from the queen."

"I was able to let the trader from the coast know that I desire that sea silk, but it has not arrived."

"That is all right. She seems to have forgotten that request. She has requested red again, a deep color that will set off her coloring. But it must be finer than anything anyone has ever seen."

"That is a tall order."

"I will embroider it all over with gold thread, and sew gems into it. But I must have the most exquisite silk you can get."

Ira nodded, and then he coughed. "I understand. The thing is, Miss, there is the small issue of payment."

"Just put it on the palace's account."

Ira shifted his weight from one foot to the other. "You see, Miss, the problem is that that account has not been paid in many months. To acquire the costly silks you require, I will need the payment for the previous orders."

"What?" Abital genuinely did not understand. "You have not been paid?"

"No, Miss. And I cannot acquire more costly fabric without that money."

"I see." Abital had no idea what to do.

"Perhaps you could let the queen know, so the account can be settled?" Ira said. "Then I would happily procure the silk you require."

Abital returned to the palace, bewildered. How would she raise such an issue with the queen? She would be livid that Abital had come back without the fabric. Was there anyone else she could approach? The men who handled the palace's money would be the ones to pay the bill, but Abital did not see how she could approach them and also did not know whether they would listen to her.

Abital sent word to the queen that she needed to see her. Jezebel sent for her later that afternoon. When Abital arrived, the queen was lounging on a cushion while Mara ran a brush through her long hair, which appeared to have been freshly washed. She wore a loose robe and had a pipe resting on a table to one side. The sweet smell of opium hung in the air.

"Well, have you found the fabric?" Jezebel asked. She looked at Abital's empty hands.

"I am afraid not," Abital said. "The merchant says the bill must be paid before more fabric can be purchased."

"What?" Jezebel sat up quickly, jerking the brush out of Mara's hand. "That cannot be. Did you tell him who it was for?"

"I did, my queen. He says he cannot get more fabric until the other cloth is paid for."

Mara silently bent down and picked up the brush.

"How dare he?" Her voice was raised now. "He cannot think we will not pay. He cannot think the king does not have the money."

"I do not know," Abital said. "I only know that he would not give me more fabric until he receives payment for the others."

Jezebel let out a string of epithets and threats, saying that she would shut down Ira's business and ruin his reputation, culminating in an order for Mara to send for the man who paid the merchants in town.

"This will be taken care of," Jezebel said. "You will go back tomorrow to retrieve the fabric for my gown, and this will be settled. And you will buy twice as much while you are there."

Abital did not sleep well that night, dreading both her return to the cloth seller's shop and the visit to the temple of Baal the next day. She could not imagine wanting to take part in the rituals performed there, but she understood that the queen producing a son was all that mattered. Until she gave the king a son, her position was not secure, which meant that none of them was secure. Abital must do whatever was necessary to help the queen.

When Abital returned to the shop the next day, Ira smiled and told her that the bill had been taken care of and that she was free to select any cloth she chose for the queen's gowns. She left with two bulging bags of heavy red Damascus silk and several spools of gold thread. Ira also showed her a bolt of smooth silk the color of the night sky. It was somewhere between a dark blue and the color of obsidian. Abital knew as soon as she saw it that the queen would love it, so she bought most of the roll. She did not know what she would make for the queen yet, but she knew she would use it soon. She tucked the dark cloth away in her workroom for later and knocked on the door to Jezebel's rooms. She found the queen in high spirits once again.

"That is the most beautiful cloth yet," she said, running her fingers over the fine red silk. Emeralds gleamed on her fingers as they moved. "You must make a gown to make him forget that horse-faced little commoner."

"I will do my best."

"She will never have had so fine a gown," Jezebel said. "She is not even royalty."

"You will look stunning."

"Of course." The queen clapped her hands. "Now run and put that away. We must leave for the temple shortly."

"Yes, my queen."

Abital was not sure what to expect at the temple, but she put on her best tunic, a light yellow wool, and returned to the queen's rooms a little later to find Jezebel and Mara wearing simple shifts of light-colored linen.

"It is too late to change," Jezebel said, shaking her head. "Come on. Let us go."

Abital followed behind the queen and Mara, and Hiram the guard and a few of the maids who cleaned the rooms also came along with them. They went out the main front doors of the palace, where a carriage pulled by two horses was waiting. Jezebel climbed into the carriage and shut the door, leaving the others to walk along behind.

The temple was located not far from the palace. It stood at the edge of a square near the market. Tall white columns framed its grand entrance, and as they entered, Abital could see a large statue of a golden man with the head of a bull in the middle of the high-ceilinged main room. People bowed down before the statue, prostrating themselves before it, while men placed around the edges of the room collected the offerings worshipers had brought to plead their cases before the gods.

"Mara, you come with me," Jezebel said. Abital did not miss the look of smug satisfaction on Mara's face. "The rest of you may stay out here and pray for the king to have a son." She indicated Mara should follow her toward the closed doors at the back of the large central room. Abital did not know what was behind those doors, but given the rumors she had heard, she was grateful she did not need to see for herself.

Abital was not sure exactly what she was meant to do, but the servant girls knelt before the statue, so Abital did the same. She heard those around her offering prayers, praising Baal's power and asking for his blessing of a good harvest, of children, of health. Baal was said to be the god of thunder and rain in addition to fertility, so it seemed like just about any prayer could fit under his areas of specialty.

She gazed up at the statue of the man with a bull's head. Did this golden statue really hear their prayers? Was it truly any different from the other gods? The queen was talking about having an Asherah pole installed in another temple. Asherah too was a fertility god. How would people know which one to pray to? Were any of the gods even real?

Abital was on her knees for quite some time, and still the queen did not return. From behind the closed doors, she heard the cries of a baby, and then a lot of shouting, followed by silence. Still, the doors did not open, and the queen did not emerge. By the time Jezebel and Mara finally came out, Abital was weary and hot and hungry, and the maids had long given up praying and were gossiping outside the temple. Hiram, like Abital, was making the effort to pray, but he too looked bored and tired.

Jezebel walked toward them, her smile wide, her face triumphant. Mara's eyes were rimmed in red and the skin around them was swollen. Abital reached out a hand to Mara, but Mara pulled away and would not look at her.

Mara said nothing as they made their way back to the palace. She went directly to the queen's chambers upon their return, and Abital did not see her again until late that night, when she lowered herself onto her mat silently, long after the others were asleep.

"Are you all right, Mara?" Abital said quietly.

Mara did not answer, but by the way her shoulders shook, Abital was sure she was crying.

"Can I help?"

Mara shook her head but did not speak. Abital decided to leave her be. As she drifted off, she was grateful that she had been spared the sight of whatever had happened in that inner room.

The next morning, the haughty look was back in Mara's eyes, and when Abital went toward the kitchen, she heard Mara telling Michal what an honor it was to be close enough to the queen to be asked to be a part of the rituals.

Abital dreaded her visits to the queen's chambers, fearing she would insist on another round of sacrifices at the altar. She worked diligently for the next month, making not only a gown embroidered with gold thread and studded with sapphires and rubies but also a matching robe for the queen, trimmed in rabbit fur. It was, as promised, the most stunning gown yet.

The days shortened, the oppressive heat beginning to give way to the cooler air of the harvesttime. The wedding would take place before the beginning of the rainy season made the roads difficult to pass, and they were blessed with more fine, sunny days as the palace prepared for the wedding.

The year's harvest was not as plentiful as in most years. Summers were always hot and dry in Jezreel, so this year's streak of unbroken sunny days did not seem unusual, but it had also been a dry spring, which led to some of the plants producing smaller fruit or fewer heads of grain. The vineyards were parched, but everyone said the long hot days made for the best wine.

In the palace, there was no sign of a meager harvest. Soraya and her cooks were busily preparing a lavish wedding feast. They slaughtered a dozen sheep and roasted quail, they ground beans into a thick paste and flavored it with lemon and oil and nuts, and they gathered fresh fruit and layered it with honey and almonds. The palace was filled with delicious smells.

The party from Samaria arrived, drawing dozens of carts and wagons loaded with the new wife's things behind them. Abital stood with many of the other servants in the garden to watch as the procession approached the palace, hoping for a glimpse of the new wife, but Keziah rode inside a covered cart drawn by a donkey, while the men rode on horses. Keziah was given a suite of rooms in the palace down the hall from the queen, and there was much noise and commotion as furniture was carried in and settled into place. Several servant girls were chosen to serve the new wife, including Channah from the kitchen. Abital was pleased to see Channah elevated to serve the new wife, though Soraya stormed around banging pots and dishes for several days, bitter at having lost one of her most reliable helpers.

Jezebel spent much of the next few days in a rage, and though Abital did her best to avoid the queen, she was summoned to help the queen dress for the marriage ceremony. Jezebel complained about the fit of the gown and about how loose it was, but once she was ready, she admired her own reflection for quite some time. Then Abital walked, alongside the guard Hiram, behind the queen toward the great hall, where she was once again instructed to wait outside in case she was needed. Just before the queen went inside, Abital adjusted the back of the gown and straightened the neck.

Standing outside the hall next to the guards Hiram and Golyat and Elon, Abital could see much of the ceremony. She saw Jezebel, arresting in her low-necked gown, her glossy hair piled on her head. The gown showed off her figure, and it glistened when she moved, encrusted with gems. She was the most beautiful woman in the land, there was no doubt about it. In that way, Jezebel had achieved her aim.

Yet it was Keziah who Abital could not help gazing at. She wore a robe of deep blue, with long sleeves that covered her arms and form, and all but a few strands of her hair were tucked beneath a matching veil. She was not a great beauty—anyone would appear dull compared to Jezebel—but her smile was placid. Abital wondered what she must be feeling, knowing the character of the man she was marrying. He had a reputation for being cruel, unjust, unkind. Did Keziah know these things? How could she appear so serene, if she did?

Abital could not help but run her eyes over the gathered crowd and pick out the face of Obadiah, the handsome brother of the king's new wife. He stood tall and proud next to his father, his robe a different shade of deep blue, as they watched the wedding proceed. Abital tried not to get caught watching him again, but she could not deny the way her heart sped up each time she glanced his way.

Jezebel showed no emotion as the ceremony culminated and the feast commenced. She sat at the long table and played her part, but Abital could see that she was somewhere else in her head. She showed little relish at the food, though Abital saw her indulge in many cups of wine. She seemed to almost fade into the background—a thing Abital could not have imagined if she had not seen it herself.

Keziah, by contrast, appeared to almost glow. Before they were seated at the center of the long table, the king touched her hand tenderly, and when she looked up at him, he seemed to almost grow taller somehow.

The meal was winding down, and Abital's feet and back were aching from standing so long. Soraya had sent up bowls of soup and some bread for the staff outside the banquet, so at least she was not hungry as she watched the king begin to say goodbye to his guests, his new bride on his arm.

"Is this where you have been hiding the whole time?"

Abital looked away from the door and saw Obadiah striding up beside her. He was taller than she remembered, but even more handsome up close. He was grinning at her as he came toward her.

"I was told to stay close, in case the queen needed help with her attire," Abital said.

"I am glad. I was hoping you would be here. Our miracle worker."

She noticed that he had a small half-moon-shaped birthmark just above his jaw, and a sprinkling of freckles over his nose and cheeks.

"I cannot imagine why you would hope that. I am nothing but a servant here. I am not invited to attend such gatherings." She hated how much it thrilled her to be talking to him. He was the brother of royalty, and she was just the queen's seamstress.

"As it happens, I am nothing but a servant here as well now," he said.

"What do you mean?"

"I am to join the household of the king. I am to manage the palace."

"Manage it how?"

"The money, mostly. Perhaps oversee some of the staff. But mostly I think I will make sure the king's money is being spent wisely."

Abital could not but let out a laugh, thinking of the exorbitant sums that were spent on cloth for the queen alone. "I wish you much luck with that."

"It sounds as though you have some ideas for how to cut back."

"It is not for me to say." She had said too much already.

He gazed at her, and she feared he was going to press her for more, but instead, he said, "I am looking forward to living at the palace. I am told it is full of interesting people."

"There are plenty of characters here, if that is what you mean."

"You are funny, Abital. Did you know that?"

"I do not mean to make light, sir." She did not know what had gotten into her. She could not speak this way to a man, especially not one who now managed the palace. "The king employs many good people, and it is an honor to be counted among them."

"I am looking forward to being a servant of the king myself," he said after a pause.

Abital should not say what came into her mind next. But something about this man made her feel as though she could speak freely. "If you are to manage the king's wealth, you will hardly be a servant. You are a royal adviser. Those are not the same."

"I will be here to serve the king, the same as you serve the queen." He smiled at her. "We are the same. That means you do not need to act like you think you should not be talking to me."

"I am not—"

"You are, but it is all right," he said. "I have always appreciated a good challenge."

Abital could not help it. She laughed out loud. "You are the brother-in-law of the king. I hardly think you will have any challenge finding people who want to talk to you."

"Yes, but the problem is that I do not want to talk to most of them," he said.

She waited for him to move along to wherever he had been headed, but instead he leaned back against the wall, as if he had no intention of going anywhere. She did not know what to make of it. He was a royal adviser. He was the brother of the king's new wife. Why was he here in the hallway, talking to her, instead of enjoying the party?

For a moment, he didn't say anything, just smiled at her.

Abital felt uncomfortable with the silence. She finally asked, "Do you have much experience managing money?"

"Let's just say that I know as much about it as you know about sewing." He scratched at his sleeve absently. "That is to say, I know a lot."

"You are not shy about it, I see."

Most men would be offended at her impertinence, but this man seemed amused by it.

"It is my father's trade, and he taught me. How else would someone like me come to be here?"

"What do you mean, someone like you?"

He shrugged. "We are not royalty. Our family is not highborn. We are just simple people. The fact that I am here is almost laughable."

Simple people with a lot of money, Abital wanted to add.

"So how *did* you end up here?" Abital said instead.

"My father has worked with the king before, in Samaria. He knew the king needed help. The wars against the Assyrians and Moabites are bleeding the nation's treasuries dry. My father proposed a solution."

"Your sister."

"Keziah. She will be a good wife to the king. She is a good woman. Kind."

"She may not like it here, in that case."

"She already likes it here." He held her gaze for a moment longer than was necessary. "As do I."

"You have only just arrived."

"But so far, I am enjoying it very much." He raised an eyebrow before he pushed himself away from the wall. "Plus, living here at the palace will allow me to stay close to my sister. And she will need allies, from what I am told."

Abital chuckled but did not say anything.

"I am hopeful you will be kind to her as well," he said. "It would make me very happy if that turned out to be the case."

Abital knew he was flattering her. He knew exactly what he was doing, trying to use his wit and charm and looks to get her on his side. And even though she knew exactly what he was doing, she could not help but allow herself to believe him.

A noise from inside signaled that the king and his new bride were about to leave the great hall, and the crowd began to cheer for them. Obadiah looked inside, and then back at Abital.

"I must go," he said. "But I hope to see you around the palace."

As he walked away, Abital hoped for the same thing.

CHAPTER SEVEN

In the weeks after the marriage ceremony, Jezebel was short tempered and on edge, and Abital did her best to stay out of her way. The king, besotted with his new wife, did not send for the queen, and she took her anger and frustration out on those around her. When Mara could not get Jezebel's hair to twist the way she wanted it to, Jezebel told Mara she was thinking of replacing her. When her soup was too hot, she threw the bowl at the wall. When the king did not call her to his bed, she drank jugs of wine and smoked from the little pipe. When her monthly bleeding arrived, staining her bedsheet, she ripped the sheet in half. She gathered the prophets of Baal to insist they pray and make sacrifices. She also went to the temple of Baal regularly herself, bringing offerings and engaging in the rituals that she believed would bring her the results she desired. Abital was required to go sometimes, though she mostly spent her time in the outer part of the temple, wondering how a golden statue could possibly hear her prayers.

Several weeks after the wedding, King Ahab departed the palace, heading to Samaria and his faltering army, newly flush with money to keep them fed and advance his campaign. Abital saw the new wife around the palace in the weeks that followed, and Keziah would duck her head or say hello. She also saw Obadiah a few times, once while he was walking with a band of the king's advisers and once on his way to visit his sister in her rooms. He caught her gaze and smiled before moving on.

While the king was away, life at the palace moved more slowly. They did not have important visitors, and the great hall was largely unused. Both of the king's wives took their meals in their own rooms, and all of the king's servants could breathe easier. Even the guards laughed and chatted in the halls sometimes. But each day he was away, Jezebel seemed to grow a little more anxious. She visited the temple often and also received groups of prophets of Baal and Asherah in her rooms. These groups of men dressed in matching linen robes and wore their beards closely trimmed, and many of them had markings—bolts of thunder or the head of a bull for the prophets of Baal, serpents or a flowering tree for the followers of Asherah—inked on their arms or necks. They would not speak to or meet the eye of anyone but the queen, and none knew what happened during their visits, as the queen allowed no one else to be inside the room when they came.

Abital worked on new everyday tunics for the queen to wear around the palace, but these did not require the same amount of careful stitching as the gowns for the big feasts, and so Abital spent her time spinning and weaving woolen cloth of her own. Though she loved working with silky-smooth, costly cloth, she would always feel more at home spinning wool into fine strands and dying it herself, then weaving it into fine pieces of cloth, as she had learned to do at her imma's side. She could not collect the wool herself here, as she had done after shearing the sheep she'd tended when she was a child. Instead, she bought the wool from a man who kept his flock in the hills outside Jezreel, and she carded it, dyed it, and spun it herself, letting her fingers feel when the thread was the right thickness. When she worked this way, she remembered the long days spent with her imma, learning from her how to know when the thread was just the right thickness, was just taut enough, was just smooth enough. No one could match the fine feel of Imma's soft yarn, nor the smooth feel of the cloth she wove, but Abital had learned as much as she could.

The days were cool now, shorter, and though the rainy season should have begun, Jezreel was still enjoying days of unbroken sunshine. The farmers waited to plant their beans and grains, hoping for the cool wet days that would allow their seeds to sprout, but few in the palace minded the extra days of sunshine.

At the beginning of the month of Tebet, the king returned to the palace, and the queen dressed with great care, making sure to always appear in her most flattering attire. During the days, she would walk through the palace garden or sit on her balcony, looking out over the city. She would often press Abital into coming to talk to her about the clothing she desired, describing gowns she had imagined and robes she dreamed of. She wanted a gown that fit tightly but had wide sleeves, and a robe trimmed in fur that had been dyed many colors, like a rainbow. Each garment she imagined was more outlandish than the next. Abital promised she would do her best, though part of her wondered if the queen even really wanted such things or was merely bored.

Some days, the nursemaids brought Jezebel's daughter, Athalia, to see her mother, and Jezebel was usually delighted to see her, at least for a few moments. The little girl toddled around, playing on the cushions and reaching for the statues that decorated the room. Jezebel would send Athalia and her nursemaids away when the child grew fussy or when she threatened to break one of the many treasures placed around the chambers.

Most nights, Abital helped her into one of her silky nightgowns, and Jezebel sipped wine while she waited to be called to the king's chambers. Sometimes she would insist that Abital and Mara wait with her. On some nights when they stayed, she ignored them and gazed at her reflection in the mirror. At other times, after several cups of wine, she would tell Abital and Mara stories of her childhood in Sidon, a large city in Phoenicia. She spoke once of the time the invaders from the North had come, trying to take the capital for themselves. Jezebel told them how she had hidden, along with her sisters, among the king's robes in his chests, and how they had cowered as soldiers found their mother and attacked her, and how much she had feared they would find them as well. Jezebel never spoke of these things unless she had consumed many glasses of wine, but while it seemed to give her no pleasure to do so now, she told them anyway.

On some nights, she asked Abital or Mara to tell her stories, and Abital would tell her about her life back in Napoth Dor, about growing up in a house surrounded by hills where her saba's sheep roamed.

"You were a shepherdess?" Jezebel had been plaiting a section of her hair but stopped, gazing at Abital. The disdain on her face was evident.

"No, my grandfather hired men to keep watch over the sheep. I really only saw them when it was shearing time. Then I would help my imma load up donkeys with the food and other supplies, and we would feed the workers as they sheared the sheep, and then Mother brought the wool back. She had grown up in that house as well, and it was she who taught me how to clean the wool and dye it, and spin it and weave it."

"Your mother worked for the late king's wife, did she not?"

"She did, my queen." When King Omri passed away and the new king had married Jezebel, four years ago, her imma had gotten her the position sewing for the new queen.

"Was your mother as good at sewing as you are?"

"Better. She taught me everything I know."

"How did a shepherdess become seamstress for the queen?"

Abital ignored the barb. "My imma did not much care for life on the farm, as it turned out." She did not want to elaborate and did not see what good it would do to tell more of the story, but Mara piped up.

"It is said that she ran off with a soldier."

Trust Mara to bring up Abital's deepest shame and mention it before the queen.

"Did she, Abital?" Jezebel asked, eyebrow cocked.

"She did." There was no point in lying. It was known by many.

"My abba was from a neighboring village, and he died of a sickness when I was very young. My imma returned to her family when he passed away. Many years later, when the king's army camped in the area, my imma fell in love with one of the high-ranking soldiers. He spoke to the commander and got her a place at the palace, sewing clothes for the queen."

"That must have been quite a scandal." The idea seemed to delight the queen.

"I suppose it was," Abital said.

"I grew up in this palace," Mara said, a bit too loudly. She pointedly turned away from Abital. "My family has always served the king. My father was one of the first to move from the capital in Samaria to here when King Omri built his palace in Jezreel."

Abital knew this history made Mara feel important, but Abital did not see why. They were both servants. Neither had a better place.

The king did not send for Jezebel that night, but he did the next. While Abital adjusted the dressing gown, Mara touched up the curls in the queen's hair, and then Jezebel made her way to the king's chambers.

Jezebel was in better spirits the next day, and when the king called for her for a few nights after that, some of her anger seemed to drain away. But soon the king returned once again to Samaria, and when Jezebel bled once again, she lay in bed for three days. She refused to leave her chambers, short-tempered with everyone who tried to help her.

The days were dark and cold. Each day, Abital looked to the sky, hoping to see clouds gathered on the horizon, but no snow fell, nor rain. There was talk of another sacrifice to Baal. Perhaps the god was angry and needed to be appeased before he would send rain.

Abital did not notice at first, but she soon began to hear the servant girls complain about the meals coming from the kitchen. There was little meat these days, and the portions of lentils and flatbread they received were smaller. The bread was served dry, with no oil.

"It cannot be helped," Soraya said. "It is that new man in charge of the money. The brother of the new wife. He says I cannot have the things I need to feed the palace well. He says I must do more with less."

"Why would he do that?" Obadiah did not seem like a man who liked to make others suffer.

"Selfish, if you ask me," Soraya said. "Wants more for himself, so there is less for everyone else."

"He is getting more?"

"Him and his sister, no doubt." Soraya sniffed.

Abital did not see why she should not believe her. Soraya knew everything that went on at this palace, and if she said it was so, she was no doubt right.

One morning, early in the month of Adar, in the coldest part of the year, Channah came to Abital's workroom and knocked on the door. Abital looked up from the loom, the same one her imma had brought from home and had used for so many years before her.

"Miss, Keziah would like to see you," Channah said.

In the months since Channah had been serving the new wife, she appeared to have grown, both in stature and in confidence. She no longer avoided the gaze of all who spoke with her, and her cheeks were fuller, her eyes brighter.

"What does she want?" Abital asked.

"I do not know, only that she asked that I summon you," Channah said.

Abital set down the piece of wood the wool was wrapped around, and she stood up, brushed off her tunic, and followed Channah upstairs.

"You look well," Abital said as they walked along the long marble hallway.

"Keziah is kind to me," Channah said.

"I am glad." Abital remembered Jezebel throwing her dish of soup at the wall but quickly pushed the image out of her mind.

When they got to the door of Keziah's rooms, Channah knocked gently.

"Come in."

Channah pushed open the door and led Abital inside. The room faced the valley, giving a view of the plains just outside the city and the rows of hills beyond. A fire roared in the hearth, chasing away the winter's chill. The room was furnished simply, with a few heavy pieces of wooden furniture and a sleeping mat. The cushions looked soft and plush but were covered in a simple linen. There were no altars and none of the golden accents that made the queen's room so decadent.

"Good afternoon, Abital." Keziah was seated on a cushion, working with a needle and thread on a piece of linen. Her curly hair hung loose around her shoulders.

Keziah set the linen and the needle and thread aside. "Come in. Have a seat." She gestured to the cushion across from her.

Abital hesitated. What was she asking her to do? Abital could not sit with her, as if she were a friend.

"Oh. I see." Keziah's cheeks reddened. "I have put you in an uncomfortable position. I am sorry. I am not used to the rules of the palace. Would it be better if I stood?"

"No—I mean, you must stay comfortable. I will stand."

"Do not be silly. These rules are ridiculous." Keziah pushed herself up. "Come. We can sit at the table. You will sit with me there, will you not?"

Abital did not move. Did Keziah really mean for her to sit with her? She glanced back at Channah, who gestured toward the table subtly.

"I feel awkward having you stand while I talk to you, and I cannot stand for too long without feeling sick, so you would be doing me a favor to sit with me." Keziah walked to the table and pulled out first one chair, then the other, and lowered herself into one.

"Are you ill, my lady?"

"Not ill, exactly," Keziah said. She indicated for Abital to sit in the other seat. "That is why I asked you here, actually. It seems I am to have a baby."

Abital gasped. "That is wonderful news." Abital did feel a thrill of excitement and genuine joy at hearing the announcement. Another child for the king was great news for the kingdom. However, she could not help but feel a stab of worry about what would happen when the queen found out. "It happened so quickly. You are very lucky."

"I am pleased, of course. I have always wanted to be a mother. Yahweh has blessed me indeed."

"When will the child be born?"

"Sometime this summer."

Channah placed mugs of mint tea in front of both of them. Abital dared not touch it, and looked up at Channah, narrowing her eyes. Channah simply smiled in return.

"Thank you, Channah." Keziah turned back to Abital. "Please, drink it. You are my guest." Keziah sipped her own tea. "It settles my stomach. I have been drinking it constantly."

Wisps of steam curled up from the surface of the tea.

"The thing is, I brought many items of clothing to my marriage, and I was thinking they would last me much longer than it seems they will." Keziah took another sip. "I thought to ask my father to send the seamstress from Samaria to come here to help me, but my brother says there is no money to have two seamstresses here at the palace. And besides, she is not half as good as you are."

Abital looked over Keziah's loose robe. It was made of very fine linen, though it was a plain flax color. Even though it was big on her, Abital could see that it was tighter across the chest than her clothing had been a few weeks ago. "That is loose enough that it will last you for a while."

"It will indeed, but I like to plan ahead. I wanted to ask if you would be able to help me with some clothes that will fit me as I grow larger."

"I—"

Abital broke off. Could she? She answered to the queen, not to the second wife. Didn't she? Would Jezebel allow it? And yet, how could Abital say no?

"My brother has spoken with the king, and he is very eager to see this happen," Keziah said. "He said I should ask you to help me."

If that was true, then there was nothing wrong with saying yes. It sounded as though she didn't have a choice anyway. Keziah was framing it as a choice to be kind, but if the king had already approved of the arrangement, there was nothing else to be done.

"If you fear you will not have the time, please say so. I know the queen asks a lot of you, and I do not want you to suffer."

Abital would have to use her time wisely, but she knew she could manage the work. That was not her concern. But truth be told, after only a few moments in Keziah's chambers, Abital found that she wanted to say yes. Though these rooms were less grand than the queen's, they felt warm and welcoming, and Keziah had a spirit of peace about her that Abital had never felt before in this palace.

"It would be a great honor. Of course I will, my lady."

"Thank you."

"What kind of clothing would you like me to make?"

"I do not need anything elaborate. Just some simple shifts that will fit me as I grow."

"You will want fine cloth, though. Maybe wool for the rest of the chilly season and then silk as the days heat up and your time grows closer."

"I do not need silk, at least not for most things. Perhaps if there is a banquet, but for most days, linen is just fine."

She did not want silk? She preferred linen?

"Then we will make sure you have the finest linen in the land. What colors do you prefer? I know where to get the most wonderful red. That blue you wore when you first came to the palace was very becoming as well, or—"

"When I am to see the king, I want to wear the deep colors he prefers, but for most days, there is no need for costly dyes."

Abital felt her mouth fall open, and she closed it quickly.

"And since I will be growing, there is no need for the fit to be tight. I will be much more comfortable with something loose that lets the air in."

It was as though she wanted her style to be different from the queen's in every way. But it did not sound like she was doing so from spite or malice, but genuine desire.

"I am told you are the one who typically chooses the cloth—that you buy it from a shop in town or weave it yourself," Keziah said.

"Yes, that is right." Abital nodded.

"My brother has asked that I have you choose less costly materials, if that can be done. Will that be all right?"

"I—" Everything about this conversation made Abital feel that the ground under her feet had shifted.

"You will let me know what you need, and I will make sure you have it, though," Keziah added.

"Yes, my lady," Abital said.

"That is good. Thank you, Abital."

Abital started to push herself up, but as she did, Keziah spoke.

"Are you happy here, Abital?"

"Happy, my lady?"

"Do you enjoy living here at the palace? Sewing for the queen?"

"I am grateful for the opportunity, my lady."

"That is not what I asked. I asked if you were happy here."

"I suppose so."

"Where did you live before this?"

"My lady?"

"You did not grow up at the palace, I am sure."

Despite herself, Abital was curious. "How can you know that, my lady?"

Keziah smiled. "You are kind. You do not spend your days trying to raise your own stature. You do not exaggerate or tell lies to advance your position."

Keziah was speaking plainly, so Abital decided to do the same. "How could you know that, my lady?"

"I pay attention. I see things," Keziah said. She wrapped her hands around the cup. "And, if I am to be truly honest, I also asked others." She nodded to the corner, where Channah was using a cloth to clean dust off the cabinet where Keziah's clothing was kept. "Channah says you can be trusted to not use my request as a reason to cause trouble with the queen."

"I will not, my lady."

"Thank you. I do not wish to upset her." She took a sip of the drink. "My guess is that you are not from one of the cities."

"No, my lady, I am not. I am from outside Napoth Dor, in the hill country near the coast."

"How did you come from the hill country to the palace, Abital?"

"My saba raised sheep, and I learned to spin and weave the wool before I could walk."

"Who taught you?"

"My imma. She was a skilled weaver and could make cloth finer and smoother than any in the land. She taught me to do the same. She also could sew with the finest stitches and make the most beautiful garments. She taught me that as well, before she got a place at the palace. Then she moved here and sewed clothes for the former queen."

"She left her husband and family behind?"

"My abba had passed away many years before," Abital said. She would not share the full story. "I stayed with my saba at the farm."

"And where is your imma now?"

"I am sorry to say she passed away too." Abital did not relish telling the story, so she said, "When King Omri passed away and

King Ahab took the throne, she suggested the palace hire me to sew for the new queen."

"Why did your mother not take on that role? Why did she not sew for Jezebel?"

"Dinah—King Ahab's mother—did not want to let her go. She did not like the new king's wife and did not want to share."

"No, I suppose one would not want to share," Keziah said. "I am surprised you were allowed to come to the palace, a young woman like you."

"Like me?"

"A beautiful woman, and a clever one. Of the age to be married. Your grandfather did not want to arrange a marriage for you?'

"He was in conversation with a few families in the area. But when the king sent for me, he did not exactly have much choice. You do not say no to the king."

"No, I suppose you do not," Keziah said. "You worked at the palace with your mother, then?"

"For a few months."

"What happened?"

Abital willed herself to keep her feelings down.

"The fever came that winter and took her, along with Dinah and many others in the king's household."

It was hard to think back on that terrible time, when so many had become sick and perished, and all were afraid they might be next. There seemed to be no pattern in who got sick and who didn't. Abital knew she was lucky to have been spared, though it had not felt so when she lost her imma.

"I am so sorry."

"The gods were not to be satisfied that year. So many were lost."

Keziah took a long drink from her cup. "Which gods did people offer sacrifices to?"

Abital did not know how to respond. She remembered that Keziah was loyal to Yahweh—did Keziah wish her to talk about Yahweh? But she had praised Abital for speaking the truth previously. "To all of them, my lady. To Yahweh and to the gods the queen brought with her when she came to the palace."

"Baal?"

"And Asherah."

Keziah adjusted in her chair. "I did not think I would ever see these false gods openly worshiped in Israel."

Abital did not know what to say. How to respond.

"What do you think, Abital?"

"About the gods?"

Keziah nodded.

"I do not know."

"Do you believe in the power of Baal and of Asherah?"

What did belief have to do with it? The gods just were, and people did their best to appease them. It did not matter what she thought about them.

"We served Yahweh at my saba's house," Abital said, hoping this was what Keziah wanted to hear. "I was raised to serve Yahweh."

"And now?"

Abital decided once again to speak truthfully. "My imma served whichever gods would help her get what she wanted. There are many gods worshiped at the palace. I saw that my imma worshiped Baal, along with Yahweh. She told me that the king would not worship other gods if they were not important."

"And do you agree with that sentiment?"

It felt like she was failing some sort of test. "I do not know, my lady."

Keziah looked as though she was far away for a moment. "The king is but a man," she finally said. "A powerful man, but he does not make gods true or false. He allows the worship of them, or he does not. And he has allowed great wickedness by letting false gods into the kingdom."

It did not sound as though she expected a reply from Abital, and in any case, Abital did not know what to say.

"Yahweh will not be mocked," Keziah said. "The One True God of Israel will make His name known in all the land."

"Yes, my lady," Abital said, to end the awkward silence that stretched out.

Just then, a knock sounded on the door.

"That will be my brother," Keziah said. "He comes to see me most days around this time."

"Yes, my lady." Abital stood just as Channah opened the door to allow Obadiah to step in. He grinned when he saw Abital.

"I am sorry, sister. I did not know you had a visitor." But he did not look sorry at all. Instead, he smiled as though he had a secret he could not wait to share. She could not help but notice how good his robe looked on him, the way it cinched in where it tied at the waist made his shoulders appear broad and strong.

"Abital has agreed to help me," Keziah said.

"I am glad." Obadiah smiled at Keziah. "My sister needs as much help as she can get."

"He thinks he is funny," Keziah said.

"I am happy to help, my lord, and so very glad for the good news that requires my help." Abital started to walk toward the door. "Thank you for the tea, my lady."

"Thank you for talking with me," Keziah said. "I find it can get lonely here in the palace, and I am always grateful to have visitors."

Abital was hardly a visitor. She was a servant, called here at the request of the king's wife. But she could not say so, and indeed she could see that Keziah truly meant what she said. It did not feel like the times when the queen demanded Mara and Abital tell her stories, as if they were there to entertain her. Instead, it had seemed as though Keziah truly did want to know about her and her thoughts.

"I hope we will be seeing more of you," Obadiah said, ducking his head as she headed for the door. As she walked past him, Abital felt his eyes on her, and she looked up at him, meeting his eyes for one long moment, before she tore her gaze away and kept walking.

All the way back to her workroom and as she worked, she replayed the strange encounter in her mind, trying to make sense of the ideas Keziah had spoken. She did not know whether the new wife was right or was speaking heresies. All Abital knew was that she wanted to hear more.

CHAPTER EIGHT

The winter turned to spring, and still no rain came. There was great consternation and much hand-wringing among the king's advisers, but the queen redoubled her efforts at pleasing the god Baal, who controlled not only fertility but also the rain and thunder. She ordered that all in the kingdom were to offer prayers and sacrifices to the god. Abital complied, but she didn't stop thinking about what Keziah had said. Was Yahweh the One True God? Were the sacrifices to Baal and Asherah worthless?

A letter from Saba reported that the year's lambs were fewer in number, and the ewes had a hard time producing enough milk to feed them. The lack of rain had dried up most of the grass they could eat. The garden too was struggling. He hoped they would not have to kill one of the sheep so they would have mutton to eat. Saba also reported that he was in talks with Gershom, a man from the village, about a potential marriage for Abital to his son Ezra. Abital remembered Ezra as a skinny little boy who said little, and her heart sank.

Though the skies remained clear, things were stormy inside the palace. Abital knew the moment she stepped into the queen's rooms one morning that Jezebel had learned of Keziah's pregnancy. Several of the jade figurines lay in pieces on the floor, and a shattered plate and cup were left by the wall, where she had thrown them. A greasy stain showed where the remains of her food had fallen. A pitcher of wine sat empty.

"My queen?" Abital said, stepping into the room.

The queen lay on her sleeping mat, facedown, all of her blankets on the floor beside her. She did not move, though she muttered for Abital to leave the gown she had brought and go. Several days passed before she moved from her bed, and when she finally did, she snapped at everyone who tried to bring her food or comfort.

Abital spent as much time as she could in her workroom, away from the noise and chaos of the queen. She wove cloth of the lightest, finest wool, and also visited Ira, who was surprised to see her choose plain linen over the more costly cloth she normally purchased.

"The new wife does not need such fine things," Abital said.

"That is good for the king's money counters but not so good for me." He grinned.

While Abital worked on new shifts for Keziah, Jezebel redoubled her efforts to catch the attention of the king. She demanded a new set of tunics and robes, which she wanted to have lower necklines and fit her more tightly than before. Abital cut and sewed the fine cloth, and she marveled at how different the gowns of the king's two wives were.

A week later, Abital sent word that she had finished the first tunic, and Keziah summoned her to bring it. When Channah admitted her to the chamber, she found the king's second wife reading from her scrolls again, and this time, her brother sat across from her, also looking at a piece of parchment.

"Oh. I am sorry. I did not mean to intrude—"

"Do not be silly. You are not interrupting." Keziah rubbed her belly with one hand as she held the parchment with the other. She set the scroll down, and Obadiah lifted his head and smiled at her as well. There appeared to be genuine warmth in his eyes.

"It is good to see you again, Abital." He lowered his gaze to the ground and then back up again. Abital was unsettled. She was not used to finding men in the wives' rooms. This was Keziah's brother, and there could be nothing untoward about that, but she was not sure how to behave in his presence. She felt her palms start to sweat and her heart beat a bit faster. But he smiled and said, "I am sorry to cause you extra work. We did not expect my sister would outgrow her wedding clothes so quickly."

"It is very good that she has," Abital said. "A child for the king is wonderful news."

"Yes, it is." He set his scroll on the table. "And we are both glad you were able to help her."

"I am eager to see what you have made," Keziah said.

"Here, please set that down." Obadiah moved the scrolls aside and cleared off a spot on the table. As Abital stepped forward to rest the bag on the table, she saw again that the parchments were covered with Hebrew letters.

"I do not know if this is what you were hoping for," Abital said, pulling the simple linen sheath out of the burlap bag. "If it is too plain—"

She held the shift up and let it unfurl.

Keziah stepped forward and touched it softly. She used two fingers to rub the fabric. "It is perfect," she said. "It will last me until the child is born." She stepped back and examined the garment, feeling the weave of its cloth. "It is very nice fabric, and cleverly sewn."

"If it pleases, I will make more like it," Abital said.

"Well done, Abital," Obadiah said. "You are indeed as clever with the needle as they say."

Abital felt the praise was unnecessary, as it was by far the simplest garment she had made since coming to the palace. But she couldn't deny the pleasure his words gave her.

"My brother is mostly pleased that the fabric did not cost the treasury dearly," Keziah said with a laugh.

"I know little about clothing," Obadiah admitted. "I wear what my sister tells me to. But I do know that if she is pleased, I am as well. And"—he turned to his sister with a smile on his face—"yes, it does not hurt that it is not made of silk imported from the East. Many farmers have no plants in the fields. They do not have enough to eat or to sell. Many people are suffering. When so many in the kingdom are hungry, it is hard to justify spending so much on one garment."

"The queen does not see it that way, unfortunately."

"There are many things the queen and I disagree on." Obadiah looked as though he wanted to say more, but he did not. But then he added, "If he wanted to, the king could stop it, but he is too interested in maintaining his own comfort, never mind that his citizens have less and less to give."

"Brother." Keziah cleared her throat.

"Why does he not stop it?" Obadiah repeated.

Keziah did not respond. Abital dared not speak.

"He does not believe me," Keziah said. "It is not that I have not tried."

"You must try harder. People are suffering."

"I know. Do you think I am not trying? You know how unreasonable he is." She took in a breath. "I will keep trying."

"How can he just close his eyes, even after he was warned?" Obadiah said.

"I am doing my best." There was an edge to Keziah's voice, one Abital had not heard before. For a moment, they seemed to have forgotten that Abital was there, and she had the sense she was witnessing a conversation the brother and sister had had many times before. "He does not believe what I say about Elijah. He does not think Yahweh is behind the drought."

"You must convince him. You must—" Obadiah was about to say more, but a cough from the corner, where Channah stood, appeared to remind him they were not alone. He sighed, turned to Abital, and said, "I am sorry. We should not be saying such things."

"You are talking about Elijah, the man who interrupted the feast of the dedication of the new temple?" Abital said.

"We are not talking about anything. Please—" Keziah stepped forward. "My brother forgets himself. Do not listen to us."

"My sister is right," Obadiah said, turning to face Abital now. "Please, forget what you have heard. It means nothing."

Abital knew it did not mean nothing, but she did not know what it did mean.

"You do wonderful work," Keziah said, holding up the new gown again. "I am most grateful to you."

"I will make you more."

"I am most grateful. Thank you, Abital." Keziah rubbed her hand over her belly. "I am so glad we can trust you."

Abital understood that Keziah was asking her to keep the conversation she'd just heard private. Abital nodded, but her mind was swirling. As she walked back to her rooms, she replayed the conversation in her mind. Was the drought truly the result of the madman who had rushed into the feast at the opening of the temple? But how could that be possible? He was nothing but a crazed lunatic, who had somehow pushed his way into the banquet. The idea that he could have been telling the truth in his warning—

It wasn't possible. He'd claimed to be a prophet of Yahweh, but none of the prophets of Yahweh knew him. He'd vanished, and no one knew where. And even if he did speak for Yahweh—which Abital was fairly certain he did not—the Hebrew god was only one of the many worshiped in the kingdom today.

No, Abital could not believe it. They had been offering sacrifices to Baal because he alone controlled the rain.

But if Keziah and Obadiah were right—if what they had suggested was true—then Yahweh was to blame for this drought. Could the god of David, of Moses, of Abraham have caused it?

And, if so, why would anyone want to worship such a god?

CHAPTER NINE

The month of Iyar brought warmer days, with more hours of light and more sunshine. Most years, the palace would be gifted with a portion of the bountiful harvest of grains and beans raised by farmers throughout the land, but this year, the spring harvest was scant, and the meals at the palace became more meager as well. Meat appeared only once a week, and most days there was scarcely enough oil made from olives to flavor the smaller portions of bread they were given.

Many blamed Obadiah, who oversaw the whole palace and approved what was spent. Some of the maids grew to resent him, believing he was cutting back on their food so he could have more for himself. But Abital had a hard time believing this, and in her own mind, she wondered if Elijah could be right and this was all the fault of Yahweh.

Each time she ventured to the kitchens and spoke to Soraya, the cook bemoaned the quantity and quality of ingredients she was given to work with and the scarcity of flour and oil. She did not care who was responsible, only that she was not able to make food that lived up to her standards.

Still, a feast was ordered on the anniversary of the dedication of the temple of Baal. Abital sewed a new gown for the queen, made of the midnight-colored cloth she had bought from Ira. Jezebel insisted her household join her to make offerings at the temple. In her excitement during the sacrifice, the queen had torn her gown, and she'd changed into a dark red gown for the feast she held for the wealthy and important in Jezreel to celebrate one year of Baal's goodness to Israel. Abital could not see what goodness he had brought to the land. The god who controlled the thunder had not made it rain, and in his role as god of fertility, he had not made the queen conceive. She could not understand what exactly Jezebel was thanking him for.

Tensions between the king's wives continued to grow as well.

"I saw the king's second wife last evening," Jezebel said one morning as soon as Abital was admitted to her chambers. On this day she wore a wine-red gown with puffed sleeves and a cord made of golden silk thread. It was one of the new garments Abital had made for the queen, based on her specifications. The dark gown was still in Abital's workroom while she repaired it.

Jezebel seeing Keziah should not have been notable, given that both sets of rooms branched off from the same hallway, but Jezebel went out of her way to avoid running into the new wife. She would have Mara make sure the hallways were clear before venturing out, so as to avoid seeing Keziah and her belly, which was growing rounder with each day. "She was wearing a new tunic, one I had not seen before."

Abital knew better than to speak but waited for Jezebel to go on. In the corner of the room, Mara was watching, a smug smile on her face.

"I did not understand where she would have gotten such a thing, since she brought all her clothing with her to her marriage. She was not to have needed more for some time."

Abital could see clearly what the queen was suggesting with this, but Abital reminded herself that the king had told Keziah to ask Abital for help. She could not be in trouble for simply following the orders she had been given.

"I am told you have been spotted coming into and out of Keziah's rooms, sometimes with garments in your arms."

"Yes, my queen."

"Have you made new tunics for her?"

Everything in her wanted to deny it, to spare herself the wrath of the queen, which she was certain would follow her admission, but she knew she must tell the truth.

"Yes, my queen. The king's second wife called me to her chambers and told me the king had said she should ask me for help. Her clothing did not fit, not with her pregnancy, and she needed new clothing."

"You work for me, not for the new wife."

"I was told the king had ordered it, my queen."

"The king would do no such thing. He knows that I need you."

Abital was not sure what the queen wanted her to say. Whatever she said, it would not cool the anger that marred Jezebel's features now.

"I do not know. I have only done what I was ordered. Perhaps the king would tell you if he did so or not?"

Jezebel looked as though she was going to argue. She opened her mouth but then closed it again and turned for the door. "Yes, let us go talk to the king," Jezebel said. "Come, Abital. We will ask him to make it clear once and for all that you will not do work for that peasant."

"My queen?"

"Come." And then, when Abital's feet remained firmly rooted to the floor, she continued, "Did you not hear me? Let us go."

She could not be serious. She planned to go, unannounced, to confront the king? And she wanted Abital to come with her? She could do no such thing.

But she was doing so, it seemed. Jezebel was already walking toward the door, and it appeared she fully expected Abital to follow her.

"Well?" Mara hissed from the corner. "Go!"

Abital did not know why these words from Mara were the thing that finally made her feet move, but she suddenly found she was hurrying to catch up with the queen, who stormed down the hallway. The queen did not actually intend to approach the king, unbidden, did she? To confront him about his other wife?

"Are you sure you—"

"You will come, and you will keep your mouth shut, if you wish to remain at the palace," Jezebel hissed.

Abital quickened her pace and followed Jezebel out of the wing of the palace where the women lived and into the far side, toward the rooms belonging to the king. Jezebel greeted the stunned guards, who appeared frozen, unsure if they should stop her. Jezebel pressed forward, and Abital followed in her wake.

Abital had never been to this part of the palace, and even in her confusion and anxiety, she marveled at the highly polished marble floors, the walls hung with intricately woven tapestries, and the gilt trimmings.

Jezebel walked to the double doors at the end of the hallway, which were flanked by another set of guards.

"The king is in a meeting with his advisers, my queen," said one guard, but Jezebel did not listen. She reached for the handle and pushed the door open.

"My queen—"

"Come!" she said to Abital just before she stepped inside. Abital followed her into a large room that opened on a balcony that looked out over the entire Jezreel valley. Pictures of men in military garb had been painted on the walls and ceilings, but most of the room was taken up by a long wooden table, around which were seated more than a dozen of the king's advisers. Abital recognized two of his top military commanders, as well as the man who managed the citizens of Jezreel. Obadiah was there too, and she saw not just confusion but concern on his face when he realized who had entered the room. The king, seated at one end of the long table, rose.

Abital bent her knees and ducked her head, and then she stayed behind the queen. Jezebel hesitated and then reluctantly bowed to show the king respect.

Abital could not believe she was here. She did not want to be here. One did not simply approach the king, and one certainly did not storm into his rooms in the middle of a meeting of his top advisers. Everything in her told her to turn and run, before she was cut down alongside the queen, but she found she was frozen. She was not sure which she feared more, the wrath of the queen or the judgment of the king, who was known for his quick temper and cruel punishments. Either way, Abital was sure this would be her last day at the palace.

"My queen," the king said. "We are in the middle of a—"

"Have you told the second wife that my servant will make clothing for her?" The queen's voice echoed around the now-silent room.

She had interrupted the king, on top of everything else. How would he respond to this?

"This is not a matter of such importance that—"

"Have you told the second wife that my seamstress will make clothing for her as well? When you know full well that she works only for me?"

It was then that the king seemed to notice Abital, hanging back. He ducked his head, and she did not detect anger or malice in his eyes, simply confusion. Then he turned his attention to the queen.

At first, Abital wasn't sure if he was going to throw them both out without another word. The king looked as if he was not sure himself. The faces that gazed at him from all around the table betrayed confusion. The king did not speak for a moment, and Abital held her breath. Then, slowly, he said, "I am told you have the best seamstress in the land right here at the palace. You always have the most beautiful clothing, my queen, so I know this to be true. Keziah needs new clothing now."

"Then she can hire her own seamstress."

Abital had never heard of anyone speaking like this to the king. Surely he would not stand for it.

"With this drought, there is less money coming in than expected," King Ahab said, as though unbothered. "We all must find ways to economize. There is no reason she cannot make outfits for both of you."

"My maid works for me, not for her. She will not make any more dresses for that peasant."

There was no sound in the room. Each man around the table seemed to be holding his breath. One did not speak to the king that way. Arguing with the king—especially in front of others—was suicide.

But the king did not order Jezebel to be taken away, nor did he tell her to watch the way she spoke to him, though all knew he would have been within his rights to do so.

"Your seamstress works for the palace. She works for me." His tone was even, his voice calm. "Step forward, maid. What is your name?"

Abital felt cold liquid course through her body. Her stomach turned, and her knees grew weak. But she forced herself to stand and to answer.

"My name is Abital, my king."

She would be sent home for certain. People like her did not speak to the king.

"Abital, will you make gowns for my new wife as well as your queen?"

What was she to say? It was an impossible question. If she said no, she was defying the king. If yes, she would anger the queen. She wished for nothing but for the ground to give way so she could disappear. She cast her gaze around the room, searching for any clue as to how she should answer, and caught the eye of Obadiah, who did not look away from her but nodded slightly. She did not know what he was trying to tell her, only that his unabashed gaze gave her courage to speak.

"I will do whatever my king commands of me," Abital said, trying to keep her voice even.

The king lifted his chin, and when he looked at her again, he appeared to really see her for the first time. She felt his eyes travel from her face to her form, lingering perhaps too long before he gazed back up at her eyes again.

"Then you will serve both of my wives," he said evenly. He gave her one last long look before he turned back to Jezebel. The queen was standing perfectly still, her fists curled, her breaths low and long. "Now, please leave us to our meeting."

Jezebel appeared as though she would speak out once again. The queen did not like to lose, especially not in front of others. But after a moment, she spun around, her robes flying out around her, and stormed out. Her footsteps echoed on the polished floor as she raced for the door.

Abital ducked her head once more before she followed the queen out of the room. She was sure Jezebel would not simply accept the king's decision. She did not know what the queen would do, but she was certain there would be consequences.

She discovered Jezebel's horrible plan for retribution a few days later, when Abital walked into the queen's chambers and found dozens of the prophets of Baal and Asherah gathered. Abital had finished a new day tunic of light purple silk trimmed in silver thread, and Jezebel had requested she bring it as soon as she had finished. Abital knocked gently on the door of the queen's chambers, but there was no answer. She heard voices inside, however, and so she quietly pushed the door open. Mara was nowhere to be seen, but the queen was seated on cushions, surrounded by the prophets.

"—must rid the land of their evil influence," Jezebel was saying. Abital stood by the door, not wanting to interrupt the meeting.

"My queen, how can we do such a thing?" one of the prophets asked. He had a long black beard and a picture of a bull inked on his bald head. "You cannot ask this of us."

"I will ask what I want, and you will do as I say, if you want to continue to live and eat without cost. The king has said we must cut back. Fewer prophets would be a boon to the palace's coffers," Jezebel said.

"The prophets of Yahweh are wily," a second one said. This man had long dark hair that hung in lank strings, and he wore the snake, the symbol of the goddess Asherah, on his arm. "They will fight back."

"Then you must attack them before they attack you," Jezebel said. "You must find the right men for this task."

"We do not like these Yahwists any more than you do," the first said. "They are proud, believing they serve the only true god, as if Baal does not help them as well."

"Asherah as well," said the second. "But I do not see how having them all killed will help Israel."

"If it is true that their god is responsible for withholding rain from the kingdom, killing the Lord's prophets will send a message to Yahweh," Jezebel said.

"You cannot threaten a god," the first said. "You must appease them."

"You can appease a god only if you believe he has power," Jezebel said. "Which this one does not. Getting rid of Yahweh's prophets will show to all of Israel that this god has no power over them."

"Is it right to shed blood for this?" the second one asked.

"Ushmuel," Jezebel said, "I have witnessed the ways you quench Baal's insatiable hunger for blood. Do not try to tell me that you have a conscience about taking a life now."

Ushmuel argued that ritual sacrifice was another matter entirely from the wholesale slaughter of Yahweh's prophets. He insisted that the children offered to Baal were lowborn—throwaways—and they were given a great honor in their sacrifice. The other prophets insisted that ignoring Yahweh's prophets was the best way to keep them from gaining power, and that offering sacrifices to Baal and Asherah was the way out of the dilemma. They argued that if Yahweh was indeed the reason for the drought, angering Him by dispatching His prophets would not help. But the queen did not listen.

The prophets did not sway Jezebel, as Abital knew they would not. They could not, for Jezebel's desire had nothing to do with ending the drought in Israel but with punishing the king's new wife, whose loyalty to Yahweh was well known. Jezebel, Abital saw, believed that in eliminating the prophets of Yahweh, she would be hurting Keziah, in some twisted kind of payback.

"You will go now. It will happen tonight. Find as many as you can and kill them."

Abital knew the queen wanted to see her. She knew that as soon as Jezebel had dismissed the prophets, she would be looking for Abital. But Abital did not think the queen had yet noticed she was in the room. She had been so absorbed in her arguments with the prophets that she had not turned toward the door, where Abital hovered. Abital weighed her options for a moment. If the queen had seen her, she would know that Abital had overheard the plot. But if she had not seen Abital standing here, Abital might be able to slip out, to send the warning before it was too late. It was a very big gamble. Surely if she was caught, Abital would not merely be dismissed from the palace. She would be killed, as surely as the prophets of Yahweh would be. But if she did nothing—

She could not bear the thought. The mention of the children sacrificed to Baal was a terrible reminder of what this queen and her gods required. She could not stop the slaughter of innocents that occurred in the temple, but she could possibly help save some of the prophets of Yahweh.

She did not know if she believed in the power of Yahweh over the other gods, but could she live with herself if she did nothing?

Abital did not realize she had made a decision until she found herself turning, slowly and carefully so as not to catch the attention of anyone in the room, and slipping out the door.

CHAPTER TEN

Abital stepped into the hallway and closed the door softly behind her. Then she hurried down the marble floors to the door of Keziah's rooms. She did not knock but flew inside. Keziah was seated on a cushion, reading from her parchments, reciting the words of King David, while Channah pulled the brush through her silky dark hair. Both looked up, their mouths open, as Abital rushed inside. Keziah's hair fell in a glossy sheet to her back.

"She is going to kill the prophets of Yahweh. You must act fast if we are to save any of them."

"What?" Keziah stood quickly, and Channah dropped the brush, though neither seemed to notice. "The queen?"

"Yes."

"How do you know?"

Abital recounted how she had been inside the queen's rooms and overheard her plot to kill the prophets of Yahweh. She still held the purple silk gown in her shaking hands. It looked incongruous here in this bright and light room, where Keziah wore a simple linen shift.

"Are you sure they did not see you?" Keziah said.

"I do not think so, but I do not know for sure."

"We must be very careful, in that case. I need to speak to my brother, but you cannot go, not if you might have been seen." Keziah asked her to wait, and asked if Channah could take a message to Obadiah. "It will put you in danger if anyone finds out about this later. Are you willing?"

"Of course, my lady. For you, and for Yahweh, I will do anything."

It had not occurred to Abital until that moment that Channah might be a Yahwist too. It made sense, actually, that Keziah wanted someone in her household who shared her loyalties. Somehow Abital had never thought to wonder. Channah was so quiet and faded into the background so often that she often went unnoticed. Hopefully this trait would help her now.

"You will need to get past the guards who oversee that part of the palace, but you must not tell them why you need to get through," Keziah said.

"That will not be a problem," Channah said. "I will make it."

"Please, tell him to come as quickly as possible," Keziah said. "And thank you, Channah."

As soon as Channah left, Keziah began to pace up and down her room, speaking quietly under her breath.

"Can I help you, my lady?"

"Do you know the story of our ancestors, how Moses led them out of Egypt and allowed them to walk across the sea on dry land?" Keziah rubbed her belly as she walked.

"Yes, my lady. My saba used to tell me the story, and we remembered it every year at the feast of the Passover."

"Tell me the story now. It will give me courage to hear it again."

So Abital told Keziah how the Lord had appeared to Moses in the shape of a burning bush, and called Moses and given him a special purpose, sending him to Egypt, where the Lord's people were enslaved, to tell the Pharoah to let the Hebrews go free.

"Moses was a murderer, and yet the Lord used him," Keziah said.

"Yes, my lady. And he had a stutter, so Yahweh sent Aaron to go along with him. But Pharoah did not agree to let the people go, so the Lord sent plagues, one after another, to get the attention of the ruler of the land."

"Some say each of the plagues the Lord sent was intended to best a false god the people in Egypt believed in," Keziah said.

"I had not heard that," Abital said.

"My father told us Yahweh sent frogs to show He was greater than the Egyptian goddess Heqet, and darkness to show His power over Ra, the Egyptian god of the sun. Each of the plagues was sent with a purpose." Keziah reached one side of the room and turned, pacing back toward Abital. "It is not so different from how He is trying to get our attention today, is it?"

Keziah was referring to the drought that now plagued their land, she felt certain. Was she right, that this drought was intended to show Yahweh's power over the other gods that supposedly controlled the rain? Were these times like the time of the ancient Hebrews? Another part of her mind kept wondering if the queen had sent for her yet, or had noticed that she was late.

"Please, go on with the story," Keziah said. "I am sorry to have interrupted."

Abital told Keziah how plague after plague did not change the mind of the Pharoah, and so Yahweh told the Israelites to paint the doors of their houses with the blood of a lamb, so the spirit of the Lord would pass over those homes when the plague on the first-borns came that night.

"The Lord passed over the houses marked with the blood, but took the firstborn from each of the houses of the Egyptians, including the Pharoah," Abital said. "And then the Pharoah finally told the Hebrews to leave, but quickly changed his mind, and sent his armies after them. The Hebrews were pressed up against the shore of the Red Sea with nowhere to run, but then the Lord dried up the water and allowed them to walk across the sea on dry land. As soon as the last Hebrew had made it across, the water came back, killing all of those in the Pharaoh's army. He led the Hebrews to safety."

"I always remember, when I hear that story, that even when something looks impossible, Yahweh will provide a way," Keziah said.

The door of the chamber flew open, and Obadiah raced in, followed by Channah. "Is it true?" he said, closing the door tightly behind him.

"I heard the queen plotting it herself," Abital said. "She intends to have the prophets of Yahweh killed tonight."

"You are sure of this?" Obadiah's eyes were wide, and he was gazing at her.

"Unless she has changed her mind, yes, that is what I heard her order. And I have never known the queen to change her mind."

"I know where some of them are, not far from here," Obadiah said, turning to his sister. "I will warn them and lead them to safety as soon as it is dark."

"Please be careful," Keziah said. They all knew what danger he would be in if he was found out. What danger they all would be in. But Abital saw that the danger would not dissuade him.

"It does not matter what happens to me," said Obadiah. "Yahweh's prophets are the last vestige of His influence in this land. We must not let faith in the One True God die out in Israel."

"May the Lord go with you," Keziah said, and she hugged her brother before he headed for the door.

"Wait," Abital said. Both Keziah and Obadiah turned to her. "I have some dark cloth in my workroom. It is a very deep purple, nearly the color of midnight. I will get that. If you keep it over your head and shoulders, like a cloak, you will blend into the night."

The brother and sister looked at one another, then at Abital. "You would lend my brother this cloth?" Keziah asked. "If he is caught, the queen will link the cloth to you. You would risk being caught as part of this scheme."

Abital realized in that moment that she would risk that and so much more to keep Obadiah safe. She did not really know how to understand it, but she just knew that she could not bear it if something happened to Obadiah.

"I am already at risk of being caught. It will not take the queen long to figure out where you have learned about the plot. This cloth will only increase the chances of success, and all of us will be safer."

"Thank you, Abital," Keziah said.

"I will go now and get it."

Abital left the chamber and fought to keep her steps slow and even as she made her way down the hallway. Rushing would only call attention to herself and make others wonder what was happening.

She found the midnight-colored gown, pulled it apart quickly, and tucked the largest piece into a burlap bag. It was long and full enough that it should cover most of Obadiah if he draped it over his shoulders. Then she returned to Keziah's chamber. Once she was inside, she set the bag on the table and unfurled the dark cloth.

"It will work perfectly," Obadiah said. "Thank you."

"You have done a very good thing," Keziah said.

"I must get back before the queen finds me gone. You will send word when it has been accomplished?" Abital asked.

Keziah nodded. "I will send for you and let you know. Thank you, Abital."

"Thank you." Obadiah pressed his lips together and looked as though he wanted to say more, but instead he just met her gaze and held it for longer than was necessary. After a moment, Abital forced herself to look away and turned for the door.

A few moments later, when Abital returned to Jezebel's rooms, she found the queen lounging on her cushions, a smug, satisfied look on her face. A jug of wine sat next to her. Abital had to fight with everything in her to keep her voice level, her breath calm.

"Do you have the gown?"

"I do, my lady."

"I expected it to be done sooner."

"I think you will find it was worth the wait." Abital held up the lavender silk dress, which unfurled and fell in long waves.

"That is pretty," Jezebel said. She pushed herself up and gestured for Abital to come closer. Abital set the dress gently next to the queen, just where Ushmuel, the prophet of Baal, had sat not long ago. She fought to keep down the sickness that threatened to rise up in her.

"It will do nicely," Jezebel said. She lowered herself back onto the cushion. "Please hang it with the others." She gestured dismissively. "I must rest now. It is to be a big night, and I must sleep now if I am to be up for it."

Abital could not bring herself to ask the queen what was special about this night, and Jezebel did not seem to mind. She lay down on the cushions, a smile on her face, and closed her eyes. Abital took one last long look, pressed her lips together, and walked out.

CHAPTER ELEVEN

O badiah waited until dusk began to fall over the land before he went to the back door of the palace, the one used to empty chamber pots and toss out scraps for the dogs, and slipped into the darkening evening. It would be safer to wait until night had fallen completely, but he did not know how long he had until Jezebel's men would attack. He had to get there first.

The camp where many of the prophets of Yahweh lived was several hours' journey on foot, but Obadiah was determined to make it in half the time. He was grateful that he had been out to see the prophets a few times since he'd arrived in Jezreel and knew the way.

He could not go out the main city gate, where the guards would see him and ask his business, so he slipped out the secret unmanned gate built into the section of the wall closest to the palace. The king had insisted on installing the gate. He wanted the freedom to have his guests come and go from the city without the notice of the nosy guards at the city gates. Obadiah had long lamented this gap in the city's protection. It made them all vulnerable. In addition, whatever guests could not be seen entering the city were not guests the king needed to associate with. But King Ahab always had been a man ruled by his desires, and there was no controlling the king. This night, however, Obadiah was glad of the king's duplicity.

He tied the dark fabric over his head, so it draped down his back, and then he slipped out the gate and quickly made his way through the parched dusty land. There was only a sliver of moon, and he thanked the Lord for that blessing. He may make it without being seen, if he was careful. The night was clear, and the air cool, but flying gnats swarmed around him, hungry, as all were these days. He swatted at them as he walked as quickly as he could to the east, toward the river and the encampment in the hills on the far side. Obadiah prayed as he walked, asking the Lord to give him success, to protect His prophets, to slow down the prophets of Baal and Asherah on their bloody mission.

As the steps wore on, he could not help his mind turning to Abital, whose bravery had set this journey in motion. He had admired her from the time he first met her, and not just because of her beauty, though that did not hurt. She did not seem to realize how pretty she was, which made her stand out in a palace full of people vying for attention. But it was her wit and her intelligence that had impressed him. She was not afraid to banter and spar with him. He had never before met a woman whose words were as quick and precise as hers. He had never met a woman who seemed to match him in that way. And Keziah had told him Abital could read, as well. He did not know how such a thing was possible, but he wanted to talk to her more and find out.

He knew it was wrong to think of her as much as he did. She was not a Yahwist but worshiped all the gods. She was a servant at the palace, and though he had told her he was also but a servant of the king, they both knew the two of them were not of equal stature. Still, she was intriguing, much more so than the noblewomen his father was constantly parading before him, their expensive clothing and alluring figures negated by their vacant stares. It made no sense, but he could not stop thinking about her. And the way she had looked at him tonight, he could not help but wonder if maybe, just maybe, she felt a connection to him as well…

Obadiah shook his head and quickened his steps. There was only one thing that mattered tonight, and that was saving those prophets. Though the path through the hills was steep, and he was forced to clamber over boulders and up precipitous vertical faces, he dared not stop for water or to catch his breath, and he was out of breath and parched when he finally approached the clearing, nestled deep in the hills, where the Yahwist prophets camped.

He found the camp mostly quiet, the fire at the center of their dwellings turned to embers, most of the men retired to their tents. Quiet conversation emanated from a few of the tents, but a hush had fallen over the encampment. Obadiah went straight to the group conversing at the far side of the fire. The altars to the Lord, set apart at the far side of the camp, were mostly in shadow.

"Where is Joram?" Obadiah asked, approaching the group. "Is he here?"

"He has just gone to his tent," one of the men said. Obadiah had met him before, but could not remember his name. He was one of the youngest of the prophets in the camp, though still many years older than Obadiah. His long beard was streaked with white.

"Tell him to come out, please. Tell him Obadiah has come, and there is no time to waste."

"What is going on?" asked one of the other men, whose white hair had grown thin on top.

He really should wait and tell Joram first. But there was no time to lose. "You must get ready to go," Obadiah said. "Tell the men to gather their things. You must leave here at once."

"Why?" asked the first man, and the second added, "What is happening?"

"Please, take me to Joram."

The younger man gestured for Obadiah to follow him. Before Obadiah followed, he called, "Start packing!"

The men did not hesitate but immediately started tearing down their tents. They knew Obadiah came from the palace, and no doubt that is why they trusted his word. The younger prophet led Obadiah through a warren of tents, one after another, until he came to the largest tent in the center of a clearing.

"Joram!" Obadiah called. "I have come from the palace. I need you to listen, gather your men, and leave."

A moment later, the leader of the prophets stepped out of his tent. "What is this?" He asked.

"The queen is sending men out here to ambush your camp," Obadiah said. "You must leave, and quickly. They will come tonight."

"What?"

Obadiah explained what Abital had told him.

"You are sure of this?" Joram asked.

"Quite sure. They will be here shortly. You must get your men and move."

"Where will we go?"

Obadiah had a plan. He had come up with the idea on the way over.

"I know of some caves not far from here," Obadiah said. "I will take your men to them, and they can hide there. They will be safe for a while."

"How many can fit in each cave?" Joram asked.

"They are big caves. I will take two large groups," Obadiah said. "I will sound the alarm."

Joram gathered several of his trusted men and gave them instructions to rouse the camp, and soon the entire area was busy with men pulling down animal skins and packing supplies in bags.

"We have a group ready to go," called the first prophet, the youngest one, from the front of the camp.

"You lot go with Obadiah," Joram called, and moments later, Obadiah was leading fifty men through the hills and up into the higher, drier parts where the caves were.

"How do you know these hills so well?" asked one of the prophets, a man with a long brown braid down his back. "It seems that you know them better than we do, and we have lived near them for many years."

"My abba's business is limestone," Obadiah explained as they walked. "He quarries it and sells it to build cities and palaces. He always needed to find new sources of the hard stone, and I spent many years exploring the whole region, searching for areas that would be good for mining. I have walked most of the land in all of the Jezreel Valley and beyond."

He had once hoped that the natural caves in this region, most carved by the hand of God directly into the hillsides, might be a rich source of the strong stone. But the remote and treacherous location made it too costly and dangerous, Abba had declared. Still, if Obadiah could find those caves once again, they would make a good hiding spot for these men.

It was difficult to find the caves in the dark, but once he located the right path, he led the fifty men into the first cave and made them step away from the mouth, where they would be less likely to be seen.

"I will return shortly with the rest of the men, and bring them to that cave," Obadiah said, pointing to another opening on the other side of a small creek.

He hurried back to the camp and found that Joram had the other fifty men ready to go. Obadiah led these men to the second cave and promised to return soon. He knew they would not be able to come out of the caves for some time, and they would need food and water.

Obadiah pulled the cloak tightly around himself. He needed to get back to Jezreel and let Keziah know that Jezebel had not succeeded in silencing Yahweh's voice.

CHAPTER TWELVE

Abital did not sleep well that night, waiting and hoping for news. Around her, she could hear the breaths and light snores coming from Michal and Tamar and Mara, but though she listened for a knock at the door, none came. The next morning, bleary-eyed, she went to Jezebel's chambers to help her dress, and Abital found the queen smiling as she sipped her tea. Her long silk robe draped onto the floor and pooled at her feet.

"You are up. I was not sure you would be awake this early, as you said you would be up late," Abital said, stepping inside the room. Mara was in the corner of the room, straightening the queen's sleeping mat and blankets. She too had a smug smile on her face.

"I am too excited to sleep. This is a very good day, indeed."

With her words, Abital felt her stomach turn. Had Obadiah been successful? Had he been caught? Had he been killed himself?

"What is the good news, my queen?" Abital walked to the rack where the queen's gowns hung, and ran her fingers along the rich fabrics. The new lavender gown was at the end of the rack. "Would you like to wear the new gown today?"

"Hmm?" The queen seemed to have already forgotten what she had said.

"The new light purple gown?"

"Yes, that will be perfect for this day of celebration." She took another sip of her tea, and said, "The prophets of Baal and Asherah have won quite a victory this day. Soon, all will see which gods are the most powerful."

"That is very good news, my queen," Abital said. She hoped Jezebel could not hear the catch in her voice, but Jezebel did not seem to be paying attention. "What victory?"

"The prophets of Yahweh have all been killed," Jezebel said. "Gone. There is no more Yahwist threat in Israel."

Abital tried her best not to show her distress. "That is…" She did not quite know what to say. "I am glad to hear it." She wanted to rip out her tongue for saying the words.

"Yes, it is very good news," Jezebel said. "Here, put the gown on me, so I will look beautiful when the news spreads throughout the palace."

Abital forced herself to focus on the task at hand and not the sick feeling that threatened to make her double over. Her hands shook as she pulled the silk robe off the rack and slipped it over the queen's shoulders.

"You look lovely," Abital said, arranging the silk so it lay flat against the queen's smooth skin.

"You have done well," the queen said. She must have been feeling generous, in her good mood. "Now, what about the green one? How is that coming?"

"I will get to work on that now," Abital said, and stepped toward the door. "Unless there is more you need from me?"

"Not right now," said the queen.

"I will leave you to your peace, then."

Instead of heading to the workroom, she went instead to Keziah's rooms and knocked on the door. Keziah herself opened the door a few moments later. She said, "I am glad it is you, Abital. We were just about to send for you. Come inside." Her skin was sallow, and there were dark shadows beneath her eyes.

She ushered Abital inside and shut the door behind her. She turned and rested her back against the door, as if to hold herself up.

"I was just with the queen, and she said all the prophets had been killed," Abital said. "Is it true?"

"Not all of them." Abital recognized Obadiah's voice and was startled to see him at the table in the room. The dark cloth was still wrapped around his shoulders.

"You are here," she said. She was not able to hide the relief in her voice. "I was worried—"

"You did not need to worry. I was kept safe, because of your cloak." He folded the cloth and set the fabric on the table. "I have you to thank for my life."

She felt a flush of pleasure, quickly followed by a rush of shame. She could not take pleasure in his attention, not now.

"And what of the prophets? What happened?"

"Please, sit." Keziah gestured toward the table. Abital sat in one of the chairs, to the left of Obadiah, and Keziah lowered herself into the chair on her other side. Channah emerged from the corner of the room carrying a pot of tea. "Tell her the story, brother."

Channah served the tea and walked away, and Obadiah wrapped his hands around his cup of tea and told them of how he had led two groups of prophets to safety.

Keziah placed her hand on her brother's. "If not for your brave actions, all of the prophets of Yahweh would have died last night. You saved one hundred of the Lord's servants. Because of you, because of your brave actions, Yahweh will not be forgotten in this land."

"It was not only my actions that saved them," Obadiah said. "Without Abital's quick thinking, they all would have been lost." He finally looked up from his cup and turned his gaze to her. "Thank you."

"I could not let them get away with it," Abital said.

"It was very brave of you," Keziah said. "Yahweh will not forget your actions, and neither will we."

Abital felt a flush of pleasure at the words, but she also felt unsettled. Once she'd heard the queen's plans, she knew she had to act. But what was it all for? What was the point of all this slaughter? So the queen should show that her gods were more powerful than Keziah's god? That Jezebel was more powerful than the king's second wife? Was so much bloodshed caused simply by an insecure woman jockeying for power?

Keziah and Obadiah began discussing the plan for Obadiah to return at nightfall with food and water for the hundred prophets split between the two caves, and while Abital was half listening, she was also trying to make sense of all that had happened.

Or were the night's events less about the queen and her vendetta, and actually a reflection of the gods' will? Terrible acts— sacrifices of children—were committed to satisfy the appetites of some of the gods worshiped in this land. It was too terrible—what kind of god could truly want the sacrifice of innocent blood in his name? Did this slaughter truly make Baal more powerful? Then again, if Yahweh truly was behind this drought, which was causing so much suffering, was He any better than the Phoenician gods? Were the gods just like young boys, playing at games to show their dominance? What good did any of it do? Was there really only One True God of Israel? If so, why had He allowed the murder of so many of His prophets? Why did He leave so many in Israel suffering?

As relieved as she was that Obadiah was safe, as drawn as she was to this man and his kind sister, Abital could not help but wonder if any of the gods were worth all of this suffering.

CHAPTER THIRTEEN

Keziah's baby was born in the heat of the summer—a beautiful girl she called Ayla. The baby had big eyes rimmed by dark lashes and perfectly formed lips. Keziah was besotted, and Abital agreed that she was the most beautiful baby she'd seen. Gifts of pomegranates and lemons and other fresh fruit they had not seen in some time poured in to congratulate the king on the new princess. Obadiah was so pleased with his new niece that he came often to visit her.

Jezebel, too, was overjoyed by the birth.

"A girl," she sneered. "She walks around the palace so smug, and yet she gives the king nothing but a girl."

Abital did not dare point out that a girl was all Jezebel had given the king as well.

Through the long, hot, dry days of that summer, the second with no rain, Obadiah continued taking food and water to the prophets, who remained hidden in the caves. Jezebel apparently believed that the attack had killed all of Yahweh's prophets, and she did not know about the hundred hiding in the hills in the Jezreel valley. Obadiah took great care to keep them hidden and to ensure word did not get back to the palace that some had survived the attack.

At Keziah's invitation, Abital had taken to working on her sewing in Keziah's rooms, which were better lit and more comfortable than her workroom. Abital had felt awkward at first, as she was but a servant and Keziah was treating her as a friend, but something seemed to have shifted between them the night Abital brought the warning about the prophets. Keziah appeared to trust her now and treated her almost as an equal. Abital knew that Keziah was lonely at the palace, and she was glad to spend time in Keziah's peaceful rooms instead of the stuffy workroom or the choked air that pervaded Jezebel's chambers. In Keziah's rooms, Abital finished sewing the midnight-colored gown and returned it to the queen's wardrobe, and the queen did not know how it had been used.

Abital also did not mind that on many days, she got to see Obadiah when he came to visit his sister and the new princess. She was careful to hide the flutter that rose in her belly when she saw him. The adviser to the king, and also the king's brother-in-law, could not possibly take notice of someone like her, a mere servant in this house. But she could not deny that it gave her pleasure when he came in and greeted her, and when he smiled at her, she sometimes thought he might feel more for her than he let on.

Some days, Obadiah brought news of things happening in the palace, such as a fight between the king's armor-bearer and his jeweler, who both wanted his blessing to marry the same woman. He told them of the visitors to the palace, men from throughout the kingdom who had come begging for extra grain for their animals, which were slowly growing thinner and thinner. He told them of the scheming of some of the king's advisers who hoped to gain money or position for themselves when the king was with his armies or at the capital in Samaria. Though they lived in the palace as well, the world of the women of the palace was so cut off from the rest of what happened that sometimes it seemed as though they lived in a different part of the kingdom altogether.

Some days, they played games Obadiah brought to Keziah's rooms. He liked a game that used a board of thin wood and stones that moved and jumped in diagonal lines. He did not mind when Abital beat him, which happened more often than not.

"How did you get to be so skilled at games?" He laughed, shaking his head.

"Just born that way, I guess," she teased. She did not understand it either, and could not explain how she was able to see the next moves she should make clearly, understanding how they would affect play two or three moves ahead.

"Abital is clever," Channah said. "She has a mind for these things."

"She is too clever." Obadiah pretended to be hurt by the loss. "But we will play again, and she will not win this time."

Other days Obadiah brought news from the prophets in the hills, telling them how they continued their worship and praising of Yahweh, even in their dire circumstances. He was encouraged by the faith of these prophets, whose undying belief in the God of Abraham, Isaac, and Moses kept the faith of their fathers alive in the land.

One afternoon in the month of Tishri, when the heat of summer was finally starting to relent, Obadiah appeared with a story so wild, Abital was sure it could not be true.

"I have heard news of the prophet Elijah," he said, placing a plate of dried figs on the table. He gestured for Abital to join him there, while Keziah reclined on the cushions, a sleeping Ayla resting on her chest. Channah never joined them at the table, though she stayed in the corner of the room. She had been invited many times, but Channah did not think it her place. Abital set down the silk robe she had been sewing for the queen and joined him at the table.

"The one who confronted the king at the feast and threatened to cut off the rain?" Abital asked.

"Elijah did not cut off the rain," Obadiah said. "He only warned the king about what Yahweh would do if the king allowed such wickedness to continue."

It did not seem to be much of a distinction to Abital, but she kept quiet. It struck her that she alone in this room had been witness to the confrontation. Neither Obadiah nor Keziah had been living at the palace at that time.

"He is alive, then?" Keziah began to push herself up a bit on her arms to see her brother better, but when Ayla began to fuss, she stayed where she was. "Where has he been?"

"He is alive, or was when he went to see the prophets in their caves two days past."

"How did Elijah find them in their caves?" Keziah asked, and Abital could see that she feared the same thing Abital worried about. If Elijah had found the prophets, would someone else find them as well?

"He told them that the Lord directed him there." Obadiah pushed the plate of figs across the wooden table toward Abital.

"Can that be true?" Abital asked.

"That is the least bizarre part of his story," Obadiah said. "Listen and you will see. I was sorry he had gone from the cave before I arrived last night, but the prophets in hiding were quite encouraged by his visit, and they told me the most incredible story that he had recounted to them. He told them that after he was released from the prison last year, after the night he passed along his message from Yahweh to the king, the Lord told him to turn eastward and hide in the ravine by the river Kerith."

"Does Yahweh speak directly to Elijah, then?" Abital asked. She knew that Moses had heard the Lord in the burning bush, and on the mountain of Sinai, and several of the other of their forefathers had heard directly from Yahweh, but the Lord did not seem to speak directly to many these days. "How does he hear Yahweh?"

"I do not know," Obadiah admitted. "That is a question you will need to ask Elijah himself someday. All I can say is that the Lord told Elijah to go to the river Kerith and to drink from the brook, and he sent ravens with food for him."

"The ravens brought him food? What kind of food do ravens bring?" Keziah asked.

"It is said they brought him bread and meat in the mornings, and bread and meat in the evenings as well." Obadiah must have seen the confusion on Abital's face, because he continued, "As strange as it sounds, it is not the first time the Lord has delivered food to His servants in need. Let us not forget the manna that kept our ancestors fed while they walked through the desert."

"Yes, but...ravens?" Keziah still seemed as confused as Abital. "Where did birds get loaves of bread? Where did they find meat?"

"You are getting caught up on the wrong thing. The story gets stranger still," Obadiah said. "Let me go on, and I will tell you."

"By all means, please tell us more," Abital said. Once again, Obadiah nudged the plate of figs toward her, and she picked up one and took a bite. It was sweet and tart and tasted like spring. She had not had such a delicacy in many months, and she savored each bite.

"Eventually the brook dried up, because of the rain."

"Elijah did not think of that, when he cursed the land?" Keziah said.

"Again, it is not Elijah who decided to withhold the rain. He was just carrying out the Lord's instructions," Obadiah said. "Anyway, the word of the Lord came to him and told him to go to Zarephath."

"Why Zarephath?" Keziah's brow wrinkled. "That is near Sidon, is it not?"

"It is," Obadiah said. "It is in the territory ruled by Ethbaal, the father of Jezebel."

"Why would the Lord send Elijah into the land where the false gods that have overtaken our land came from?" Keziah asked.

"I do not know, but that is what the Lord instructed Elijah to do. So he went to Zarephath, and at the city gate, he found a widow there, gathering sticks. He asked her to bring him some water, and as she was going to get it, he asked also for some bread. 'I have no bread,' she told him. 'Only a little oil and a little flour. I am gathering sticks so that I may make a meal for myself and my son. It will be our last, as there is no more.' And Elijah said to her, 'Do not be afraid. Go home and do as you have said, and make a small cake for me, and bring it to me, and then make something for you and your son. The Lord God of Israel will not allow your jug of oil to run dry, not your jar of flour to be used up, until the day the Lord gives rain.'"

"Did she do it?" Keziah asked.

"She did. She went off, made the cakes, and brought one to Elijah, and after that there was food every day for her and her son. He took a room in the upper part of the house and stayed there, and the oil did not run dry and the flour did not run out."

"That is incredible." It was so incredible, in fact, that Abital found it hard to believe.

"Did she turn from her false gods and worship Yahweh after that?" Keziah asked.

"I do not know," Obadiah said. "But I do know that—"

"Did the Lord do the same for the others who are starving in this drought?" Abital asked. "Why does He not feed all those who remain true to Him?" Abital thought about her saba, killing his sheep to have something to eat.

"The two of you are conspiring to make sure I never get to finish telling this story," Obadiah said. Abital did not know if his exasperation was real or feigned, but she found it funny nonetheless.

"Please go on," Abital said, trying to make her face show contrition.

"We are sorry, brother," Keziah said, smiling. "Go on."

"Sometime later, the son of the widow fell ill and died."

"That is a terrible ending," Keziah said. She rubbed her fingers gently down the back of her sleeping child. "Now I am sorry we let you finish."

"That would be a terrible ending, but that is not the end of the story," Obadiah said. "The widow brought the boy to him, and Elijah carried him to the upper room, where he was staying, and laid him on the bed. Then he cried out to the Lord, 'O Lord my God, have You brought tragedy also upon this widow that I am staying with, by causing her son to die?' Then he stretched himself out on the boy three times and cried to the Lord, 'O Lord my God, let this boy's life return to him!' The Lord heard Elijah's cry, and the boy's life returned, and Elijah carried the child down to his mother and said, 'Look, your son is alive!'"

Keziah pushed herself up again. "You are right that this story gets stranger. Do you mean to tell us that Elijah brought this woman's child back from the dead?"

"That is the story Elijah told the prophets," Obadiah said.

"But that is unbelievable," Abital said. It could not happen.

"And yet it is true, all the same," Obadiah said.

"What happened to the woman and child after that?" Keziah asked.

"The woman told Elijah, 'Now I know that you are a man of God and that the word of the Lord from your mouth is the truth.'"

"Praise God," Keziah said.

Abital still had so many questions. Had the woman not seen that to be true when Elijah had made the flour and oil replenish themselves? Why had it taken the raising to life of her son for her to understand that Elijah's words were true?

"Is Elijah still living with the widow in Zarephath?" Abital asked. If that was the case, how had he come upon the caves of the prophets?

"He lives still in the room above the widow, but said he heard word of the prophets of the Lord being attacked and killed. The king

Ethbaal held a celebration in Sidon to celebrate Israel being rid of Yahweh's prophets. But the Lord told Elijah that some had survived, and sent him to encourage them that Yahweh has not forgotten them. He is still powerful, brave, and true, and when Israel turns from her wicked ways and returns to Yahweh, all will see the glory of the Lord."

Abital was quiet for a moment, thinking over what Obadiah had just told them. He had been right. It was an unbelievable story. And yet, he clearly believed it. He had hope that someday Yahweh would end this drought, that Yahweh's glory would be revealed.

"But how do we get Israel to turn from the worship of Baal and back to Yahweh?" Keziah said. "I have tried everything I know to get the king to end the queen's wickedness, but she has too strong a grip on him. He says he cannot tell her not to worship Baal. The queen's father wants to keep her happy, and the security of the northern border that he provides is too valuable."

"But what good is a secured border if all your people die from starvation?" Obadiah said.

"I am doing my best, brother," Keziah said. "He does not actually ask my opinion when I am with him. I must work hard to get him to talk to me about anything beyond the superficial. It is not conversation that he wants from his wives. I will try everything I know to do, but it is not up to us. Yahweh will make His name known in Israel, one way or another."

Abital only wondered how many more must die before the Lord made it so.

Obadiah needed to return to his work, and Abital left the room shortly after that, marveling at the story he had told.

Abital continued to work on new gowns for the queen, though cloth from the East was harder to get these days, and costlier. When so many in the land were hungry, Abital did not understand how the queen could spend so much on clothes, but nothing appeared to quench the queen's thirst for new, costly garments.

Abital was careful not to let the queen catch her working in Keziah's room, but Jezebel was distracted anyway. She was busy arranging a day of repentance for all of Jezreel to make sacrifices to Baal in order to persuade the god to send rain. King Ahab was away from the palace, but Jezebel declared that she did not need the king's help or approval to arrange for the day. She was so absorbed in her meetings with Baal's prophets and planning for the day that she did not have as much time to spend scheming against Keziah. Planning for the event, the queen seemed happier than Abital had seen her in some time. Despite her unease about the festival, Abital was grateful—Jezebel snapped at her and Mara less and was more content in general.

It soon became clear the queen had another reason for her good spirits. Her belly began to swell again, and this time she was sure that she was carrying the king's son. She required a new set of outfits that would accommodate her changing body. Abital got to work.

The queen may not have noticed how much time Abital was spending with the second wife, but Mara did. She approached Abital one morning, after Jezebel was dressed and was gathering the prophets of Baal in her chambers to plan the coming sacrifice. Abital went to leave the room to get to work, but Mara cornered her before she reached the doorway.

"I know where you are spending your days," Mara said, her chin lifted high. "The queen will not like to hear how much time you are spending with the second wife."

Abital's heart raced. If Mara had noticed, she was sure to tell the queen, and it would be the end for Abital.

"I do not know what you mean." Abital fought to keep her voice even.

"You know as well as I do that if I tell the queen you are in league with this Yahwist, she will send you back before dinner to that speck of a town where you were born."

"I am not in league with any Yahwists. I serve both of the king's wives, as directed by the king. I must spend time in Keziah's room, as I do in here, to help her dress and make clothing for her."

"That wife has not had new clothing since her brat was born. You cannot be meeting with her about her tunics for so long."

Abital moved toward the door, but Mara did not step aside. "If the queen wishes to have the king reconsider the work I do for Keziah, she should take it up with him. Until I am instructed otherwise, I will continue to do as I have been ordered."

"I know what you are up to," Mara sneered. "And when the time is right the queen will too."

"I am not up to anything, I assure you," Abital said. "Now if you will excuse me, I must get to work."

Abital waited all day for the news to come, saying she was dismissed from the palace. But she did not receive any such word, and so she went about her work, though she could not relax. She knew Mara would not let the matter drop. She would tell the queen when it suited her, and Abital was afraid it would not end well.

Soraya also knew that Abital was spending time in Keziah's room. "Be careful," Soraya warned her one morning when Abital went down for tea. "You need to be careful about aligning yourself with those Yahwists."

"I am not aligning myself with anyone," Abital said.

Soraya made a noise at the back of her throat. "There are many in this palace who would love to see the Yahwists and any associated with them gone. You do not want to be caught up if it comes to that."

"I am not caught up with them," Abital insisted. Soraya acted as though she did not hear, and returned to work.

The mood in the palace was somber as the second summer with no rain turned to fall. The crops had withered in the fields, and all were saying there would be almost nothing to harvest this year. There were reports that some in the countryside were eating mud to fill their bellies. Obadiah could no longer find enough food in the palace to bring to the Yahwist prophets without being noticed, so he helped them move out of the caves and establish a settlement on the edge of the desert, where they were able to eke out enough food due to a small stream that still flowed. Because Jezebel believed they were dead, they hoped she would not catch wind of them. They did not have much, but they were surviving, Obadiah reported when he came back from his regular visits.

Saba wrote to say farmers had taken to slaughtering their animals, which were too malnourished to give milk, simply to survive. He had slaughtered a few of the sheep but was hoping to avoid taking any more. Abital took to asking Soraya to make less for her and instead put aside a few dried lentils and grains. Reluctantly, Soraya complied after Abital made a new tunic to give to her daughter.

Each week, Abital gathered the dried food Soraya had saved and packaged it up to give to Ira to send to Saba, along with her notes.

Abital continued to do her work in Keziah's room, even despite the threat of Mara's meddling. She found great comfort and enjoyment in their daily talks and had come to think of Keziah as something of a friend. As the day approached when Jezebel had decreed that all were to attend the sacrifice at the temple, Abital asked Keziah what she intended to do.

"I will not go, of course." Keziah looked surprised, as though this had been obvious. She was lounging on the cushions and feeding Ayla. Keziah had refused to let a wet nurse care for the baby, insisting on keeping her by her side. "I will not offer sacrifices to any but Yahweh."

"But all in the palace are required to attend."

"The king's first wife does not tell me what I must do. I answer to the king, and to the Lord."

"And what does the king say?" Abital asked.

"The king is busy with his armies near the southern border. He does not even know what Jezebel has planned. But even if he knew, he would say I did not have to attend. He knew from the beginning that I would worship no god but Yahweh. It was one of the conditions of the betrothal."

"Really?" Abital realized she had no idea how such things worked. "Your father negotiated that?"

"He did. He was very upset, as were we all, about the introduction of the false gods into Israel by the king's first wife. The king should be more loyal to Yahweh than anyone else, not less, and so my father made sure I would not have to worship any god but Yahweh.

His greater hope is that I will be able to persuade the king to stop the worship of the other gods altogether, though that is proving more challenging than he had hoped. Still, we will not go, and you do not have to attend either," Keziah said.

Abital marveled at this. She wondered exactly how rich Keziah's father must be if he was willing to wed her to the king with a condition of this sort. But such musings did not solve her immediate problem.

"I do not see how I can avoid it, my lady. She has said all must go. I do not have the same kind of arrangement with the king. I work also for Jezebel. She will notice if I am not in attendance."

"The queen does not have the authority to make decrees such as this. Only the king has the power to do such things."

"She may not technically have the authority, but all will listen to what she says, regardless. The king does not stand up to her, and so she does what she wants, and he goes along with it. She may not have the crown, but she has the power to make those in the kingdom do as she demands."

"Do you desire to worship the false god?" Keziah asked.

"Not particularly." The more time she spent talking to Keziah and Obadiah, the more she found herself drawn to the Lord, Yahweh. To the faith of her ancestors.

"Then do not go. I will see that you are not punished for it."

Abital did not think Keziah, as kind as she was, had that sort of power.

"My brother will protect you if I cannot," Keziah said, as if seeing her thoughts. "He would not want you to be sent away."

Abital knew it was foolish, but she was pleased by the words.

"He would tell you the same if he were here. He had a meeting with the tax collectors this afternoon. He will be sorry to have missed you."

"I am sure your brother does not notice whether I am in the room when he comes to see you, my lady."

Keziah laughed. "It is not me he comes to see, Abital. My brother cares for me, but not so much that he would neglect his work to visit me each day. He did not, before you started working here. Do you truly not see this?"

Abital felt her cheeks flush, and everything in her wanted to shout, but she could do nothing of the sort.

"You are flattering me, my lady."

Keziah had a small smile on her face. "Just wait. You will see."

CHAPTER FOURTEEN

The day of the sacrifice arrived, and Abital left her rooms, uncertain. She wanted to believe Keziah and believe that she would not be punished if she did not attend the ceremony, but too much was at risk. The palace was one of the few places in the land left with consistent access to food, and if she lost her place at the palace, she would have nothing to send home to Saba.

The king returned to the palace less than a week before the planned sacrifice, and the queen demanded Abital help with her gown that evening, hoping he would send for her. Down the hall, Keziah would also be slipping on a clean shift, in case he sent for her, but Abital was certain the second wife did not spend as much time preparing as the queen. Abital helped Jezebel into a rose-colored gown that clung tightly to her top but was loose over her belly.

"Make sure it is tight up here," Jezebel said, gesturing at her bust. "And low enough to catch his attention."

"You look stunning, my queen. He will not be able to take his eyes off you."

But when a knock came at the door that evening, it was not the king's servant sent to summon her to his chambers but the king himself who strode into the room, wearing a dark blue robe trimmed in gold. Mara gasped, and both she and Abital ducked their heads and stepped back. Abital had never seen Ahab enter the chamber of one of his wives, and she wondered what had prompted this visit.

"My king." Jezebel masked her surprise with a seductive smile. "I see you could not wait."

"Is it true, what I have heard? Have you declared that all in the land must attend a sacrifice to Baal?"

He had stridden into the room and now spoke as though he and the queen were the only two in it. He was used to overlooking the servants, forgetting that they would hear or see all that went on.

"Yes." Jezebel did not hesitate. "There is nothing more important than ending this drought. You must know how many in the land are suffering. The god of thunder must be appeased."

King Ahab said nothing for a moment. He gazed at his wife, not with the lust the queen had been hoping for, but with something like exasperation.

"You do not make decrees about what people must do," he said finally.

"I just thought—"

"I am the king. I am the only one who can compel our people to do anything. Do you understand?" He did not raise his voice. He did not have to.

Abital watched the exchange with growing unease. Part of her was hopeful, believing that the king's words truly might mean that she did not have to attend. But at the same time, she understood that Jezebel was losing this exchange, and they would all pay for it.

"How are we to end this drought unless we are all in this together?" Jezebel said. "What is her god doing to bring the rain?"

The king did not answer for a moment. Then, he spoke.

"I will send a notice that all who wish to attend the sacrifice to Baal are welcome to do so but that the king does not compel it," Ahab said.

Why did he not tell her to end this madness? Abital wondered. He was the king. As he had said, he was the one who made decrees. If he did not want her to go through with this communal sacrifice, he should tell her so, and she would have to listen. But he did not. He was not just cruel, he was weak.

"You will be sorry," Jezebel said. "Do you not want this drought to end?"

"I want nothing more."

"Then you must do this. For me, and for our son." Jezebel pressed her hands to her belly, revealing its round form.

The king's eyes widened. "You will have a child?"

"Yes, my king. This spring."

A grin spread slowly across his face. "That is very good news."

"You are glad?"

"Of course I am glad." The frustration that had been there a moment before seemed to fade away.

Jezebel reached out to touch the king's cheek. "I had hoped you would be happy. I am happy as well. I am sure it is a boy this time." She trailed her fingers down his cheek, to his chest, and she took a step closer to him. "I am so glad you are home. I have been waiting to welcome you."

For a moment, the queen's attempt at distraction seemed to have worked. The king appeared to have forgotten the anger he had felt a moment before. But as Jezebel placed her other hand on his shoulder, attempting to pull him closer, the king stepped back.

"It is good to see you, as always, my queen." King Ahab ducked his head, and then he walked to the door and strode out, leaving all in the room in stunned silence.

Jezebel flew into a rage that night like nothing Abital had seen before. She screamed at Mara and Abital and tossed bowls and cups off the balcony, watching them smash on the ground far below. She threw a jug of wine at the wall and tore from top to bottom the gown she had been wearing. Only her opium pipe eventually seemed to calm her. When the rage had finally passed and she rested peacefully on her mat, they helped her into a nightgown and to bed.

The preparations for the sacrifice continued as planned. Jezebel did not change the message that had been sent out in the city, but nonetheless word spread through the palace that the king would not require all to attend.

Abital was quite certain that did not mean her. Jezebel would know if she was not there, and she would be punished for it.

On the day of the sacrifice, there was much activity at the palace, as all prepared to make the journey to the temple of Baal. Abital helped Jezebel dress in a new scarlet gown, and then she followed the queen along the hallway and out the palace doors. She met the king on the palace steps, and together they rode to the temple, the members of their household following on foot.

The temple was writhing with people, all shouting and crying and bowing down before the statue of the god. The temple guards held boxes full of gold jewelry, jugs of oil, and every other valuable thing the people in Jezreel had brought as offerings to the god. The offerings helped feed and pay for the housing of the prophets, but she wondered how much also made it into the pockets of the prophets themselves. The crowds parted as the queen and king made their way to the center of the room, next to the statue, and asked the prophets who stood around the edges of the crowd to bring the sacrifice. The terrible sounds and the smells of the offering were something Abital would not soon forget.

As she returned to the palace, Jezebel told Abital she would need help undressing, and Abital promised she would be there shortly, after she stopped in her own room.

And then, instead of going to her room, she went to see Keziah. She was not sure exactly what it was that compelled her. She knew she was asking for trouble by not doing exactly as the queen asked. But after what she had witnessed today, Abital felt drawn there. She felt unclean, and needed the peace and purity the Yahwists offered.

Keziah opened the door and ushered Abital inside.

"Oh, Abital, you look awful. Was it horrible?"

Keziah ushered Abital in and wrapped her in a hug. Obadiah was there at the table, and Channah sat in the corner, holding Ayla.

"Tell me what happened," Keziah said.

"I would rather not," Abital said. "I would rather not ever think of it again."

"It seems nearly everyone in the palace attended," Keziah said.

"Even the king," Obadiah said. "It is terrible. The king of Israel, worshiping false gods."

"That is nothing new," Keziah said. "It is indeed terrible, but you cannot act surprised. We knew who he was."

"I will never forgive Abba for giving you to such an evil man."

"You will watch your tongue," Keziah said to her brother. Her voice said that she would not be argued with. "You will show respect to Abba. I may not have chosen this life for myself, but I would not have Ayla without him. And if anyone in the palace overhears you saying such things, it will be all over for both of us."

Obadiah bent his head, chastened. "I am sorry, my sister."

"Let us return to the story," Keziah said. Then she turned to Abital and explained, "We were telling the stories of our people, lest they be forgotten this day."

"I was just sharing how Joshua led the Israelites into the land Yahweh had promised them," Obadiah said. "And how the Lord delivered their enemies into the hands of God's people so they could claim their homeland."

"This land," Channah said from the corner. She was so quiet that Abital often forgot that she was there, listening.

"Though some have forgotten it, Yahweh's gift will not be forgotten," Obadiah said. "His people will not let His name be forgotten, even on this wicked day."

Abital sat down with them and listened as Obadiah continued his story, reminding them of how the Lord had made the walls of Jericho tumble to the ground, and how He had guided the stones of the small shepherd boy who would one day become king as he fought the giant, and how He had brought much wealth and power to God's people.

"May we never forget that this land was given to our people by Yahweh," Keziah said. "And He alone rules, though many have forgotten."

"If only He would show the people a sign, that would bring them back to Yahweh," Channah said. "The people of this generation have not walked across the sea on dry land, nor seen the walls of their enemies tumble down, and they have forgotten that Yahweh is all-powerful. If only He would show them, they would turn from these false gods."

"But He has shown them, and they still have not turned from the false gods," Obadiah said. "It has been a year and a half with no rain. It is just as the prophet Elijah said. What more do they need to see to believe?"

"It is not enough," Keziah said. "Perhaps Channah is right, and we should pray that Yahweh will find a way to make His power known, so none can question."

"Or we can pray that the people will remember who they are, and leave the worship of these false gods and turn back to Yahweh, and He will end this drought for good," Obadiah said.

"True repentance," Keziah said. "Everything that has passed will be forgotten with true repentance."

Abital wanted to stay and hear more about the goodness of Yahweh all evening. But she knew she could not. With each moment that passed, the queen no doubt grew more agitated.

"I must return to the queen's chambers," Abital said sadly. "I have already been gone too long. She will be upset."

"Stay strong, Abital," Keziah said, pressing her hand into Abital's. "She is powerful for now, but a day will come when Israel will remember her for who she truly is."

Abital thanked her. She hoped what Keziah said was true, but even if it was, it did nothing to change the terrible things that were happening now.

"Where have you been?" Jezebel said from her cushions. She still wore the scarlet gown she had worn earlier, though her hair hung loose around her shoulders. She rubbed her belly absently, while Mara sat at her feet and rubbed a sweet-smelling oil into her toes.

She could not tell the queen the truth.

"I was not feeling well, my queen."

"I am sorry to hear that. You are better now?"

"Yes, thank you."

"Someone thought they saw you with the Yahwists after the sacrifice," Jezebel said. "The ones who ignored my decree and stayed behind. I said there was no way that could be true. My servants do as their queen commands."

Mara kept her eyes firmly on the queen's feet.

"I did go to the room of the queen's second wife. That is true," Abital said. There was no use denying it if Mara had reported it. "And then I came straight here."

"Why did you not come here directly, like I requested?"

"I needed to check on the second wife, as I had been gone all day, my queen."

"You must remember, Abital, that I demand loyalty from those in my household," Jezebel said. "If you want to stay here in the palace, you will have to choose who you will serve. You serve me first. Do you understand?"

"Yes, my queen."

As she walked away. Abital understood that things could not go on as they were. But she did not know what would happen to her when she could no longer work for the queen.

CHAPTER FIFTEEN

The sacrifice to Baal did not work. Baal was not appeased. The days grew shorter and cooler, but still no rain fell. Some days, the sky filled with gray clouds, but they did nothing except raise false hopes and dampen spirits in the palace.

The queen's belly grew rounder, and she demanded more from her servants with each passing day. They had to help her get out of bed, bathe, use the chamber pots. She insisted that the king's son must be protected at all times. She spent most of her days in bed, but that did not stop her demand for more gowns. Abital spent her days in Keziah's rooms working when she could. Obadiah still appeared most days.

A letter came from Saba with news.

> *Thank you for the new grain. Every bit helps, and it was much appreciated. Things are lean here, but we are getting by. There was no wheat harvest this year, nor barley or grapes. The sheep are thin, and we lost a few, but we dried the meat and ate what we could, so perhaps that was a blessing after all. Yahweh is providing for us, as He always does.*
>
> *I am nearing an agreement with Gershom, though the thinning of the herd is presenting some challenges on that*

front. I do not have as many sheep left as he wants for your dowry, but the Lord will provide. I will not allow this drought to keep me from seeing you settled.

I know these days are hard, but stay firm in your faith, my child. Yahweh is the God over Israel, and He alone knows when the rain will return.

Abital found comfort in the fact that the food from the palace was sustaining her saba and his workers, but, though she was sure Saba had meant the note to be encouraging, it instead filled her with dread. She did not want to marry Ezra, and yet the fact that her saba could not afford the dowry Ezra's abba required did not feel like a reprieve, only as if things were getting truly desperate in Napoth Dor. She packed up another bundle of dried beans and grains and sent it, along with a note telling him all was well.

As the weeks dragged by, sacrifices to Baal continued, but when the drought wore on, with no end in sight, the king grew discouraged. His armies in the South were losing. Emaciated and weak, they had not the strength to fight. At the order of the king, they raided homes and demanded food and drink from the people living along the border, but these people too had nothing to eat. Reddish-brown dust, blown about by the wind with no grass to keep it grounded, caked every surface, no matter how many times the servants wiped it off.

"He is looking for Elijah," Obadiah reported one afternoon in Keziah's room. Ayla was sitting on a blanket on the floor, and Keziah sat beside her, handing her interesting stones to examine. "The king now believes that he is responsible for the drought."

"That is good news," Abital said. "Perhaps the sacrifices to Baal will cease."

"I do not know about that. The queen must still be convinced," Keziah said from the floor.

"The soldiers have been sent all around the nation, and even to the kings of other nations, looking for him, but they have not found him," Obadiah said.

"He must be hiding very well," Abital said.

"But why is he still hiding?" Keziah asked. "If Elijah will come to the palace, King Ahab can get him to put an end to the drought."

"I do not know," Obadiah said. "I think it is just as likely the king will kill him as talk to him. I am sure that is why he does not want to be found."

"You must send word to him," Keziah said.

"I do not know where he is," Obadiah said.

"Is he not in Zarephath?" Abital asked.

"Soldiers have searched the town, and met with King Ethbaal, who insists Elijah is nowhere within his borders."

"You could send word through the prophets."

"They do not know where he is either, I am afraid," Obadiah said. "No one does."

"Yahweh will tell him to return," Keziah said.

"Let us hope he does," Obadiah said. "I do not know how much longer the kingdom can survive with no rain."

Early in the month of Shebat, Jezebel's labor pains began, and after a long night, with much crying and groaning, a baby boy was born. The king named him Ahaziah and paraded him around the room, pleasure evident on his face. Ahaziah was small, with a pinched face and a head of dark hair that stuck up in places, but the king beamed with pride. Jezebel lay back against the pillows, spent, exhausted, but with a smile on her face. She had given the king a son. Her place in the palace was finally secure.

After a few days in his mother's room, the baby was sent to the nursery to join his sister, and Jezebel threw herself into the task of getting her body back to its normal desirable shape. She had only one goal, and that was to deliver another son to the king, and that meant tempting him to her bed once again.

Abital was sent to Ira's shop to buy new fabric—brocades and silks and fine linens—for a new wardrobe for the queen. After Keziah's daughter had been born, she returned to wearing the clothes she had brought into the marriage, but Jezebel required new clothes, always.

Abital packed up more lentils and grains that Soraya had kept for her and went to take them to Ira. But when Abital got to Ira's shop, she found it closed. Abital had never seen it closed before.

"Do you know where he's gone?" she asked the man who ran the leather stall next to Ira's.

"Closed up. Done." He had a thick, unruly beard and dark eyes, and a deep scar on one cheek. "No one can afford to buy silk these days."

There was still one place that could, though. There must have been a misunderstanding of some kind.

"Do you know where I can find him?"

The man shrugged. "He lives over by the market. Near the king's armory. You could see if he is there."

Abital knew of the area. The armory was a foul-smelling place where leather was tanned and metal heated and shaped to make weapons and armor for soldiers.

"Thank you," she said, and she started off toward the market. As she walked, taking in the familiar smells and the narrow alleys, she noticed that the streets were not as crowded as they usually were. Truthfully, she had noticed the last few times she had come into town that there were fewer people about, but it was even more pronounced now. It was almost eerie. Where had everyone gone?

When she got to the market, fewer than half the stalls were occupied, and the tables that were set up were not laden with goods, as they normally were. The fruit and vegetable sellers were not here, and the stalls that had sold fish and quail and rabbit now only had a few scraps of dried meat to sell. The man who sold rugs had a large stack, but no one came by to see him. She pushed her way past hurriedly.

The stench of the armory greeted her as she neared the part of town where Ira lived. The houses here were grimmer than she remembered, small boxes crowded one on top of another, each pressed up against the next, and the streets were covered in muck and smelled of offal. And yet from here, all could see the palace perched high on the hill, gleaming in the sun like ivory.

"Can you tell me where Ira lives?" Abital asked an older woman hunched over a cart filled with broken pieces of pottery.

"Who?" The woman looked her up and down.

"Ira. The cloth merchant."

"Over there," she said, indicating a house in the middle of the row. "The one with the boy in front."

Abital saw a small child wearing nothing but a dirty cloth around his waist standing before a dirty doorway. She could see each of the child's ribs, though his belly appeared to be swollen. Abital thanked the woman and walked to the house.

"Is your father at home?" she asked the child. The boy looked up at her and turned, without saying a word, and went inside. A moment later, Ira came out, wearing a dusty robe.

"Abital. What are you doing here?" He shook his head. "You should not be in this part of town dressed like that."

"Dressed like what?" She was wearing her everyday tunic and robe, made of undyed linen.

"No one around here can afford such fine cloth these days. You should be more careful."

Abital did not understand. "There is nothing nice about this."

Ira shook his head. "You of all people should know better than that, Abital. Even the servants at the palace wear clothing finer than most can afford these days."

Abital realized this was likely true. The meals at the palace, meager as they were, were also likely more filling than what most people ate, judging by what she had seen in town.

"I went to your shop, and it was closed."

"There is no point in staying open these days. Not when there is no one to buy costly fabrics."

"But I have an order from the queen."

Ira cocked his head. "I am afraid not."

"What do you mean?"

"The palace has not paid its bill in many months. I cannot sell you any more cloth until the bill is paid. And since the palace was the only customer buying fine fabrics these days, it did not make sense to keep the shop open."

"That cannot be true." How had this happened?

"It is true, I assure you. I cannot afford to feed and clothe my own children unless the bill is paid."

"I will go now and take care of it, just like the last time this happened. The queen requires new gowns."

"I do not think so, Miss. They did not tell you? When I appealed at the palace for payment, I was told that no more cloth would be required. They agreed to pay what was already owed, but payment has been slow in coming. I do not know if the bill will ever be paid in full. So you see, I cannot give you anything more."

"The queen will be very upset." She said it more to herself than to him, but he nodded.

"Perhaps that is true. But also maybe it is for the best. The people of Jezreel do not think much of the queen buying new silks and costly dyes when the people down here are starving."

Ira took her bundle of food for Saba, and she insisted he must take some of it for himself and his children before he passed it to the trader. Abital did not know if the trader would still come to town with Ira's shop closed. She did not know whether the rest of the food would ever make it to Saba.

Abital walked away from the house feeling completely bewildered. She had known things in the kingdom were bad, that people were hungry and hurting, but it was far worse than she had realized. How had she not seen? Was she so protected and coddled up at the palace that she had missed this level of suffering completely?

Her heart ached for the people in Jezreel who were suffering. But more immediately, she feared what would happen when she told the queen about the cloth.

Jezebel received the news more calmly than Abital had expected, and Abital hoped for a moment that she might not cause a fuss. But the story that she heard later, from Obadiah, chilled her.

"She did not storm in, as she had before," Obadiah said. "But she waited until there was a break, and then she approached the king, pulled him to the side, and explained that there must be a misunderstanding. All could hear what she was saying to the king. When he told her that there was no money to buy new silks, that what little money coming in must be spent on keeping the government running and people in the palace and the armies fed, and that she would have to live with what she had for now, she told the king that most at the palace and the armies could starve for all she cared.

"She said it was not her concern whether they lived or died. It was her job to show the people that all was well in Israel, to inspire confidence, to appear perfectly attired at all times so that all would respect and envy the king."

"How did he take that?"

Obadiah hesitated. "He knows that there are no taxes coming in, and that the army has taken to plundering villages just to find enough food to survive. He knows how she would howl if those who cook her food or clean her rooms were gone from the palace. He told her once again that there was no money for new cloth, and she would need to be content with what she already had."

"What did she do?" Keziah, Abital noticed, was careful not to take too much interest in stories about the queen, but even she could not help being drawn in by this one.

"She told him he would be sorry. He replied, 'I have no doubt of that, but it cannot be helped.' And then he told her that he was hopeful that things might soon change, that something may soon happen to help make things better in Israel."

"What did he mean by that?" Abital asked.

"We will have to wait and see," Obadiah said. He looked over at his sister, and Abital was sure she detected a sadness or tenderness in his gaze. A sense of dread began to work its way through Abital.

A few weeks later, the news was announced. The kingdom needed an infusion of money, weapons, and livestock to survive, and the king also desired an ally to the south, which could help Israel fight off the Moabites. The king had found a way to solve each of these problems.

Aaliyah, daughter of the king of the Ammonites, would become King Ahab's third wife.

CHAPTER SIXTEEN

The king married his third wife with far less celebration than he had the last one. There was a banquet after his wedding to Aaliyah, but after two full years of drought, Soraya did not have much to work with. She cooked up the last of the mutton and roasted quails and pheasants. She also found fresh melon to serve with the sweets, though Abital did not know how she managed it. They had not seen fresh fruit in many months. Despite Soraya's resourcefulness, most of what was served at the banquet was provided by Aaliyah's father. There had been plenty of rain in Rabbah, and the country was fruitful and prosperous.

Aaliyah took up residence in a set of rooms across the hall from Keziah. Anu from the kitchen was sent to work for her, and Abital was assigned to help her with her clothing. There was no money for fabric, and besides, the new wife had brought a full wardrobe with her to Jezreel, but Abital went to her rooms each day and helped her nonetheless. Aaliyah had brought rich silks, gowns made of fabric that had been finely woven in intricate patterns, and heavy robes trimmed in fur. Abital had not seen such fine cloth in many months, not since Ira's shop shut down. The sight of the beautiful clothing made Jezebel all the more jealous of this new wife.

Aaliyah was quiet, and she appeared to be haughty at first, but it only took Abital a few days to understand that she was actually quite shy. She was kind enough, but she kept mostly to herself. She enjoyed playing music on a small harp, and when she spoke, she talked of her two older sisters, who had each married the king of a powerful city, and how much she missed them.

After more than two years with no rain, many were in despair.

The king's desire to see Elijah only grew stronger, and he sent out a demand across the land, insisting that Elijah present himself. Day after day, there was no response. The prophet either did not know or did not care that the king had demanded his return.

Abital still spent much time in Keziah's rooms, though Obadiah was busy trying to acquire food from foreign lands to feed the people of Israel and was not able to come most days. Ayla was crawling now, and Keziah was kept busy following after her.

Each day there seemed to be fewer people at the palace. The king must reduce the staff, Obadiah said. The king could not feed and clothe so many, and with so little food to cook, many of the kitchen maids were let go. Soraya cried for her maids but did not complain. Each worker knew they could be next.

"You must get him to stop providing for the prophets of Baal," Keziah said to her brother one afternoon. "How many hundreds does the queen feed? Men who sit around and do nothing but talk about how much gold the queen's forced offerings bring in, while the poor kitchen maids go home to starve."

"I thought the offerings brought in at the temple were used to feed the prophets," Abital said.

"That is how it should work," Obadiah said. "But in actuality, their food is provided by the king, who also pays for their home."

"That cannot be true," Abital said. "What of the offerings, then?"

Keziah shook her head. "No one knows what the prophets do with the riches brought to the temple. There must be a storeroom somewhere full of treasures offered to the false god."

"Why does the king allow it?" Abital asked, though she realized she already knew the answer.

"I have told him the care of the prophets at the expense of the crown must end, but he will not stand up to Jezebel," Obadiah said. "Even though it is sinking the kingdom even further into debt."

Abital feared each day that she would be told her services were no longer needed. What good was a seamstress when there was no cloth to be had? If she was let go, she would not be able to send her meager bits to Saba, and what would happen to him then? And yet, each day, she somehow was not let go.

Jezebel's temper grew worse as the spring drew out, one unbroken blue sky after another. She was called to the king's rooms even less, and the portions of food served at the palace dwindled even further. A thick layer of dust choked every surface.

"I cannot stand it," Jezebel said one day, looking down at her dish of lentils and a dry crust of flatbread. There was no yogurt or oil or cheese to offer flavor and substance. Soraya had run out of those many months back. "We are eating like peasants."

"Most in the kingdom have nothing," Abital said, trying to cheer her. "We are lucky to have as much as we do."

"We are not like most in the kingdom, though," Jezebel insisted. "We are meant to have more. I am the queen. Why should I not have more than most?"

Neither Abital nor Mara answered.

"I thought the point of marrying the new wife was to get money for things like food," Jezebel said another day, lifting her spoon so the mashed grains in milk ran off it. "And yet we eat this garbage."

"Much of the grain that the king received went to feed his armies, and what was left was distributed to those in the kingdom who had none." Obadiah had said that it was not nearly enough, that it would stretch out only a few days for most, but it was all they had. Saba had written to say that his allotment of flour from the king was most welcome, though it was gone quickly. He was still working on arranging her engagement to Ezra, and if this year's crop of lambs was healthy, they should be able to strike a deal. Her heart sank at the news.

"It is the fault of that manager," Jezebel said another time, looking down at her bowl of cooked grains. "He keeps the best for himself and his sister, and he starves the rest of us."

"Keziah does not get any more than you do," Abital said, and immediately regretted it. She always tried not to compare the two. "I see what she gets, and it is the same as you. She is not getting any special treatment, I assure you."

"Then he is keeping it all for himself."

Abital did not argue, though nothing could have been further from the truth. She dared not tell the queen that because of her care and feeding of the prophets of Baal and Asherah, there was not enough to go around for everyone else.

"She is so smug, sitting there with her little scrolls, saying her prayers to Yahweh." Abital understood that Jezebel was still speaking of Keziah. This was a familiar pattern of refrain. "If her God is so powerful, why does He not make it rain?"

Abital again bit her tongue. It was not as though Yahweh were some obscure deity. Yahweh had been the God of Israel, worshiped throughout the kingdom, for many generations before the kings turned to false idols. Israel had forgotten her covenant with Yahweh, who had given them this land, but that did not make Him any less powerful. Abital also did not point out what was becoming ever clearer to her—that Yahweh would send rain only when Israel turned from its wicked ways and acknowledged Him as the One True God. Perhaps all the time she spent with the Yahwists was beginning to change her.

As the queen's moods grew worse, she talked of home more and more, of the feasts they had there, and how well they dressed, and how much better her father was at managing a nation than King Ahab. Finally, one morning, as Abital arranged the folds of a lightweight silk gown from last summer that Jezebel had called "worse than what the paupers wear," Abital dared to make a suggestion.

"Perhaps you could visit your family."

"The king would never let me go." Jezebel turned her head, trying to get a better angle as she looked in the mirror. "He depends on me."

Abital was not sure this was true. She tried again. "The king wants you to be happy. A visit to your father's house would make you happy, would it not?"

"But who would care for Ahaziah if I was gone?"

Though she was confused by the question, Abital tried not to show it. Jezebel did not care for Ahaziah herself. She often did not see him for days on end. "Perhaps the future king could come with you to meet his Phoenician family."

Jezebel dismissed the idea at first, but soon it seemed to take hold, and before the summer arrived, she was preparing for her journey. The king had approved the idea of her visit to her homeland and even appeared pleased by the idea, according to Obadiah.

"He will be glad to go a few weeks without hearing complaints from her," Obadiah said.

"Obadiah. Be kind." Keziah cut him a look with her eyes.

"You are right. I am sorry." But Obadiah did not act sorry. While his sister's back was turned, reaching for Ayla, he grinned at Abital. "I am sure he sees that it will be good for her to see her family. And no doubt it will not hurt that she will take several members of her household with her. There will be fewer mouths to feed. Let King Ethbaal feed her entourage for a while."

"Is she taking a lot of her household with her?" Suddenly Abital was filled with dread. Would she be required to leave the palace with the queen?

"Mara will go with her, of course, and the nurse," Obadiah said. "She wanted to bring you as well, but I said it would be unfair to the other wives, since you serve all three. The king agreed."

"I am most grateful."

"It is entirely selfish, I assure you." He quirked an eyebrow and smiled at her.

When Abital went to Jezebel's room the next day, the queen's clothes were in a large pile on the floor.

"We must pack all the newest clothes," Jezebel said, throwing aside a blue linen tunic for a scarlet silk. "They are nowhere near new enough, but they will have to do."

Abital helped the queen sort through her clothes and pack them neatly in a trunk, and Jezebel declared she could not possibly manage without Abital's help. She would talk to the king, Jezebel said. Abital must accompany them. Abital feared she would be dragged into the queen's trip after all, but two days later, the queen and her entourage set off, packed into carts piled high with trunks and cartons of all sizes. Abital feared for the donkeys that had to pull so much weight as she stood in the palace garden to see them off. Or, truly, what was left of the garden. The plants were brown stalks, the trees withered, the grass long dead. The vineyard outside the palace walls, the one belonging to Naboth, was nothing but gnarled brown vines.

The palace was quieter with the queen gone, and it almost felt like everyone could finally exhale. Abital did not have to hide the time she spent in Keziah's rooms, and the more afternoons she spent there, the more she got to know the brother and sister, and the more she began to understand their reliance on the God of their ancestors.

"Abba gives generously at the temple, not to show off or to become recognized for his generosity, but because it is a way of showing that all he has belongs to Yahweh," Obadiah explained one day.

She learned that Obadiah and Keziah had a different mother than their much older brothers, who were born to a daughter from the tribe of Benjamin. She had passed away from a fever that swept through Samaria many years ago, and their father had taken a new wife, whose family were deeply devoted followers of Yahweh, and whose influence had brought all of their family to trust in the Lord. Obadiah and Keziah had always been close, and Keziah could not imagine life at the palace without her brother's company.

As the weeks went on without the presence of the queen, Abital's workroom was abandoned completely, her sewing things and her loom moved into Keziah's quarters.

The long, hot summer days drew out. With the queen gone, and with Obadiah appearing most days, they were some of the happiest Abital had spent at the palace. She sometimes found herself alone in the room with Obadiah, Keziah having vanished to take care of one task or another. Channah always managed to disappear at such times as well, though Abital never saw where she went. Abital and Obadiah played strategy games, and they spoke about many things—about Abital's saba and the hills where she had grown up, about what Obadiah was like as a child, and about the Hebrew Scriptures. Abital was impressed by how deeply he knew the Scriptures, and how his knowledge of them guided the choices he made each day. Every time he had to leave, Abital felt as though a small part of her was leaving as well.

When the long summer began turning to autumn, the queen returned to the palace, shattering the fragile peace she had left in her absence. She came back with stories about the fashions worn by the women in Sidon and the lavish meals they had enjoyed there. She was deprived, she said, of all good things, stuck here in this provincial palace in this tiny city. She demanded new gowns in the style of the women up north, but there was nothing to be done. There was no silk to be had now that Ira's shop was gone. One could not eat damask.

A few weeks later, Obadiah told her he was leaving on an errand for the king and would be gone for several weeks.

"Where will you go?" Abital asked.

"The army's horses and donkeys are withering and dying in the fields. The king has ordered me to go out into the kingdom and find grass for the animals."

"Find grass? Where?"

"Anywhere. We must find food for the king's animals, or they will starve."

"People are starving each day. Don't they need the grass for their own animals?" She thought of Saba, whose remaining sheep were all he had left. If the king took the grass they fed on to feed his own animals, Saba would not survive long. "How can he do this to his people?"

"The king's soldiers need the animals to push back the Moabites in the South. I suppose the king thinks the lives of his soldiers are worth more than the lives of the farmers in the field. The farmers have not been paying much in taxes, so I imagine it makes sense, to his way of thinking."

"And you?" Abital lifted her chin. "What do you think?"

"I think it is a despicable plan. One man's life is not worth more than another's. The farmers have not paid taxes because they have grown nothing, and that is because of the king's unrepentance."

"Have you said as much to the king?"

"I have, and more. And still the king insists I must go."

"Why you? You are in charge of the palace, not his soldiers or the livestock." There were plenty of men at the palace who could be spared for such a task.

"The king says he is sending me because he trusts me the most."

"You sound as though you do not believe it."

He was quiet for a moment. "I do know this land better than most. I have walked most of it at one point or another."

"But that is not the real reason either."

"No, I don't think it is. I am not oblivious to the queen's hatred for me and for my position. She blames me for losing so many of the things she loved about her life at the palace."

Abital knew that he meant not just the loss of fine clothing and rich food but also her position as the king's sole wife. Obadiah was not responsible for his sister's marriage, but Jezebel hated everyone associated with Keziah, including him.

"Surely the king has not agreed to send you on this dangerous mission because of his wife's jealousy."

Obadiah shrugged. "Have you ever seen him stand up to her? She does not always get what she wants, but it is not because of Ahab. He is too afraid of her anger to say no. I suspect she might have had something to do with his decision to send me."

"She is truly horrible."

"She is still your queen, Abital," Keziah said from the corner, where she had been listening to the conversation.

Though she was right, Abital did not like to be reminded of it. She wished she had the graciousness that seemed to come so easily to Keziah.

"Where will you go?" Abital asked.

"Come," he said. "I will show you."

Abital stood to follow him. He led her out to the balcony, which looked over the valley. The town of Jezreel spilled out down the hill to one side, buildings built one after another along the steep and narrow streets. To the other side, there was the vineyard, dry and withered from the endless days of sun, and beyond that, the whole of the Jezreel Valley. What had once been a lush, fertile valley, filled with farmland and fruit trees and threaded through with streams and creeks, was now a dry brown wasteland. At the far side of the valley, hills rose, covered in brown grass and dotted with craggy rocks and outcroppings. The caves that had hidden the prophets of Yahweh were somewhere in those hills.

"Do you see that dry riverbed?" Obadiah asked, pointing to a thin line that snaked its way along the center of the valley. "I will follow it to the east, where it joins the Jordan River. There are many creeks and streams that branch off, and I will search until I find water and grass."

"And if you do not?"

Obadiah shrugged. His face was silhouetted against the sun, and she was struck once again by how handsome he was. She would never grow tired of looking at him, though that was not what she loved most about him.

"Then we must pray for Elijah to return quickly and end this drought." He leaned forward on his forearms.

"What if you run into him out there?"

"If I saw Elijah, I would no doubt run in fear."

"In fear? Of the prophet Elijah?" Abital called to mind the image of the old prophet, with his ragged clothes, his crazy, unwashed hair, and the unhinged look in his eyes. "You are certainly better suited in a fight."

"I am not afraid of Elijah himself," Obadiah said. "Though I do have a few things I would like to say to him, since he is but the Lord's messenger. None of this is his fault. No, I would be afraid of the king, who has declared that any person caught associating with the prophet is subject to death. He has already hinted to me many times over the years that he thinks I know where Elijah is hiding."

"But you do not know."

"I do not. But that does not mean the king believes me. He knows I am a Yahwist and assumes I must therefore know where Elijah hides. I have insisted I do not, but if I turn up with the prophet now, he will think I was lying."

"Surely if you came across him in the desert, you could explain, and—"

"When it comes to Elijah, I believe the king would attack first and ask questions later. He mentions daily what he would do if he saw the old man. I believe anyone near Elijah is in danger when the king finally meets him."

"Then let us hope you do not come across him."

"I hope I do not meet him. But I do hope he returns soon. I do not know how much longer we can last with no rain. I fear what will happen to Israel if something does not change soon. It will not be long before we too starve, so many already have," Obadiah said. "The king will be overthrown, almost certainly, or Israel conquered. In any case, it seems certain the land that was given to our forefathers will soon fall into the hands of foreign invaders if nothing changes."

"Yahweh will not let that happen." Abital did not know if she believed it.

"It is not up to us to know what Yahweh will and will not do. Look at what He has done already to try and get the nation to turn back to Him. Hundreds are dying each day. There is no reason He would not turn His back on this wicked generation."

Abital pondered this. Was it possible? Would this drought go on so long that Israel might simply cease to exist? She could not imagine such a thing. But that did not mean it could not happen.

"Do you like it, working for the king?" she asked a few moments later.

"Do I like it?" He used his forearms to push himself up and angled his body toward her. "I do not know that I have ever thought about that, really. It is not as though we get to choose these things. I do what I am told to do because that is my job."

"But you do not have to work for the king, do you? Could you not be working with your father back in Samaria?"

"I suppose so, but he thought I could do more good here, in the palace, where I can keep an eye on my sister and work to keep Yahweh's name before the king, so here I am. But we will see."

"What do you mean? You will see about what?"

Obadiah didn't speak for a moment. He seemed to be gazing at something very far away.

"My father is pressing for me to marry," he eventually said. "He is hoping to find some nice young woman from Samaria to send up here."

The words made her belly clench and her knees weak. She fought to keep her voice level, to not show how they affected her.

"That will no doubt be a good thing for you."

"Will it?" A lock of his hair caught in the breeze, and he brushed it back. "I am not so sure."

"Your sister would be happy for you." It felt like the right thing to say, and was the best she could do.

"No, she would not. She would not want me to marry one woman when my heart is with another."

Abital felt that she could not breathe. A flame of hope leaped inside her. Had he just—did he mean—

"You do not need to look so shocked, Abital. You are so clever, I know you cannot have missed this. I have not exactly hidden my feelings for you. And my sister is well aware, which is why she is gracious enough to occupy herself otherwise so often." He reached over and touched her hand. When she did not pull her hand away, he covered it with his. "If I were to marry, it would not be fair to my wife, because I would still be thinking of you, day and night."

Abital did not say anything. She did not know what to say. She felt like her legs were turning to jelly beneath her. Her belly felt warm, and his touch awakened every part of her. She had longed to hear him say such things for so long. She had suspected how he felt—as he had said, she was not blind. And she knew that she felt the same way, that if she married another, it would not change her feelings for him, and she would simply long for him instead.

But she also understood what he hadn't said. He had not suggested he could marry her. They both understood that could not be. His father would never agree to such a marriage, and her saba could never afford a dowry of the size that would be required. He did not see a future where they could be together, and though she knew this too, it still stung to hear it from him.

"I do not know what will happen when I go out searching for grass, and I do not know what will happen to Israel if I do not, so I wanted to make sure you heard me say it." Obadiah ran his thumb across the back of her hand. He was looking at her as if he wanted to say more, to do more, but he dared not. "No matter what happens, I will be thinking of you."

It was everything Abital had wanted to hear, and yet now she did not know what to say in response.

"I will be thinking of you as well," she said after a moment, turning her palm up to meet his. "And I will wait eagerly for your return."

CHAPTER SEVENTEEN

Obadiah returned from his journey a week later. When Abital saw him enter Keziah's room, she wanted to run to him and throw her arms around him, but she merely looked up from her sewing, meeting his eyes and then gazing down.

He reported that he had found a brook to the east where there was a little water still flowing. He, along with several of the other men from the palace, drove dozens of donkeys and horses to the brook, where they quickly ate the little bit of green grass that had surrounded the trickle of a creek. The animals returned to the stables tired but healthier than they had been in some time.

"He will send you again, you know," Keziah said. "Because you have succeeded once, he will send you again, and he will expect success a second time."

"There is no more grass to be found. I have searched everywhere, and there isn't any."

"That does not mean he won't want you to find some," Keziah said.

Ayla crawled around the room, playing with a small bowl and cup, muttering to herself. Now and then she uttered a word or two, stringing them together with delight. Her dark curls framed her face, and her wide eyes took in everything around her.

"Let us hope he does not send me out again," Obadiah said.

As the long days of autumn turned to winter, the temperature dropped and the skies grew cloudy some days, but still no rain fell. It had been two and a half years now, and big chunks of cracked earth dotted the land where lush fields had been. The vineyard near the palace was completely dead. The wine was running low, and there was little to eat. Still, Abital sent parcels to her saba as often as she could, and he wrote back and reported that he did not know how he would survive without them. Ira also took a small portion of the food for his help, as did the trader who carried it, so Abital knew that the amount that got to her saba was scant. Still, it seemed to help. Each day, Abital feared her services would no longer be required, and she would be sent home.

As Keziah had predicted, the king was so pleased that Obadiah had found grass for the animals to eat that he sent him out again to look for more. Obadiah did not know how long he would be gone, but when he said goodbye to Abital, she got the sense that he believed he would be going on quite a long journey.

The king sent out more spies to hunt for Elijah, but they returned with no news of the mad prophet. Keziah reported that she did her best to convince the king that repentance was the only thing that would bring Elijah back and end this drought, but he would not outlaw the worship of idols, not now when he needed help from any god who would send the rain. In addition, he dared not upset Jezebel, Keziah reported, not now when his armies were so weak and he required the help of the king of the North. If he were to outlaw the idols, he would lose the support of her father that he so desperately needed.

Ahab spent most of his days in the capital of Samaria, but though he seemed to spend little time at the palace, both Keziah and Aaliyah's bellies began to swell that winter. Both were very pleased, but Jezebel grew more and more agitated by the day. Though Abital was no longer making new clothing for the queen, she still made plenty of alterations and fixes to the old clothes to try to make them look new. Jezebel had not given up her vanity, even when all of Israel was slowly wasting away.

Obadiah returned several weeks later and reported that he had found grass for the king's animals once again, only this time he had not come across it on his own. He had gone to see his father, who sent Obadiah to talk to a shepherd outside of Samaria, and the shepherd had traded his knowledge of a secret brook high in the hills for a hefty fee.

"Ahab was willing to pay this fee for the knowledge of the brook?" Abital asked.

"Oh no." Obadiah shook his head. "No, it was not the king who paid the fee."

No one spoke for a moment.

"Our father paid it," Keziah said.

"I did not know what else to do," Obadiah said. He looked thinner than he had been before, and more worn out. "The king had warned that there would be punishment for failure."

"Our father is now supporting the king." Keziah shook her head.

"Only this one time."

"You know he will send you out again," Keziah said. "And will our father have to pay again?"

"He will not, because I will not go to him."

"But if the king will not tolerate failure—"

"I will not. Our father said he would not help again unless—"

He broke off suddenly and shook his head.

"Unless what?" Keziah narrowed her eyes.

Obadiah sighed. "He still wants me to marry. He has spoken to Maryam's father, and they are anxious to work out a deal."

Abital held her breath and looked down, focusing on her stitching.

"And will you?" Keziah asked. "Marry Maryam?"

"I have told Abba I do not wish to. I have said there is too much to do at the palace and I could not possibly handle a marriage right now."

Keziah looked like she wanted to say more, but after a quick glance at Abital, she changed the subject. "Did you hear any news of Elijah on your journey?"

"The prophets do not know where he is," Obadiah said. "They have not seen him in more than a year."

At the beginning of the month of Tebet, at the coldest part of the year, Obadiah was sent out once again, but this time he returned three weeks later with no new source of grass. The king raged, but Obadiah simply told him that there was no more grass to be had in the area. Abital could not help the relief that flooded through her at this news. Obadiah had not gone to his father, then. He had not agreed to marry the girl from Samaria.

The days began to grow longer. It had now been three years since Elijah told Ahab there would be no rain until he repented, and not a drop had fallen from the sky in that time. Each day, there were more reports of children starving and farmers dropping dead from exhaustion as they tried to coax any living thing out of the dry ground.

Abital had long given up trying to understand why Yahweh would allow suffering of this sort. Keziah and Obadiah did their best to make sense of it.

"Yahweh did not cause the suffering, but He allows it," Obadiah said. "In order to turn Israel to repentance."

"But so many suffer and die," Abital said. She wanted to trust Yahweh completely, the way Keziah and Obadiah and Channah did. She saw and understood their faith in many ways, but in this way, she could not quite convince herself all was well. How could any god be just and still allow such terrible suffering among his people?

"Yahweh will not be mocked," Keziah said. "You will see. Because of this, His power will be made known."

The answer did not satisfy Abital the way Keziah seemed to think it would.

Abital hoped that there would be another chance for her and Obadiah to talk together, to hear him say that he cared for her, though she knew that it was probably better if they did not. No good could come out of hearing that he cared for her but could not marry her. Still, she longed to hear the words anyway.

The Feast of Baal approached. Jezebel would hold a celebration, as she had each year. It would be a pitiful affair this year, but Jezebel insisted that it must happen, so she kept Soraya busy with instructions on the food she wanted served. Soraya smiled to her face but laughed behind her back.

"Where does she think I am going to get lambs to roast?" Soraya said. "Or cheese? She is living in a dream."

"She does not care about the suffering of others," Abital said. "Only about herself."

Though she could not have a new gown for the feast, Jezebel demanded that Abital remake something she already had. Abital had been working for weeks on refreshing one of the queen's many red silk gowns, but then Jezebel called Abital to her room.

"The dark gown," Jezebel said. "The one the color of midnight. You can make a new gown from that one, lower and tighter."

"I—" Abital started and then faltered. The gown had been made loose, with long sleeves and a flowing skirt. Maybe it could work. The way the fabric had been cut, would there be enough of it?

"I will do my best."

Abital retrieved the gown from her chest. The fabric was still smooth and shiny and moved under her hand like freshly poured milk. She set to work on it, planning how she would cut the silk to refresh the gown. It might work, but barely. She started to undo the seams before setting it aside for the day. She would have to work carefully, but what the queen asked might be possible.

Later that day, Obadiah reported that he was being sent out again, though this time the king's orders were different.

"The king has said that he and I will both go out to find grass," Obadiah reported. "He will go one way, and I will go the other."

"I thought the creeks were all dry," Keziah said. "Except the one Abba paid for you to find out about."

"Perhaps there are some that are not," Obadiah said. "Let us hope we will find them."

"Why has the king decided to go himself?" Abital asked. He had never done so before but always sent others.

"He does not believe that there is no grass. He says he wants to see for himself." Obadiah sipped the tea from the cup he cradled in his hands. It was little more than warmed water with a few mint leaves that had been used many times.

"How can he not believe this to be true?" Keziah said. "Does he think you are lying? That everyone in the kingdom is lying to him?"

But Abital thought she understood. "It is not really grass the king is after, is it?"

"He would be happy to find some grass, but no, I do not think that is what he is truly seeking," Obadiah said. "I believe he grows weary of his spies returning empty-handed. He is going to try to find Elijah himself."

"And what if he finds him?" Keziah said.

"He will kill him, I am sure of it," Obadiah said.

"In that case," Abital said, "let us pray that he will not be found."

CHAPTER EIGHTEEN

Obadiah had been walking for almost two weeks. He had nearly reached Sidon, searching for any source of water, any scrap of green grass left, but there was nothing. He was hot and tired, and his feet hurt, and even if he had managed to find grass up this way, it would do no good. The king's animals would never survive the journey, as weak as they were. He would turn around and start for home in the morning. He would simply have to tell the king he had failed again. The king would not be pleased. Obadiah would likely be sent away from the palace, and then he would not get to see Abital. Or his sister and niece. He could only pray that the king would be merciful.

Obadiah camped outside the town of Tyre, in what must once have been a beautiful grove of trees alongside a bubbling brook. Now the trees were dead and brown, the ground was nothing but hard-packed dirt, and the riverbed completely dry. Obadiah dared not light a fire. If a stray spark escaped, this whole area would quickly go up in flames. He ate dried figs and a bit of jerky, and spent a restless night dreaming of Abital. All day, he thought of things he wanted to say to her. He wanted to tell her about every encounter. Even when they were apart, she filled his mind and his thoughts, and he could not wait to get back to the palace to see her again.

He rose early, ate a little more of the remaining jerky, and started off. He would take a direct route this time, staying along the main roads, and it should only take a week, at most, to make it back to Jezreel. The road was quiet this morning. He had seen fewer people than normal during his travels. Most people did not have food and water to sustain them over a long journey, and fewer had places to go. So much trade had been erased in the past three years. There was nothing to sell and no money to buy it with anyway. Unless it could be eaten, no one was interested, and most stayed at home to conserve their energy.

Obadiah had been walking for less than an hour when he saw him. The man had wiry gray hair that spilled down his back in unbrushed clumps, and his grizzled beard was in a similar state of disarray. His robe was a dull, dusty brown, and his feet were bare. But his eyes told Obadiah who he was immediately. The way he was looking at Obadiah—like he knew exactly who he was, like he already knew all of his secrets—made Obadiah realize immediately that this was Elijah.

Obadiah's first instinct was to run. He knew, as sure as day, that the king would not believe he was not in league with the prophet. He knew he was putting his life at risk by even being near him. But he found he could not make himself run away. He could not turn. He was walking, as if it had been ordained, directly toward Elijah. The prophet did not look away from Obadiah as he approached.

"It is really you, Elijah?" Obadiah said. He could sense, even now, that the spirit of the Lord was with this man. That he was indeed a true prophet, sent by Yahweh.

"Yes. I am Elijah, and I have been waiting for you." His voice was higher than Obadiah had expected, and it warbled and almost squeaked.

"For me?"

"You are from the palace," Elijah said. It was not a question. "You will take a message to the king. Go tell your master that Elijah is here."

Obadiah faltered.

"Did you hear me?"

"I heard you," Obadiah said.

"Well?" Elijah said. "Why are you not going?"

Obadiah tried to find the words to explain the fear that coursed through his body. "What have I done, that you are handing me over to Ahab to be put to death?"

"What are you going on about? How am I handing you over to death?"

"The king has searched everywhere for you. As surely as the Lord your God lives, there is no nation to which the king has not sent someone to search for you. When the men have not found you, he has asked the king of each nation to swear you had not been found within that nation's borders. And now you want me to go to the king and say, 'Elijah is here'?" Obadiah felt the years of frustration and fear rising in him as he spoke, and he found his voice choking with emotion.

"Go to the king. Bring him to me."

Obadiah took a deep breath. How could Elijah simply show up after all this time and start making demands? After all they had suffered? Did he not understand what he was asking? And this man had evaded capture for the past three years. How could Obadiah trust that he would stay here and wait while he went to get the king?

"I do not know where the spirit of the Lord will carry you," Obadiah said. "You have managed to evade the king for three years. No one knows how you managed to hide so well. What is to say that you will not change your mind and evade him again now?"

The old man did not answer for a moment. Instead, he cocked his head and watched Obadiah. Then, he spoke. "Do you trust the Lord?"

"I have feared the Lord from my youth." Who was he, to ask this? "You know of the hundred prophets of Yahweh who escaped Jezebel's slaughter? I led them out of the camp. I hid them in caves, fifty in each. I brought them food and water for months. I have served the Lord as well as I could. And now you want me to go to the king and tell him Elijah wants to speak with him? When I do not even know if you will be here when I come back?"

"As surely as the Lord lives, I will be standing in this very spot when you return with the king. My servant and I will remain." He gestured to a gangly young man in tattered robes sitting a few yards away under a dead cypress tree. Obadiah had not noticed him before. "I will present myself to Ahab."

Obadiah did not see what choice he had. The prophet who spoke for Yahweh could not be denied. Obadiah did not know whether he could be trusted. He did not know whether he was risking his own life in doing as the prophet commanded. But he saw that he had no real choice.

"I will go now," he said.

CHAPTER NINETEEN

Two weeks had passed since Obadiah left, and there was no word from him. Abital feared, as did Keziah, that something bad had happened to him. Why had he not returned? The days were long and hot and dry, and tempers were frayed. The Feast of Baal was only days away, and the queen was not happy with the changes Abital had made to the night-colored gown. She had sent it back, insisting Abital cut the neckline lower and have it skim her body more.

The king returned to the palace after a week, tired and hot and frustrated. He had found no water and no grass for the animals. He had also, it seemed, not found Elijah.

Keziah encouraged Abital and Channah to pray, and Abital spent her days praying, as much as she was able, to Yahweh. With every day that dragged out, she grew more fearful. What would keep Obadiah from the palace for this long? Why was there no word from him?

Abital was getting ready to lie down on her mat that night when Channah came to find her. The night was hot, the air still and unbearably dry.

"You must come," Channah said quietly but insistently. "Quickly."

Abital pulled on a tunic and robe quickly and followed Channah through the quiet hallways.

"What is it?" Abital whispered. "What has happened?"

"You will see," Channah said. "But you must come now."

"Is Keziah all right? Is it the baby?" If she had lost the baby, she would be devastated.

"The baby is fine," Channah said. "But Keziah needs you."

When Channah led her into Keziah's rooms, she found Keziah in her nightgown, and in the light of the oil lamp, she did not see the other figure in the room at first.

"Abital."

Her heart skipped when she saw that it was Obadiah.

"You are back." He was safe. Praise God he was safe. He was walking toward her. He was as handsome as ever, but something was wrong. There was a look on his face that she had not seen before.

"I am very glad to see you," he said. "But I am afraid I have a terrible favor to ask."

Fear. Obadiah was afraid.

"What happened?" Abital asked.

"I am so sorry. I said I cannot ask it, but—"

"Elijah is back. My brother has found him," Keziah said. "And we fear what the king might do. We need your help."

Abital listened to the strange tale Obadiah told of how he had come upon Elijah the prophet. Of how the prophet had been waiting for him and had ordered him to tell the king to meet him.

"But the king will be upset with you."

Obadiah laughed. "I suspect he will be more than upset. Even if Elijah remains outside of Tyre, where I left him, if Ahab does appear and find him, Ahab will assume I have known for these past few years where Elijah has been. If I now turn up with the prophet in tow, he will believe I have lied to him, and he will have me killed."

"I see." Surely there was a way to make the king believe Obadiah knew nothing. Surely he would listen to reason. Elijah would vouch for him, wouldn't he?

"Obadiah must go tell the king now," Keziah said. "But we are preparing for the worst to happen. If the king really does try to have Obadiah killed, he must be ready to run away."

Abital felt her heart skip. He could run away. She might not see him again after tonight. Of course, that would be better than having him killed. It would be much better. But after tonight, he could be gone. And she would be left here, heartbroken.

"How can I help?" she asked. If she could help save his life, she would do anything.

"May my brother use that black cloth?" Keziah gestured at the large pieces on Abital's work table on the far side of the room. "Only long enough to get him safely out of the city. Could it be sewn up so it could be used again, just for tonight?"

Abital did not know what to say. She had started to reassemble the gown, but she could take it apart again so he could use a large piece to cover himself. Of course she wanted to give it to them. Anything to help Obadiah. But if the queen found out... Abital did not like to think about that.

Keziah hesitated. "I do not like to ask it, Abital, but I fear for my brother. If he must run, that cloth will keep him from being seen and perhaps save his life."

If the queen found out, she would have Abital sent home that night, as surely as the king would have Obadiah killed. Being sent home would be the same as being killed, for without the rations from the palace, both Abital and her saba would starve. It was madness. She could not do such a thing.

And yet, had not Obadiah risked everything when he had saved the prophets from Jezebel? No one, including Abital, had thought that wrong. Without the cloak, Obadiah would surely be at greater risk. And if he left the garment outside the city gates, in a place where Abital could retrieve it, the queen would never have to know.

She looked at Obadiah, at his strong chin, the curve of his cheek, those soft lips. At the kind eyes that were gazing at her now with so much love and tenderness. She cared for him, more than she had been willing to admit to herself. Even if they could not see each other, just knowing he was alive would keep Abital satisfied for the rest of her days. She would hold in her heart the way he was looking at her now so that when the hunger pains hit, it would be worth it. If taking the cloth gave Obadiah a chance to survive the king's rage, she would risk the queen's anger.

"I will work on it now."

"Thank you, Abital." Keziah carried a lamp over to the worktable, and as she pulled the larger pieces apart again, Keziah and Obadiah knelt and began to pray. They thanked Yahweh for His love and His mercy, and for sending Elijah to bring repentance to Israel. They asked for the Lord's protection for Obadiah, and for Abital, and asked that Yahweh would make His name known and bring His people back to Him. They asked that whatever happened, His name would be glorified.

Abital had heard Keziah and Obadiah pray many times, but something about seeing them here together hit her in a way it had not before. They asked for safety, yes, but mostly they asked for Yahweh's name to be known. Their faith was not about demanding what they wanted from God, about making offerings to appease Him, a kind of bribe to get what they were asking for. Their prayers, she realized, were a genuine expression of love and gratitude to a God they believed loved and cared for them. Who knew them by name. Who was just and whose power was unmatched. Who did not want their offerings, but their hearts.

Hearing their prayers now, she understood Him in a way she had not before. Yahweh was not only God, He was the true God. Abital could not explain it, but that night, as the shadows danced across the fabric in the flickering light of the oil lamp, she knew for sure that Saba had been right all along. Yahweh was God.

Abital felt like she was in a daze as she finished up her stitches and held out the cloak to Obadiah. It was sloppily done, but it would hold long enough for him to make it out of the city.

"Thank you, Abital." Keziah smiled gratefully. "You are risking much to help us."

"I am risking much to see the Lord's name be known once again in Israel," Abital said. The words had come to her unbidden, but she realized in that moment that they were true. "You cannot fail. I will do whatever it takes to help."

"I will go to the king first thing in the morning," Obadiah said. "If I must run, I will leave the cloak in the grove of cypress trees just outside the city gate. Come, I will show you."

He started toward the balcony, and Abital followed. Keziah stayed where she was. Obadiah and Abital walked out onto the balcony, and he gestured down at the trees outside the city's gates. "There."

"I will look for it there," Abital said. "But let us hope it will not come to that."

"I will not forget what you have done," Obadiah said. The sky was dark velvet, unfurling like a banner above them, and dotted with thousands of stars. Somehow, impossibly, the scent of jasmine and juniper hung in the air. "I will not forget you."

He reached for her hand, and Abital let him take it. "You will be all right. Yahweh will protect His servant."

"I hope we have not put you in danger by what we have asked of you tonight," Obadiah said.

"I would do it all over again, despite the risk. The most important thing is that you are kept safe."

"No," he said, shaking his head. "The most important thing is that Yahweh is glorified. Only He knows what will happen, but even if I spend my life in hiding, it will be worth it if it helps end this suffering. If Elijah is able to return Israel to Yahweh."

"Yahweh will protect His servant," Abital repeated, willing the words to be true.

"Whether He does or not, I will serve Him."

He rubbed the back of her hand with his thumb. Neither one of them said anything for a very long time. There was nothing to say. Abital knew this fragile relationship could not last. That it was built on a set of circumstances that would someday cease. There would come a time when one of them had to move on, to marry, to change roles. Abital had always known how this would end. But that still did not make it any less difficult now that it had.

They stayed there for a long time before Obadiah finally leaned forward, pulled her into a hug, and held her for a moment before releasing her.

"I will be thinking of you every day," he promised. Abital could not speak as tears filled her eyes, but she pushed them back. She knew she would think of him too.

CHAPTER TWENTY

The next morning, as Abital helped the queen and Aaliyah dress, she waited for news. Jezebel chose one of her more comfortable robes, saying that the king was leaving the palace that morning, but that was all. When Abital got to Keziah's room, she learned that Obadiah had appeared before the king early that morning and reported that Elijah wanted to meet him. The king had grown angry, as feared, and had suggested again that Obadiah was in league with the prophet, but he had quickly prepared for a journey and followed Obadiah out of the palace.

"He did not have to flee?" Abital said.

"The king went with him," Keziah confirmed.

Then he should have left the cloak. Would he have been able to leave it, though, if he was with the king? She would check. Abital hoped Jezebel did not ask to see her progress on the midnight-hued gown this morning.

After Keziah was dressed, Abital left the palace and walked through the quiet streets to the city gates. The guards at the gates asked where she was going but did not stop her when she left the king's protection behind and walked to the grove of cypress trees. They were now nothing but brown sticks, dead limbs against the blue sky. The cloak was not there.

Jezebel would be incensed if Abital did not have it.

She prayed Obadiah would not need it.

Abital returned to Keziah's room and reported that Obadiah still had the cloak.

Keziah thanked her and then spent much of the morning pacing up and down the balcony. Abital waited until the time of day when Jezebel usually napped, drowsy from the effects of the opium pipe, and she went into the queen's room and took another of her gowns, one of her red silks, from her trunk. Mara looked up as she came in, but when Abital explained she was having trouble with the black gown and wanted to prepare another gown in case she could not get it to work, Mara nodded and went back to lounging on the mat. Abital returned to Keziah's chambers and did her best to focus on her sewing. She prayed that the queen would believe that she could not get the black gown to look like what the queen had requested. She worked hard on the gown, so it would impress the queen so much that she did not mind that it was not what she had asked for. But she found that her hands shook, and she pricked her finger again and again. She feared for Obadiah. Was he safe? Would he be safe? She worked through the day and into the night and then again the next morning, finishing the gown for the queen on the morning of the feast.

"This is not the black gown," Jezebel said, surveying the red silk Abital held up.

"The cut on that one is still not working the way I want it to," Abital said. "I could not allow my queen to wear a garment that was less than perfection, so I reworked this one instead. It is one of your finest silks, and it turned out beautifully, did it not?"

The queen's face showed her dismay but then, also, a softening as she examined the red gown.

"I always did look fine in this gown," Jezebel said.

"And you will look even more stunning now that I have lowered the neckline and tightened the cut around the waist. Come, let us try it on and see how pretty you look."

Jezebel let Abital dress her and surveyed her reflection in the mirror.

"You have done good work," Jezebel said, surveying the new garment. "It is flattering, isn't it?"

"You look marvelous in it," Abital said. "We must hurry and get your hair dressed and your jewelry on, though, so you are not late."

Abital had been working so frantically, so afraid of what might happen, that she had not even thought about what the Feast of Baal meant. Jezebel would be making another sacrifice to a god that Abital now knew was false. Her stomach turned.

"This will do for today," Jezebel said, and Abital tried not to show her relief. "Keep working on the black gown, though."

"I will, my queen." If she ever got it back, she would. For now, though, she thanked Yahweh for the queen's pleasure in the red gown. If she had insisted on the black one, things could have gone very differently. But now she had a different problem before her. She could not attend the sacrifice, not now that she knew the truth.

Mara styled the queen's hair, and soon she was ready to set off for the temple.

"Come." The queen swept toward the door. "We must go."

Mara followed the queen, but Abital was rooted to the floor. She found she could not make her feet move.

"Abital, come. We cannot be late."

And yet, Abital did not move. She could not. She did not want to.

"I will not be going to the temple." Abital had not realized she would say the words until they came out of her mouth.

"What?" Jezebel turned back to her, her brow wrinkled.

"I am not coming," Abital repeated, more forcefully this time. "I will not worship Baal. I cannot, now that I know the truth." Abital felt like she was outside her body, and she was watching the scene from above. "I know that Yahweh is the One True God, and I will not worship any god but Him."

"I—" Jezebel seemed at a loss for words. Abital had never seen her as flustered as she was now. "You cannot mean that."

"But I do." Abital had not intended to do this, but she had never been more certain of anything in her life. "I will not be going to the temple of Baal, today or ever again."

"But you must. All in my household have to."

"But I cannot." Even as she said the words, she knew what they could cost her. She had avoided the queen's wrath over the black gown, but she would not avoid it now. She would be sent home, at best. She would soon starve. Saba would starve. But even knowing everything that lay ahead and what it would cost her, she could not make herself change course. Not now that she knew the truth.

Jezebel's mouth fell open. "This is the doing of those Yahwists."

"She spends each day with them," Mara volunteered from the doorway. "She works in the second wife's rooms and sleeps there sometimes. Who knows what those Yahwists do with the doors closed, but she likes it enough that she does not ever want to leave." Her face was smug.

Abital found that she could not even bring herself to be upset about Mara's words. They were salacious and intended for cruelty, but aside from a terrible insinuation, they were not untrue.

Jezebel narrowed her eyes at Mara and shook her head. "Do you think I am blind, child? Did you honestly think I had not seen that? Did you believe you were telling me something I did not know?"

Mara shrank back and cast her eyes to the floor.

"I have known for some time that you were in league with the Yahwists, and have I not always been willing to overlook that?" Jezebel narrowed her eyes at Abital.

"You have been most gracious, my queen." Abital bowed her head.

"I have not complained, even when you ignored your duties to me in order to serve the king's other wives."

"When have I—"

Abital started to argue back, but Jezebel raised her hand. She would not be interrupted.

"You were brought here to serve me. I allowed you to work for the other wives, but your first duty was always to be to me."

This was not true, nor was it fair. The king had expressly given his permission—his blessing, even—for her to help dress his other wives. But Jezebel either did not remember that or did not care.

"I have kept you around, even when there was no more cloth to be had and no need for your service. But this is too far," Jezebel said. "I will give you one chance to take back your words." She lifted her chin.

"And yet I will not," Abital said. "It is true that I have learned to love and serve Yahweh by spending time with the king's second wife." And her brother. She grew bolder, thinking of him and his faith in her. "And it is because of my devotion to the deliverer of Israel that I will not go to the temple or the feast of Baal ever again."

There was a moment of silence. Jezebel could not seem to believe what had just happened. Abital knew she herself could not.

"In that case, you will leave." Jezebel's words were icy. "You will leave here today."

"I will not. I do not work only for you."

"You will leave the palace today. You may be friends with the Yahwists, but I am still queen, and mother of the future king. You will leave here by nightfall, or you will bear the consequences. In either case, you will not see the sun come up from inside this palace again. Go, now, before I change my mind and have you killed today."

Keziah cried when she heard the news.

"I will send a message to the king. He will not stand for this."

But the king had left to meet Elijah. He would not get the message, let alone be able to send back his own message, before Abital must be gone, or risk her life.

"I am afraid I must go before the king can help," Abital said.

"Surely you can hide—"

"I believe her when she says she will kill me," Abital said.

"Then you must go. We cannot risk your life on top of everything else. But I will send for you. You will not be abandoned, Abital."

Keziah packed up a bundle of things for Abital to take with her—clothing that she no longer needed, a gold bracelet she instructed Abital to sell, a bag of tea leaves. Abital thanked her but did not say that what she and Saba needed most would be food. Without the rations from the palace, they would surely starve.

"You will take a donkey, of course. I will have my father send one to replace it. You cannot walk the whole way. And you cannot go alone, in any case. If only Obadiah were here, he would be able to see you safely home."

If Obadiah were here, everything would be different. He probably could have prevented her dismissal, but as it was, there was nothing they could think to do.

"But since he is not here, I must make sure you get home. I will come along with you on the journey to keep you safe."

Abital had to laugh at the image of the heavily pregnant, soft-spoken wife of the king protecting her on the journey. "You are carrying the king's child. They will not allow you to simply walk out of the palace on a dangerous journey."

"Who will stop me?" Keziah said brazenly.

"The dozens of armed guards," Abital answered.

Keziah considered this for a moment and then nodded, realizing the truth of her words.

"I will send Elon with you."

"I will be fine. It is only two days' journey from here."

"I think you do not understand quite how desperate things are out there. A pretty woman like yourself cannot travel alone, especially not one carrying a bundle of food and gold."

Keziah arranged to have Elon escort Abital on the journey home. Channah helped her pack up her things, and Keziah took Abital to the kitchen and told Soraya to pack up enough food to last her and Saba for several weeks. Soraya cried when she heard the news, and asked whether the queen might change her mind.

"I am afraid not," Abital said.

Soraya pressed her lips together, and Abital was reminded of Soraya's warning to keep her distance from the Yahwists, whom she had thought would cause nothing but trouble in the palace. She had been right, in one way. Abital would not be in this predicament had she not aligned herself with the people who served the One True God. And yet she could not see that as a bad thing now. Knowing Yahweh, the Lord of Israel, was all that truly mattered. Understanding His undying love for His people—love that stretched even to allowing suffering, if it turned their hearts back to Him—had changed her life, and she would not trade anything for it.

"Please be safe," Soraya said, pressing the bundle of dried grain and some flour and lentils. She even included a little oil and some preserved cheese. Abital knew this cheese had been intended for the feast of Baal later today, and she felt pleased at taking it with her now.

Abital gathered her things from Keziah's room. She folded her loom as best she could, and Elon carried it out to be loaded into the wagon. By the time Abital was packed and ready to go, the group had returned from the temple, and Jezebel had gone to her room to prepare herself for the feast. Abital started down the hall one last time, Keziah just a few steps behind. She would never see these marble floors again, these high walls. There was some relief in that. Knowing she would never have to respond to another of Jezebel's unreasonable and selfish demands was freeing, in a way.

As she passed the queen's doors, she felt eyes on her, though she could not see how, as the door was closed. But as Keziah walked her down the hallway, the door opened, and Jezebel stepped out. She wore the scarlet robe that clung to her, her dark hair loose around her shoulders. She was beautiful, as always. The queen was many things, but there was no denying her beauty. Still, in the waning afternoon light, dressed in silk and finery, while most in the palace wore plain linen and many in the kingdom starved, Abital saw Jezebel differently.

She looked pathetic. She was trying too hard, and not succeeding. It was no wonder the king preferred his other wives. Neither was as pretty as the queen, but the queen reeked of a kind of desperation that made her difficult to take seriously.

"Mara reports that there is a donkey being made ready," Jezebel said. "That cannot be. You do not have permission to take one of the king's donkeys with you."

"I have given her permission," Keziah said. "I insisted she take one, in fact."

"You do not have the authority to do so," Jezebel. "I will tell the stable to send the donkey back to the stall."

"You may try, but I am afraid the stable master does not report to you," Keziah said coldly.

"He reports to the king, and as the queen—"

"He reports to my brother, and if forced to choose, I am certain which of the king's wives Obadiah will listen to." Keziah did not raise her voice, but she said it with so much authority that Jezebel paused. Abital held her breath. She was witnessing a power struggle between the wives.

"You do not have the authority—" Jezebel tried again.

But Keziah cut her off. "Neither of us does, Jezebel. We are just wives. Our entire duty is to make the king look good. You have no more authority than I do. But I have one thing you do not. The king values my words and opinions. Abital will take a donkey, and that is the end of it."

Keziah lifted her chin and proceeded down the hallway, and Abital followed closely behind her. She waited for Jezebel to say more, or to follow them, but she did nothing. Abital could not believe what she had seen. Keziah had just matched Jezebel in a battle of wills, and won. Abital wanted to laugh and shout, despite everything. She followed Keziah through the halls and outside at the rear of the palace.

"At least we know you will have fine weather for your journey," Keziah joked as she watched Elon help Keziah onto her donkey. They were at the back of the palace, near the stables, where the king's few remaining animals were kept. "You will not need to worry about rain making the road impassable."

Abital smiled and wondered what would happen when the king met Elijah. "You will send word when you hear?"

"Of course I will," Keziah promised. Then she took in a breath and said, "Do not worry, Abital. Yahweh will not be mocked. He will show His power and His might, and all of Israel will see His power and recognize that He is the One True God. You will see."

Abital knew that Keziah believed this with all of her being. Abital hoped she was right.

Abital told Keziah how to get a letter to her, through Ira and his trading partners. They moved around far less than they used to, but letters still made it through eventually, Abital promised. Keziah gave Abital one last hug before Elon said they must be going.

The donkey drew away from the palace, and they went slowly down the hill and into the town of Jezreel. The streets were filthy, covered in dust and trash and muck, and Abital was grateful once again for the donkey. There were few people around, and those she saw were painfully thin. They gazed at Abital and Elon from doorways, their eyes vacant. Abital felt suddenly grateful for the presence of the palace guard beside her, and understood Keziah's wisdom in sending Elon. These people looked desperate enough to do whatever it took to get food into their bellies, but none would attack her as long as she had the king's guard at her side. Would she soon be one of these people, driven to desperation by hunger?

Abital looked back as they went through the city gates and saw the palace, perched on top of the hill, cast in an orange glow by the setting sun. It was strange to think that just a few hours ago she had been a part of its workings, seen and known by the most powerful people in the land, and now she was on her way home, and likely to her death. She prayed that all inside would be well, and that the king would turn Israel back to Yahweh before it was too late.

Elon said little, aside from giving directions, so Abital had plenty of time to think as they went as far as they could before darkness overtook them. Abital thought about home, wondering what she would find there. She thought about Saba and prayed he was well. She wondered how he would react when she told him why she had been let go. He would be proud of her for standing up for the truth, she felt sure.

Once the light was gone from the sky and they could ride no farther, Elon found a place for them to set up camp by the side of the road. He tied up the donkey next to a streambed that had only a trickle of water running through it, and while he made a fire, she set out the blankets Keziah had sent with her.

"No sense setting up a covering over the sleeping area," he said, "since it will not rain." They ate a meal of lentils warmed over the fire before they settled onto their sleeping mats for the night. Abital was grateful for Elon's presence. He might not have been the best conversationalist, but he was big, and he had a knife, and he kept everyone else away. Without him, Abital would have been at a loss. She had never camped by the side of the road in her life. She was not sure she could light a fire. She would not know where a good place to camp would have been. Her years at the palace, with everything made ready for her, had spoiled her.

It felt strange to be away from the palace. She had thought she would miss it, thought she would miss the security of those solid walls around her. Even if it wasn't an easy life, working for the queen, it was a good one. Keziah and Obadiah had made her feel at home there. And yet there was something freeing about looking up at the sky to see so many tiny stars scattered across the dark sky. Yahweh had created every one of those stars and hung them in their places. Seeing it all now, she could not believe she hadn't always understood that Yahweh alone was God. Who else could have made something so vast, so unknowable? As she drifted off to sleep, Abital could not help but wonder if somewhere out there, Obadiah was looking up at the same stars.

When the first light of dawn broke over the horizon, Elon woke her. They ate a bit of dried meat and packed up, then started off on their journey once more. Abital scarcely recognized the land that she had ridden through when she'd come to the palace all those years ago. What had once been lush farmland studded with trees was now dry and choked with dust. There was little green to break up the brown, and the few animals left standing in the fields were so thin you could see their bones through their skin. They saw few travelers, and though one or two did eye Abital as they passed, one glance from Elon was enough to make them pass quickly.

When they reached the hills around Napoth Dor, Abital's heart began to race. She was coming home. She could not believe it. The place was much changed, but her spirit still knew it. The smell of eucalyptus and juniper filled her with nostalgia. There was the hill where she had played as a child; there was the tamarisk tree, now brown and leafless in the unrelenting heat, that she had climbed on long summer days. And there, ahead, was the land her family had farmed for many generations. There were only a few thin sheep where there should have been an entire wooly flock, but it was still here. It was strange to see it all still here after so much had changed. After *she* had changed. It felt, strangely, good to be home.

As they made their way down the road, the house came into view, and the stone barn behind it, and tears stung her eyes. This beautiful little home that she thought she might never see again. As they neared the house, she saw a figure emerge from the barn, a sharp blade clutched in his hand. The man was very thin, and his shoulders were stooped. Was it—

He was older and more hunched. His beard had grown long and white, and he was so very thin.

Could that really be Saba? Why was he holding a knife like that? For a moment, she was struck with a terrible fear. Her saba was a gregarious and welcoming man. He was not afraid of anything, let alone a woman on a donkey. This could not be Saba. Someone new had come and was living in his home.

But the man squinted, lowered his knife, and took a step forward.

"Abital?" he called. "Is that you?"

Abital ran toward him. "Saba!"

He was here, and he was alive.

Saba laughed and held out his arms, and she ran into them. He wrapped his arms around her and held her and they both laughed until they had tears streaming down their faces.

"It is so good to see you," Saba said. "I am so glad you are home, Abital."

"It is wonderful to see you as well," she said. "Though you are too thin. I should have sent more—"

"You are the reason I am still here, Abital. I and the others around here would not have made it without your help."

Hearing these words, Abital realized that Saba had not kept the food she'd sent for himself but had shared it with his friends and neighbors. Of course he had. She should have known that was what he would do. But at the same moment, she was gripped by a familiar fear. The provisions she had brought from the palace would not last

for long, especially if they were shared with the families on the surrounding hills.

"Yahweh has answered my prayers and has brought you home.
I am so glad to see you," Saba repeated. "But I am also curious to
know what has brought you here now."

"Come," she said, indicating they should go to the house. "Come
inside, and I will tell you the whole story."

"I cannot wait to hear it. First, let us take care of our visitor,"
Saba said, indicating Elon. He walked toward him and tucked the
knife into a leather belt at his waist. "It seems I owe you a debt of
gratitude for bringing my granddaughter safely to me."

Abital introduced Elon, and Saba invited him into the house for
a meal and to refresh himself, but Elon declined, asking instead only
to be allowed to spend the night in the barn before he returned to
the palace the next day. Saba insisted on sending him with a cup of
water from the stream, which had not totally ceased to flow, and
bread made from the flour Abital had sent. Elon led the donkey to
the barn and settled in, and Saba led Abital into the house.

The familiar smell of cloves and lanolin filled her with a deep
sense of peace. Saba lit a fire and heated cups of water for mint tea,
and then, when the heat from the cup warmed her hands, he said,
"So, child. Tell me what has happened."

Abital told him about all that had happened at the palace. She
had told him some of it in her letters, but she could not say much
about what life at the palace was truly like, for fear that her message
would be intercepted. So now she told him about Jezebel, about her
whims and her insecurities, and how she took out her own fears on
those around her. He asked her about the temples to the false gods

that the king and queen had introduced, and Abital confirmed that the queen had tried to have Yahweh's prophets wiped out and the worship of Yahweh banned.

"She is as wicked as they say," Saba said, shaking his head. "But the king's second wife—was she kind to you?"

"More than kind. She has become like a sister to me," Abital said. "She and her brother Obadiah—"

"You mentioned him. He manages the palace, does he not?"

"He does. They have both been kind to me." Abital told him how Obadiah had rescued one hundred of the Lord's prophets and hid them in caves and fed them, and how he had managed the king's palace carefully so that there was enough for all.

"Among the many things that he cut back were the funds for the queen's wardrobe," Abital said.

"I am sure she did not like that," Saba said.

"No, indeed, she fought against it as hard as she could. But with so many suffering, it could not be borne. She was forced to make do with older clothing."

"And yet you retained your place at the palace?" He raised an eyebrow.

"Obadiah saw to that," Abital said.

Saba watched her but did not say anything.

Abital went on to tell him about Obadiah's search for fresh grass for the palace's animals and coming upon the prophet Elijah, and about the fear that the king would have him killed for bringing the prophet to him.

"You said that he serves Yahweh," Saba said.

She nodded.

"Yahweh will keep him safe." He said it with such certainty and such authority in his voice that it was hard not to believe him.

Abital then explained how Jezebel had responded to the king's departure to meet Elijah with a demand that all in the palace must make a sacrifice to Baal, and how this time Abital had finally refused.

"You did not obey the queen?" Saba asked.

"How could I, when I know that only Yahweh is God?" Abital said.

Saba pressed his lips together, his chin shaking. "You truly believe that?" he finally asked.

"I do," Abital said. "It took me far too long to see it, but I know that it is true. There is no God but Yahweh."

"If that is the case, then all of this has been worth it," Saba said. "It is worth every moment of suffering to know that you acknowledge Yahweh as the One True God."

Abital had never seen her saba cry, but now there were tears pooling in his eyes. "I was not able to see the same come true for your imma, but I am satisfied to see that it is true for you."

Abital told him how Jezebel had refused to accept that she would not worship false gods and sent her home.

"I worry that without the provisions from the palace, there will not be enough to eat."

"All will be well," he said. "The Lord has always provided, and He will provide now. Perhaps now that Elijah has returned, we will soon see the end of this drought."

"More likely Ahab has had him killed by now, and all those associated with him as well."

"You say you trust in the Lord. Let us see that now," Saba said. "I believe the Lord will declare His glory and His power in a way that none will be able to deny."

Abital did not know what to think. It was what Keziah had said as well. She wished she had their faith.

Saba and Abital talked for hours that day, catching up on many years' worth of news. She greeted Elkanah, who helped her abba with the animals, and Ofir, his wife, who cooked for Saba and cared for the garden. They lived in a little cottage behind the house, and Abital was glad to see them. They welcomed her home warmly.

"This place has been too quiet without you," Ofir said.

"Though we are very grateful for the food you have sent us," Elkanah added.

That night Abital fell into a deep sleep, warm and safe in the home of her childhood. Her saba, who loved her more than anyone, was here, his presence like a comforting blanket. She was far away from the backstabbing and gossip-filled world of the palace, and it was more satisfying than she could have imagined possible.

There were still so many things to fear. There was little food, and the bit she had brought from the palace would not last long. They may not survive more than a few weeks. She did not know what had happened to Obadiah, whether the king had killed him in a rage, or what Elijah had told the king about when the drought would end.

But she found that, like Saba and like Keziah, she was beginning to believe that she could trust that Yahweh would provide what they needed.

CHAPTER TWENTY-ONE

Obadiah quickly grew tired of hearing King Ahab complain about the difficulty of the journey. The king was hot, tired, and thirsty—as was everyone in the king's retinue—and as each hour passed, he made sure to remind Obadiah of his growing discomfort. He was not used to walking such long distances, and he was not used to carrying his own things. Even though the guards who traveled with them and set up his tent and laid out his mat each night bore most of the effort, he complained as though he were being treated unfairly. Obadiah had hoped that seeing how thin and weak the people in the villages were might soften the king's heart, but the sight of his starving subjects only seemed to make him angrier.

On the second day, as they set out again, the sun seemed to beat down even brighter. Obadiah grew weary of trying to placate the king, and stopped answering when he found one more thing to complain about. Obadiah was consumed with his own thoughts and fears. What would happen if Elijah was waiting for them, just as he said he would be? Would the king kill him on sight? Would Elijah fight back? What would Yahweh do to a man who dared lay a hand on His prophet?

Or what if Elijah was not there? Would the king kill Obadiah on the spot, or would he drag him back to Jezreel to make a spectacle of him before he executed him? Would he be able to escape, to use the dark cloak to vanish into the hills come nightfall? Obadiah hated that he still carried the cloak. He worried he had put Abital at risk by holding on to it. He prayed she would be safe. He prayed he could see her again someday soon.

As they drew near to the spot where Obadiah had left Elijah, he prayed all the more. When they rounded a bend in the road, and the spot where he had left Elijah came into view, he saw that Elijah stood there, looking down the road toward them, waiting. He appeared to be in the exact spot where they had parted. It was as if Elijah had not moved. It was impossible, of course. He must have rested, and eaten, but for a moment, Obadiah almost believed that Elijah had meant it literally when he had said he would be waiting in that very spot.

"He is there, my lord," Obadiah said, gesturing toward the place where Elijah waited. The king looked, and seeing him, drew his sword.

"My lord!" Obadiah spoke quickly. "If you kill him, how will he end the drought?"

"This man is responsible for very great evil in our land," King Ahab said. "He must be stopped."

"He is a prophet of the Most High God," Obadiah said. "If you kill him now, surely Yahweh will punish all in the land, even more than He has done for the past three years. Please, I beg of you, speak to the prophet, and hear what he has summoned you here to say."

Ahab did not answer. He just kept walking, his hand on the sword at his side. Elijah did not seem at all frightened as he watched the king, surrounded by his guards and Obadiah, approach.

"Is that you, O troubler of Israel?" the king called as they approached. His voice was loud and deep, and though he intended it to intimidate, Elijah did not seem to be bothered in the slightest.

"I have not troubled Israel," Elijah replied. "You and your father's house have brought this suffering on Israel." His voice, higher and less booming, was no less sure. "You have forsaken the commandments of the Lord and have followed the baals."

"*I* have brought this on Israel?" Ahab said. He took another step forward. "I have done no such thing."

"You have, you and your false gods," Elijah said. "You pray to statues and images that are nothing but metal and stone. Instead, you must turn back to Yahweh and forsake the false gods. There is no other way to end this drought."

"How can you say I pray to false gods and that you pray to the only real one? How can you know your God is the most powerful? How can you say that He will be the one to end this drought?"

Elijah's eyes widened. "Do you truly not see? Even now, do you not understand that Yahweh allowed this drought to turn your heart back to Him? He alone controls the rain. He alone has the power to send the thunder. After all this time, do you really still not understand?"

"Who is to say who is most powerful?" the king said again.

"If you still refuse to believe, even in the face of everything you have seen, then let us settle this for good," Elijah said. "We will see whether Yahweh is truly the most powerful god. Summon all of Israel to meet me on Mount Carmel. Bring along four hundred and fifty prophets of Baal and the four hundred prophets of Asherah who eat at Jezebel's palace. Come, bring them all, and we will all see who is the One True God."

The king did not seem to know how to respond to that. He did not argue.

"In two weeks' time," Elijah said, "I will see you all on Mount Carmel." And then he turned, his robes flying out behind him, and started off down the road. For a moment, no one else moved. King Ahab did not seem to know what to do. Obadiah was afraid to breathe, lest the king remember himself and run the prophet down and stick a sword through him. The guards stood around them, waiting for the king's command.

"Come," King Ahab finally said. "We must hurry if we are to gather so many on Mount Carmel in only two weeks' time."

CHAPTER TWENTY-TWO

The next few weeks at Abital's family home followed an easy rhythm. They rose with the sun and took care of their remaining animals. There were a few scrawny chickens who produced very few eggs, as well as the goat and the donkey, and ten sheep that slept in the pen at night but roamed the hills by day. When she had last been here, there had been dozens of sheep, but she was pleased to see there were still some left. Few were so fortunate. The brook that ran through the back of the property still contained a trickle of fresh water, though the well had long since run dry. The plum and apricot trees no longer bore fruit, and the vines had died off, but the olive tree still dropped its hard, fatty fruit, and Abital gathered them each day and set them to cure.

Each morning, after caring for the animals, they would sit down to prayers and then a meager meal of boiled grains and sometimes an egg or two. Saba would work around the property, pruning back trees and repairing fences while Elkanah took the animals to the hills to gather what little grass they could. Abital helped wherever she was needed, walking far into the hills to gather grasses and find nuts and fruit. She cleaned and helped Ofir cook, and tried to make herself useful. The loom stayed in a corner of the barn. There was no point in weaving cloth or making clothing now. None could afford to purchase it, and few would spend precious money on something you could not eat.

Each morning, Abital woke hoping for news from the palace, but none came. She had forgotten how cut off this place felt. Maybe that was not right, though. This was how most of the people in the land lived, with no idea and very little interest in what was happening at the palace. It did not matter to their everyday lives whether the queen had a new gown or the king a new wife. She had forgotten, being in the thick of it for so long, that the palace was not like the rest of the world.

There, she had heard that people in the land were suffering because of the drought. Here, she saw it every single day. She saw how thin they all were, how hard they fought to make the food stretch. She saw the fear in the eyes of the mothers in the market with nothing to feed their children. As one week passed and then two, the world of the palace began to feel very far away. She found she did not miss being summoned by Jezebel at all hours and forced to cower and fear her. She did not miss sleeping with three others in a small room tormented by her fellow maid. She had thought she might miss the heady feeling of power that came from living at the center of the king's court and needed by the queen, but she did not. Somehow, it already felt like it had happened in another lifetime.

Of course, there were things about the palace that she did miss. She missed sitting with Keziah and talking about their lives. She wondered when Keziah would have her baby, and whether it was a boy or a girl. She missed going to visit Soraya in the kitchen, and sweet Channah. And of course she missed Obadiah. She felt his absence like an ache in her spirit. Each day she found herself brimming with things she wanted to tell him, and longing for news.

Was he running from the king's anger? Was he alive? Had he returned to the palace, safe, and merely forgotten about her? Perhaps he no longer cared, and that was why she heard nothing.

But she reminded herself that it was far more likely he was hiding in a cave somewhere, as the prophets of Yahweh had done. Still, that thought didn't comfort her much. As each day turned into the next, she grew more concerned. Why didn't Keziah write to her? Surely she could manage that. She could write, if only to say that there was no news. The only reason she might not write was if she believed Abital did not want to hear the news she had to share. The longer the delay, the more tortured Abital became.

Now that she was home, Saba was talking again about finding her a husband. He apologized again and again for not having lined up a marriage yet, thinking Abital was surely upset about not becoming a wife and imma by now. She insisted, again and again, that she did not want to marry anyone from the village, but Saba could not hear it. A young woman must be married, he insisted, and promised to arrange for it as soon as he could scrape together what was needed for the dowry.

Abital could see now that there was none, and had not been for some time. It would not be long before they had to slaughter the remaining sheep, and then her saba would have nothing. No abba would take on a bride for his son—as well as the cost of feeding, housing, and clothing her—without a dowry. When everyone was a few meals away from starvation, none would take on such a burden. Abital was grateful for the delay, though she tried her best not to show it. She could not imagine giving herself to another man when there was only one she wanted.

Each evening, Saba led the little group in prayers, thanking Yahweh for His provision. Abital thanked Him as well, finding herself more and more sure with each passing day of the decision she had made. Yahweh was the only true God. She could not see how she did not know it before. Baal and Asherah were nothing but false idols, powerless against the might of the One True God. This drought was proof of that. If the people of Israel could not understand now that it was Yahweh who controlled the thunder and the rain, they would never see it.

Day by day, Abital settled in more and it began to feel more comfortable. She felt her spirit coming back to life. Each new day revealed its small blessings, from the discovery of a patch of grass to the curl of a sow bug in the soil to the way the light hit the hillside as the sun sank behind the horizon. She felt each day more and more that she was home.

Then, one evening, just as the sky was beginning to darken, hoofbeats echoed on the road. Someone was approaching at a fast pace. Someone was riding toward them on a horse. Abital stepped out of the house and gazed up the road. She realized she was holding her breath as the rider neared.

No one bearing good news approached at such speed.

No one in these parts had a horse.

Whoever this was, they had come a long distance. Across the yard, she saw Saba step out of the barn, the knife clutched in his hand once again. Even Elkanah, tiny stooped Elkanah, came out with a whip in his hand.

When the rider came into view, all they could see was a man wearing a dark cloak, hunched over his horse. His hood hid his features, and the horse was not familiar to any of them. But as the man slowed the horse, he sat up, and Abital's breath caught. His hood fell back, and even in the shadows, she was sure it was him. He squinted toward the house, as if trying to discern whether he had the right place.

"Obadiah!" she cried. She could not help herself. Women did not cry out like this, but she could do nothing else. He was alive. He was alive, and he was here.

His gaze snapped to her, and a wide smile spread across his face. Obadiah pulled the reins and the horse stopped short. Across the yard, she saw Saba lower the knife.

Abital could not believe that Obadiah was here, and she did not know why he had come. Maybe he brought terrible news. But in that moment, she did not care. She was so glad to see him that she ran toward him, and as he smiled at her, she knew everything was going to be all right.

CHAPTER TWENTY-THREE

Y ou know this man?" Saba called to Abital.

"Yes, Saba. This is Obadiah, who I have told you about." She walked forward and greeted him, bowing her head as she got closer. A hundred questions filled her mind, but she simply said, "It is good to see you."

Obadiah swung his leg over the back of the horse and hopped off. When he stood in the road, he still towered over her.

"I had to come. When I returned to the palace and you were not there, I knew I had to find you." Up close, she could see the light flecks in his eyes, the strong bones of his cheeks, the lines around his lips when he smiled. His hair hung around his shoulders, but his beard was neatly trimmed.

"What happened?" Abital said. "How are you alive and standing here?"

"It is quite a story," Obadiah said. "But first, perhaps you could introduce me to your grandfather and ask that older man to set down his weapon?"

Abital laughed, still trying to process the truth that he was actually here.

"Of course," she said. "Follow me."

Abital introduced Obadiah to Elkanah. "This is Obadiah," she said. "He manages the palace and is the brother of Keziah, the king's wife." Elkanah's eyes widened, and he set the whip down without a word.

Then she led him to Saba, who bowed before him. "My granddaughter has told me about you," he said. "Most importantly, she has told me that you serve Yahweh and are loyal to Him. That you saved the prophets who speak in His name. For that, you will always be welcome in this home."

Obadiah responded by returning the bow. "Your granddaughter has told me many things about you as well," he said. "She says you instructed her in the ways of our Lord. She respects and cares for you deeply. It is an honor to meet you."

Saba led Obadiah inside the house, and for a moment Abital feared that it would not be enough for him. He was used to the finest things. His father was very wealthy, and he had so many resources at his disposal. But Obadiah commented on how charming the room was, with its beamed ceilings and its large fireplace, and complimented the view of the hills from the windows.

"They shine like gold in the sun," Obadiah said, gazing out at the hills that receded, one after another, before him.

"In better years, they have been lush and green during the rainy season," Saba said. "Though it has been a few years since we have seen that. I have always loved the golden cast of the drier months, myself."

Saba insisted they sit, and he made cups of tea for all of them. Then, when they were seated, warm cups clasped in their hands, Abital could not wait any longer.

"We are so glad you are here," she said. It was a vast understatement. She felt like her heart would burst. "But how is it that you have come?"

"It is a strange story," Obadiah said. "And one that shows me without a doubt that Yahweh is the Lord."

Obadiah then told them about how he'd gone back to Tyre with the king, and that Elijah was indeed waiting there, just as he'd promised. He told them how the king had wanted to kill the prophet but instead had agreed to appear on Mount Carmel two weeks later, along with the prophets of Baal and Asherah.

Abital knew the name of the mountain a day's ride north of here, at the edge of the sea. She had never seen the place but had heard that the hills were studded with caves and fields of vineyards and olive trees.

"Why did Elijah want to meet the king and his prophets there?" Saba asked.

"I do not know," Obadiah said. "But the king has agreed to go, and to spread the word throughout all of Israel. Elijah wants the whole nation to be there to witness whatever he has planned."

"That is not much time," Saba said.

"And that was nearly two weeks ago. I had to stay at the palace to help the king prepare, and to help my sister prepare, and then I begged leave to make the journey here. It took me some days to find you," Obadiah said. "It seems that Elon's directions were not as clear as he thought they were. But I knew I needed to make sure you heard the news. I knew you needed to be there."

"To be there?" Abital was stunned.

"Yes, of course. Like I said, the king has summoned all of Israel."

"But surely not all in Israel will go to Mount Carmel." How could the whole nation fit on one mountain? And how could everyone leave behind their homes, their animals, and journey with their families to the coast?

"I imagine not everyone," Obadiah confirmed. "But you must go, Abital. After all you risked, you should be there to see Yahweh's power displayed before the nation."

She was excited by the idea, of course. She could not deny that she would love to see Yahweh proved to be the One True God. But could she really go to see it? She looked over at Saba.

"What will happen?" Saba asked. "What will Elijah do?"

"Yahweh will finally show His power," Obadiah said. "He will finally show that He is the God who controls the thunder and the rain."

"But how?" Saba asked, trying to make sense of it. "What will He *do*?"

Obadiah shook his head. "I do not know. I do not know if Elijah knows. I know only that I will be there to see it. And I am asking the both of you to come with me."

He wanted her to come with him. To journey together with him. With Saba, too, of course. She would be lying if she said the thought of traveling with Obadiah, of having the chance to talk with him as they journeyed together, to enjoy being near him, did not have its appeal. But there was more to it than that. If what he said was true, and whatever happened on Mount Carmel could show all of Israel that Yahweh was God, then she wanted to be there. She had to be there.

When neither spoke, Obadiah continued. "I do not know what will happen. I only know that Israel will never forget whatever occurs on that mountain. I know that our God will be victorious and that His people will tell the story of His victory through the ages. Please, be there beside me."

Abital looked at Saba, who nodded. "We will come," Saba said. "We will see the glory of the Lord in that place."

CHAPTER TWENTY-FOUR

They packed that afternoon for the journey, which would begin in the morning. Abital tucked some oatcakes and a little bread into a leather traveling bag and filled a skin with water from the creek. They would soon use the last of the supplies here, but there was no telling what they might find on the journey. Elkanah and Ofir did not think they were strong enough to make the trip, so they would stay at the farm to care for the sheep.

That night, Saba broke out the last of the wine, and he and Obadiah and Abital ate some of the dried meat and hard cheese Obadiah had brought with him, along with the lentils and boiled grains, and together they talked and laughed. Obadiah shared stories from his childhood in Samaria, and Saba asked him about working for the king, and though Obadiah spoke truthfully, he was careful not to speak ill of the king. Abital could see that Saba liked and respected Obadiah. No one said aloud what they all knew— that Obadiah spending this time with them was out of the ordinary, that his concern for their well-being was most welcome but confusing. His interest in their little family was flattering, but they all knew it could never lead anywhere.

That evening after the meal, Obadiah asked Abital if she would show him the vineyard, and Saba agreed that they could walk together among the vines until it started to grow dark. He warned them not to stay outside too long and told them they must get to bed so they could leave early in the morning. She led Obadiah across the yard and up the hillside, bathed in the golden light of the setting sun.

"This place is beautiful," Obadiah said. "The fresh air is nice after so long closed up in the palace."

"It is nice," Abital said. She led him down one of the rows of vines, which had baked to a muddy brown color in the unrelenting sun. "Or it was, once."

"And will be again," Obadiah said. "Soon."

"Do you really think this drought will end soon?" His face was framed in silhouette in the golden evening light. Her belly fluttered. She could never tire of looking at that face.

"I believe that whatever happens at Mount Carmel, nothing will be the same afterward."

"You did not answer the question."

He stopped walking and smiled at her. "That's because there are things I am far more interested in than rain right now. When this is all over, when Yahweh's might has been proved and the rain comes again, everything will be different." He stepped forward to stand close to her, and reached out for her hand. Her breath caught in her throat. His hand was warm and soft, and her mind raced. She fought for the words to answer him.

"We will have food again, for one."

"Yes. That will be nice. But that is not what I mean, and you know it."

Abital understood what he was trying to suggest, but she did not believe it. He interlaced his fingers with hers.

"When the rain finally comes," she said quietly, "it will not change the rules of our society."

"It will, though. Do you not see? When all in Israel declare the name of Yahweh, nothing else will matter."

She let out a chuckle. "You have always been idealistic, Obadiah. It is one of your best qualities, but I think it sometimes causes you to miss the truth. We must be clear-eyed about this."

"I do not want to be clear-eyed. I want you."

She had known how he felt about her. He had never tried to hide his feelings. And yet, hearing them spoken aloud, she still felt a thrill.

"If you do not want me too, I will drop it and not bother you again. But I do not believe that is what you want, Abital."

She did not say anything. She gazed out over the valley below. The house and the barn sat in shadows in the gathering evening, but the sun splayed out across the hills, illuminating row after golden row.

"Do you want me to go away, to leave you in peace?" Obadiah said.

"No," Abital finally said. "That is not what I want."

He squeezed her hand. "Then let us hope."

"Your father would not agree to a match with a penniless seamstress. It will not happen."

"Have faith, Abital. When the glory of God is revealed, all will be changed."

She did not want to argue with him. He was a hopeless dreamer and was not used to being told no. She knew he did not want to believe that his dream would not survive. But she kept the words to herself for now. It was a beautiful dream. For tonight she would let him hold it. She would even try to believe it herself. She squeezed his hand, and he smiled.

"Just wait, Abital. You will see."

They stood there together on the hill, listening to the cicadas fill the night with sound and watching the swallows dip through the sky, returning to their homes, until the sun was nearly gone, dreaming of a life that could never be.

⁂

Obadiah spent the night on a pallet sleeping on the far side of Saba, and Abital spent much of the night awake, staring up at the ceiling, trying to believe that he was truly here in this house. He was alive, and he had come for her.

When morning broke, Obadiah rose early and helped Saba with chores around the farm. He cleaned up after the animals and fed the sheep. Abital had to laugh. She was sure Obadiah, reared in luxury in Samaria, with nursemaids and tutors and servants, had never mucked out a stall in his life, but he did it with surprising dignity and grace, caring not for his fine clothes or the smell that would surely follow him. Then they ate a simple meal and set out. They piled their things on the back of the king's horse and walked. Obadiah tried to insist that Saba ride, but he refused, saying he was strong enough to walk yet.

The road was busy, choked with neighbors and other people from Napoth Dor heading toward Mount Carmel. Though each face they met looked weary and every frame too thin, there was also a sense of optimism and expectation among the travelers on the road. None knew what lay ahead, but all hoped it would bring change.

As they walked, Obadiah asked Saba about his life on the land, and Saba told him stories Abital had never heard about his father and his sisters, who had each married men in other parts of the nation and who he had not seen in many years. The closer they drew to Mount Carmel, the more crowded the road became, as thousands gathered to see what would happen. Many sang songs and recited Scripture as they jostled along. The heat of the summer day beat down, making each sweaty step difficult.

They arrived at the foothills of the mountain that afternoon and slowly made their way up the narrow path toward the top.

"We should probably pick somewhere to camp," Saba said as the day wore on and their steps grew heavier. People had set up camp on each side of the road, in the shadow of the largest peak, finding any space they could.

"Let us keep going for a while longer," Obadiah said. "I think we will find a better place farther ahead."

Saba did not argue, though he did not look convinced. Abital wondered whether it was simply Obadiah's optimism speaking, or whether there was something he knew that they did not. They followed the small path up the hill, and the crowds grew denser the farther they walked. The light was starting to fade from the sky when they reached a flat clearing not far from the summit. Every bit of the flat plane was packed with people crowded into tents and cooking meals over fires. Abital wondered how they would find space to camp here, where all the available space had seemingly been taken. Obadiah led them through the crowd to a large tent that had been set up at the edge of the clearing. The smell of roasting meat coming from the fire before it made her belly groan. Armed guards surrounded the tent. Elon nodded at her as she approached.

"You made it!"

Abital turned at the familiar voice. Keziah was rushing toward her, her belly straining against the fabric of her linen tunic. Behind her, Channah held Ayla in her arms. Abital bowed her head. "Abital!" the child cried, kicking her arms and legs to get free. She ran up to Abital and threw her arms around her knees. "We missed you!"

"I did not want to leave you," Abital assured the child. Abital turned to Keziah, who threw her arms around her, and they both laughed and hugged and held each other.

"My brother said he would not come until he found you. I am so glad you are here."

"It is good to see you. How have you made it this far with your belly so large?"

"I would not have missed this for anything. Now, this must be your grandfather. You must introduce me."

Abital introduced Saba to Keziah, and her saba bowed deeply. "It is an honor to meet you."

"Your granddaughter has become a dear friend. Come. Settle in. There is a place for you over here."

"I—" Abital faltered. They could not stay here, in the king's wife's tent. But Keziah was ushering them inside of what did truly seem to be an overly large tent.

"There is room for both of you. Come, lay out your sleeping mats here."

As if in a daze, Abital obeyed Keziah.

"You do not need to worry," Keziah said under her breath as Abital unfurled the thin mats. "The queen did not come. She said she could not make such a difficult journey, though I believe she was afraid of what might happen if her gods were proved false, as I believe they will be. You will not run into her here."

Abital felt grateful to hear that. She did not relish seeing Jezebel again.

"Where has my brother gone?" Keziah asked once they were settled. In the excitement of the greeting, he had somehow vanished.

"He has gone to greet your father," Channah said quietly. She nodded toward the front of the tent.

"Ah. That is good. Abba will be glad to see him."

"Your parents have come?" Abital asked.

"Of course. They have a tent across the way. They would not have missed this. All of Israel will see Yahweh's name glorified," Keziah said.

After Saba had been introduced to Channah and met Ayla, they went back outside, and Keziah pointed out the tent that belonged to her father. It was large, made of the highest-quality goat hair, and set up with a view over the valley. Abital could not see if anyone was inside, though Obadiah must have been in there.

Once the meal was ready, they gathered around the fire at the front of the tent and talked and laughed and ate the first fresh meat Abital had had in weeks. Keziah asked Saba about the sheep and about the land he worked, and he thanked her for taking an interest in Abital.

"She has become like a sister to me," Keziah said.

When night fell, they retreated into the tent and set up oil lamps inside, which cast shadows that danced across the surface of the skins. Not long afterward, Obadiah emerged from his father's tent and entered Keziah's tent, his face grim. "I must go to see the king," he told his sister.

Keziah wished him luck. "The king was in quite a state when I saw him earlier," she said. "He does not know what Elijah will do, and he is worried he will be humiliated in front of the nation."

"He will not be humiliated as long as he does not bet against Yahweh," Obadiah said. He gazed at Abital, gave her a shy smile, and then turned and let the tent flap fall closed as he stepped into the night.

Obadiah had not returned by the time they lay down on their mats and blew out the lamps. The thick woven goat hair deadened the noises that echoed all around them, and the king's guards stationed outside gave them all a sense of security. Saba snored softly on the mat beside her. Inside the tent, though the air should have felt hot and sticky, it instead felt cozy and quiet, and Abital quickly fell into a deep sleep. She awoke in the morning to the smell of meat cooking and tea brewing. Abital stretched, refreshed. Saba was still asleep, and Obadiah was not there. She wondered where he was and what had kept him so busy.

"We had better eat," Keziah said when she saw that Abital was awake. "We do not know when Elijah will summon everyone to the top."

They sat outside the tent, and after Saba thanked Yahweh for his provision, they ate the lamb and oat cakes and drank tea. Keziah asked Saba more about the sheep on the farm and about how he liked living there.

"It is a good place," Saba said. "It is not large, but it suits us just fine that way. When I was a child, my brothers and I did much of the work of planting and reaping and tilling, but my wife and I were only blessed with one child, and we could not plant and harvest as much as my father had managed. That was all right. We bred more sheep, and that has been a blessing in itself."

"Your one child was Abital's mother?" Keziah asked. Her hand stroked her belly absently.

"That is right. My Devorah. We wanted children so badly, and had long since given up on it, when she arrived, our own little gift from God. She was such a blessing to us and gave her imma great comfort. Marta grew sick when Devorah was still small, and passed when she was only ten. Devorah was never the same afterward."

"I would imagine not," Keziah said. "Losing a mother would affect a child deeply."

"She was a good girl," Saba said. His gaze was far off, as though he were seeing scenes the rest of them could not see. "She was clever, like Abital, and so good at weaving and sewing. But she was stubborn, with a wild streak from the day she was born. She could shimmy up a tree faster than any other child in the area." Abital had not heard these stories before and loved hearing more about her imma. "When she grew older, she did not want to marry the man I chose for her. I told her again and again that Ilai was a good man who worshiped the Lord and would provide for her, but she did not think he was handsome enough. She refused to eat for a week leading up to the wedding."

Abital barely remembered her abba. She could not picture him in her mind, nor did she know his voice or his smile. She only had the vague memory that she was calmed by his presence.

"Did she think that would help her cause?" Keziah asked.

"I do not know. I suppose so. Or perhaps she thought it would make her so weak we would change our minds. But she married him and moved to Jezreel with him and his family. And beautiful Abital is the result."

"She came home when her husband died?" Keziah asked.

"That is right," Saba said. "I was so glad to have her back. Having Devorah and Abital home was like a dream come true in some ways. Though she did not see it the same way, I suppose."

"She always loved you, Saba," Abital said.

"I know she did. But she did not like being stuck on a farm when she dreamed of being in the city. She missed the pace and the life she had had in Jezreel. A soldier who came through caught her eye and convinced her she needed to return to Jezreel. While she was there before, she had done some sewing work for the queen—the former one—and so, once she was back home and itching to get out, wrote to the queen asking her for more work."

"The wife of King Omri invited her to the palace," Keziah said.

"And she never came home again. Abital was only twelve at the time. My friends said I should be grateful that I did not have to feed and clothe her. Taking in a widow can be very expensive. But I did not mind. I never minded. She was my precious daughter," Saba said. "At least she left me her little one. Abital is the joy of my heart."

"Abital is pretty special," Keziah said, smiling kindly at her. "Thank you for lending her to us at the palace."

"It was not what I would have willed, but the Lord knows best," Saba said.

Keziah looked as though she was going to say more, but just then, a man and a woman approached, and Abital jumped to her feet when she saw the man she recognized from the day Keziah's wedding had been announced. His hair was gray, his robes fine, his beard oiled, and his face was warm, his cheeks pink. His wife was tall, like Keziah, and had a regal bearing. Abital bowed low, and Saba did the same. Keziah too pushed herself to her feet and bowed before her parents.

"Good morning, Abba," Keziah said. "Imma."

"Good morning, my dear. We wanted to be sure to greet your guests." Keziah's father turned to Saba and nodded his head. "I am Azra of Samaria. It is an honor to meet you." He nodded at Abital. "I have heard much about you, Abital." He had? "I know it is in part due to your quick thinking that any of the prophets of Yahweh are alive today, and I have also heard that my son owes his life to you as well. For that, I will always be in your debt."

Abital did not think it was completely accurate to say that Obadiah owed her his life—all she had done was provide a dark cloak—but she dared not say that now.

"It is an honor to meet you," she said, ducking her head. "Thank you for all you have done for Israel."

He held her gaze for a moment, and then he looked her over from head to toe, sizing her up. She felt embarrassed by her ragged shift and robe but did her best not to show it.

"Abital has become a dear friend and a devoted follower of Yahweh," Keziah said softly.

Then a smile spread over his face. "I believe Obadiah was right," he said.

Abital puzzled over this, wondering what Obadiah was right about, but his father did not seem inclined to elaborate. Then, before anyone else could say anything, Elon approached.

"It is time," he said. "Elijah says that he will begin, and Ahab has requested that all of Israel gather."

"I suppose we must go," Keziah said. She started to push herself up, and Abital reached out to help her to her feet.

"Let us see what the Lord is about to do," Keziah's father said.

"Whatever happens up there on that mountain"—Saba pushed himself up, his knees popping as he stood—"I am quite sure that Israel will never be the same."

CHAPTER TWENTY-FIVE

They ascended the hill, led by the hundreds ahead of them and the many hundreds behind. All of the people who had responded to the king's call to gather at Mount Carmel trudged up the mountain. Though the sun was yet low in the sky, the day was already hot, and Abital's throat was parched as she walked, step by slow step, along with the crowd. Keziah did not complain, though her swollen belly must have made it hard for her. Channah carried Ayla, who struggled to be put down. They dared not let the young child loose, for fear she would break free and be trampled by the crowd. Elon helped Saba when he stumbled, steadying the older man, and slowly, they made their way to the wide flat place where the king was waiting. The king was surrounded by his armed guards and ministers, including Obadiah, who stood, impassive, at his side.

To the king's left, gathered along a ridge lined with cypress trees, the prophets of Baal stood in their long robes. To the king's right, Elijah stood alone. Abital had not seen him since the night he had rushed into the banquet, but she knew him immediately. His unkempt gray hair blew in the breeze that whipped up off the sea, and he seemed to be wearing the same dirty robes he'd been wearing the night he'd announced it would not rain again until he gave the word. His feet were bare, his beard long and grizzled, and he was scanning the crowds that assembled as though looking for someone. Beyond him, behind the mountain, was the sea, a vast, blue expanse that seemed unbroken from here. It was as beautiful as Abital had imagined it would be.

"Come," Elon said, and led the group to a flat clearing toward the front of the crowd. Abital saw Aaliyah and her household standing nearby, her belly swollen as well, and recognized several other members of the king's palace guard standing across from her. Abital wondered that both of the king's wives who were with child had managed to make the journey while Jezebel had thought it too arduous. Several other groups of people stood in favored places, wearing fine linen robes and cloaks. Keziah and Obadiah's mother and father walked over to stand with this crowd. She supposed that around them were other wealthy businessmen from Samaria and beyond.

Slowly, the great crowd filed in, and it grew more difficult to move. They were pressed in on all sides, even here at the front of the crowd. The heat and the smell of so many bodies made it difficult to breathe, even with the soft breeze that drifted in off the water. As the crowds closed in, Elijah gathered wood from nearby trees and made two piles, one on each side of the king. A young man, with long, unkempt hair and a tattered robe, helped him.

When the area was so crowded Abital was not sure they would be able to fit many more, Elijah stepped forward and addressed the king.

"It is time to begin," Elijah said.

Abital wondered if Ahab knew what was coming. Judging by the bewildered look on his face, she guessed he did not. He only knew, she assumed, that this man had announced the beginning of the drought, and only he could put an end to it.

"You may address the crowd," King Ahab said. Elijah stepped into the middle of the clearing, turned to face the crowd, and spoke. The young man who had been with him withdrew. "How long will you waver between two opinions?" he said without preamble. His voice was loud, and he almost seemed to shake as she shouted the words over the gathered group. "If the Lord is God, follow Him," he declared. "But if Baal is God, follow him."

The crowd was eerily quiet as they watched the scene unfold. Abital glanced over at the prophets of Baal who were gathered here. Obadiah had said there were four hundred and fifty of them, and seeing them now, Abital felt a sense of cold fear start to work its way through her. There were so many of them, and on the Lord's side there was only Elijah. Did he truly mean to take on all of these prophets on his own? Was there any chance that the Lord would not win after all? What would He do?

"Well?" Elijah shouted. "Which is it? Is it Yahweh, or is it Baal?"

Again, the crowd was quiet. A few shouted one thing or another, but most stood still, simply waiting to see what would happen.

Elijah looked around, and, spotting a rock at the base of an outcropping, quickly climbed up it so he could be better seen. He moved with a jerky, almost unsteady kind of step, but he never stumbled.

"I am the only one of the Lord's prophets left," he said, addressing the crowd. Abital knew this was not quite true, as there were the hundred that Obadiah had saved, who now lived in the desert. But he was the only one here, and he was indeed the most prominent and well-known. "Baal has four hundred and fifty prophets here."

Elijah addressed the king. "Get two bulls for us. Let them choose one for themselves, and let them cut it into pieces and put it on the wood but not set fire to it. I will put the other bull on the pile of wood."

She saw now what the two piles of wood were—they were altars.

He was suggesting, Abital knew, that each side make an offering on an altar to their god. But a sacrifice was typically set alight. Why was he suggesting that they should not light the altars?

Elijah turned to the prophets. "Then you will call on the name of your god, and I will call on the name of the Lord. The god who answers by fire—he is God."

The sinking fear that had started in Abital earlier now spread through her whole being. Baal was represented by a bull. Didn't his prophets have that very symbol tattooed on their arms? How could Elijah ask for a bull to be a part of this test he had planned?

"What is he doing?" Keziah whispered as a murmur went through the crowd.

"He cannot be serious," Channah whispered beside her. Even Obadiah, standing next to the king, shifting from his right foot to his left, seemed uneasy.

"Our Lord rides the thunderstorms as His chariot," Saba said calmly. "Thunder is His voice, and lightning His staff. He will answer by fire."

"These prophets of Baal also believe that their god is the god of thunder," Channah said quietly. "And the bull is the symbol of their god."

"Do not fear," Saba said quietly. "These prophets may believe in their false god, but our Lord is true. Elijah is His messenger. We have nothing to worry about."

Even so, it did not make her feel better as Elijah shouted at the crowd once again.

"Does this sound fair?" Elijah asked the crowd, and several in the crowd shouted that it did. The prophets of Baal did not try to hide their pleasure.

"This sounds fair," Ahab answered.

The king dispatched several of his guards to go down the hill to find two bulls and bring them up. Abital wondered how long this would take. The men walked off, pushing their way through the crowd to get to the path that led down the rocky slope.

The people of Israel waited. They stood there, baking in the hot sun. Abital grew hungrier and thirstier with each moment, and still the guards did not return. The king sat in a chair that was shaded with a piece of fabric. The set of his jaw betrayed his anxious feelings about what was happening.

Ahab turned to the prophets, talking quietly with several of the men at the front. Whatever he was saying to them, it was working them into a state of excitement. Only Elijah appeared unaffected by what was happening. He sat down on the rock and pulled one of his knees up, resting his foot against the rock, and seemed to be studying the ground.

"Where will they find bulls?" Saba asked. "We passed only a few sheep grazing on the hillside on the way here. It could be hours or even days before they return."

The crowd began to grow restless. Few had brought food up the hill with them, and all were hot and thirsty. A mother held a small child in her arms to Abital's left. Abital smiled at the child, who cried in response. Abital heard some people begin to grumble. They had not expected to be standing in the sun all day. Would the guards ever come back? What was to happen? Many sat where they were, while others complained and debated returning down the mountain.

Obadiah left the king's side and brought a chair for Keziah. He set it under a sunshade, and before he returned to the king's side, he leaned in and whispered to Abital, "Jehovah Jirah. The Lord will provide."

She recognized the name of God from hearing it in Keziah's chambers. It was the name Abraham had given to the place where he had taken his son Isaac to be laid on the altar. When Isaac had asked where they would find a ram to offer to the Lord, Abraham had promised the Lord would provide, and He had, stopping Abraham's hand at the last moment. Abital understood that in recalling that name now, Obadiah was reminding her that this was not the first time the Lord had used a sacrifice on an altar to declare His might and His power. The words strengthened her heart, and as she watched him stride back to the king, she felt hope once more.

Finally, after the morning was half gone, Abital heard shouts at the rear of the crowd, and people began to press apart. Abital turned and saw the men leading two bulls, each with a ring through its nose to which the men had tied thick leather straps. People pushed back, pressing together as the bulls got close, making a path where there was no room for a path. None wished to be trampled or gored by a bucking bull, and as the men led the animals to the area before the king, even the prophets of Baal shrank back. But Elijah approached, appearing unconcerned. The bulls strained against the ties that held them, but even as he walked closer to them, they did not lunge at Elijah.

"Choose one of the bulls and prepare it first, since there are so many of you," he said to the prophets. "Call on the name of your god, but do not light the fire. You must call on the name of your god, and ask him to light it."

"We will take that one," one of the prophets said, pointing to the largest of the bulls. Abital recognized him as Ushmuel, the leader of the prophets.

Once the pieces of the bull had been laid on the wood of the altar to Baal, Elijah stepped forward and shouted, "So, then. Tell your god to light the fire."

The prophets circled the altar. They began chanting, calling on the name of their god. As more and more prophets joined in the chant, Abital held her breath. Would they do it? She knew Baal was a false god, that he held no power, but she still could not help but fear that they might be successful. There were so many of them. Surely if there was any truth in this god, he would hear them and respond.

"Oh, Baal, answer us," they shouted. "Baal, show your power."

The men danced around the altar, their cries growing more and more insistent as the moments wore on and nothing happened.

"We need to try chanting all together," Ushmuel cried, holding up his hand. The other prophets agreed, and at his call, they began chanting together. There were so many men dancing around the altar that Abital could not even see the spot where the bull had been laid, but judging by the growing frenzy of the men's dancing, she was sure their god was not answering the way they had hoped.

The king watched, his face unreadable. Obadiah stood still and tall by his side. Elijah, seated once again on the rock, had gone back to looking at the ground.

The chanting went on for several hours. With each passing chant, with each new dance, the prophets grew more frantic, but nothing they did seemed to spur the interest of their god.

The people began to grow restless. It was hot, and they were hungry and thirsty. Ayla cried for milk, before finally falling asleep in her mother's arms.

When the sun was directly overhead and the heat of the day pressed down, Elijah put his feet back on the ground, stood up, and wandered over to the prophets, as if noticing them for the first time.

"Shout louder," he called. "Surely Baal is god. Perhaps he is busy, or deep in thought, or traveling."

Abital realized with a shock that he was mocking them. The prophets seemed to realize this as well, as their dancing and shaking began to take on more urgency.

"Well?" the king asked. "Does your god control the lightning, or does he not?"

"He does indeed," Ushmuel said. "He will answer any moment now."

As the prophets went back to their chanting, the king settled in his chair, his arms crossed over his chest.

"Maybe your god is sleeping. Perhaps someone needs to wake him up!" Elijah shouted, undeterred.

Many people in the crowd cheered, laughing at his words. This seemed to only rile the prophets up more. They chanted louder and danced more and used spears and swords to slash their own skin so that the blood dripped down their arms and onto the ground. Elijah's taunts continued, but though the prophets paid him no mind, the crowd loved it. They cheered after each barb he threw toward the prophets.

The afternoon wore on, the sun sliding slowly across the clear blue sky, and the prophets whipped themselves up into an ecstatic chant, and still Baal did not show. Baal did not answer his prophets. He did not come.

When the afternoon began to edge into evening, Elijah stepped forward.

"Enough." He held up one hand. "Baal is nowhere to be seen. It is time for the Lord to show Himself. Is anyone willing to help me?"

Several men stepped forward. "See these stones?" Elijah said, pointing to a slab of rock that had been broken into pieces. "This was an altar to the Lord God, the ruler of Israel. It was built by Yahweh's people, but it was destroyed by the king and queen when they tried to purge the nation of Yahweh.

"Jezebel, the most wicked queen Israel has ever seen, killed hundreds of the prophets of the Lord," Elijah called. "It is only through the bravery of the Lord's servant Obadiah that any were saved."

The king turned to Obadiah, who looked as though he wanted nothing more than to disappear.

"You did what?" the king started, but Elijah rushed on.

"Who will help me rebuild this altar now?"

He directed the volunteers to take twelve stones. "There is one stone for each of the tribes of Israel," Elijah cried. "One stone for each of the twelve tribes descended from Jacob, whose name Yahweh changed to Israel."

None in the crowd could miss what he was doing, Abital thought. Elijah was reminding the people of the covenant Yahweh had made to His people—to all twelve tribes, not just the tribes of the Northern Kingdom.

The men helped him place the heavy stones, and together they repaired the altar. "This is an altar to the Yahweh, the One True God of Israel," Elijah declared.

Then, taking a shovel from behind a large stone, Elijah dug a deep trench around the altar. Next he arranged the wood that had been lying on the ground, slaughtered the second bull, and laid the pieces on the altar. Then he called out, "Fill four large jars with water and pour it on the offering and on the wood."

What was he talking about now? Abital wondered. Where would they get four large jars of water up on this hilltop? Where would they even get the water? It had not rained in three and a half years. There could be no spring with water here. And if there was water, why had he not said so, and let the people of Israel slake their thirst? They had been standing in this heat all day long. Why had Elijah told no one of its presence?

The men who had helped him build the altar obediently took the jars and followed his directions to a spring, which he said flowed a little way farther up the path. They returned quickly, carrying the jugs in their arms. Water splashed out of the top of one as the man set it down.

"Now pour the water all over the bull and the wood," Elijah repeated. The men obeyed, dumping the water over the offering. She had not seen so much water all together in one place in more than a year. Abital's thirst rose as she watched the water pour down and soak the offering. "Now do it again," Elijah ordered.

The men once again took the jugs to the hidden spring and filled them, and dumped the sweet cold water over the offering to the Lord. The crowd began to murmur, wondering what he was doing.

"Do it a third time," Elijah declared, and once again, the men filled the jugs and poured the water over the offering. The water ran down over the altar and filled the trench. This time the people began to jeer, saying that Elijah was a madman.

Abital's heart pounded in her chest. She did not doubt that Yahweh was the Lord. She knew that with her whole heart. She knew that He was the same God who spoke all of creation into place. Who hung the stars in their places and set the boundaries of the oceans. This was the God who had parted the Red Sea, who had led His people to miraculously conquer their enemies to claim the land that He had promised them, who sent the walls of Jericho tumbling down. Yahweh had enabled a little shepherd to fell a giant with nothing more than a stone, and to establish His kingdom in Israel. Yahweh had also used Elijah to bring a child back from the dead and to make oil and flour never run out. She knew that Yahweh was all-powerful and could do whatever Elijah asked of Him.

And yet she still held her breath, hoping that He would do something miraculous now.

Then the prophet Elijah stepped forward and raised his hand, and a hush fell over the crowd. "O Lord, God of Abraham, Isaac, and Israel, let it be known today that You are God in Israel and that I am Your servant and have done all these things at Your command. Answer me, O Lord, answer me so these people will know that You, O Lord, are God, and that You are turning their hearts to You again."

He stepped back and closed his eyes.

And all of Israel waited.

CHAPTER TWENTY-SIX

The people of Israel did not have to wait long.

Only moments after Elijah had stepped away from the altar, a bolt of lightning flashed down from the clear sky. The light was so bright it was nearly blinding, and the sound was like nothing Abital had ever heard. Like metal scraping against metal, but louder, and somehow brimming with life. Almost at the exact same instant, a peal of thunder shot through the air, slicing the stillness with its deafening roar. The air filled with a metallic smell, and the altar to the Lord burst into flames.

"The Lord alone is God!" Elijah shouted, lifting his hands in the air. "See, all of Israel, and know that Yahweh is the Lord your God!"

A cry rose up from the crowd, and one by one, they fell down, putting their faces to the ground. Abital felt herself shouting as well, a cry that welled up from somewhere deep inside her. It was so shocking, so incredible, and so intensely undeniable. The Lord had done it. She bowed down, along with those around her, in reverence. Glancing up, she saw that Obadiah was already on his knees, as were several of the king's other attendants. Obadiah's parents had also fallen to their knees, along with all the wealthy and powerful families in Samaria.

The flames roared, and the air quickly became choked with a thick black smoke. The wood and the pieces of the bull, though drenched in water, were instantly burning with a heat so intense that those closest to the flames had to push back into the crowd. The flames burned so fiercely that Abital feared they might jump from the altar and spread, but she could not make herself look away. The fire burned so hot, so strong, that the flames were blue, and they danced and spun and popped, sending up sparks and waves of heat that fanned out to the crowd. The darkening evening was as bright as midday.

Abital tore her eyes away and looked over at the king. His mouth was pressed into a thin line, his eyes wide, his hands clenched.

All around her, on the ground, people were shouting and crying and raising their hands.

"Jehovah Jireh," Keziah said, over and over, tears streaming down her cheeks.

"The Lord is God," Saba said, nodding his head.

The fire's intensity began to diminish and then began to burn itself out. As the flame dwindled and died, she saw that the fire had burned up not only the bull and the wood but also the very stones. The fire sent by the Lord had licked up all the water in the trough until there was nothing left.

Around her, one by one, the people began to call out, "Jehovah is God." The man next to her echoed her cry. "Jehovah is God!"

Abital echoed the cry. "Jehovah is God!" It did not take long before all in the crowd were crying out to the Lord.

After everything she'd been through—after all that she had seen and experienced in the king's palace, Abital had thought she might feel elated to be on the winning side. But as much as she wanted to, she took no pleasure in the king's confusion and consternation. She had thought she might feel clever for having reached this conclusion before so many others, and justified in her refusal to worship at the altar of Baal, but she felt none of these things. Watching the people of Israel fall on their faces and worship the Lord, all she felt was a sense that something holy had happened here and that the presence of the Lord of Hosts was in this place.

She felt small, humbled, honored to have been allowed to see the might of the Lord. She was nothing. He was everything. And in that moment, she knew that she would worship Him until the day she died.

Tears streamed down her cheeks and blurred her sight, and it was some time before she could look away from the blackened spot on the ground and see what was happening around her. She could barely make out what was going on at the far side of the clearing. The prophets of Baal were running. They were scrambling down the side of the hill, grasping onto scrubby bushes and bracing against rocks, quickly trying to make their escape.

"Stop them!" Elijah shouted. "Gather up all the prophets of Baal. Do not let any escape!"

The king's guards did not hesitate. Though just hours before they had regarded Elijah with skepticism, now they sprang into action at his command. There was quite a lot of shouting as the guards chased down the escaping prophets. Many of the men in the crowd joined in the chase, scaling rocks and climbing over steep hillsides to bring back the false prophets.

Elijah, meanwhile, stood in the center of all the chaos, his arms raised, his head thrust up so his wild hair splayed down his back. His eyes were closed, and his face appeared as though he was listening to some song or conversation none of the rest of them could hear.

It took some time, and the sky was quite dark by the time the crowd had finally rounded up the prophets of Baal. Elijah opened his eyes, glanced around, and declared, "Take them to the brook Kishon and kill them."

Many in the crowd cheered at this, but Abital could find no joy in this order. These prophets had led Israel astray and worshiped at the altar of a false god. But they were not the ones who had introduced Baal worship into this land. They were not the ones who had elevated the false god above Yahweh within Israel and broken the covenant the Lord had made with their forefathers. They were the soldiers but not the commander of the army.

She gazed over at the king, who was watching the proceedings absently. It was as though he were watching some drama unfold before him but had no part in it.

"Go on, then!" Elijah called out to the king. "Eat and drink. For I already hear the sound of a heavy rain."

Could it really be? Abital looked up at the sky, fading now into night. The first stars were just beginning to appear in the deep blue velvet of the sky. There were no clouds to be seen.

The people of the Lord began to make their way down the hill, led by men with torches made of pitch. Because they stood near the front, Abital and Saba and Keziah waited until much of the crowd had cleared and made its way to their camps on the hill before they began. While they waited, Abital watched King Ahab, who sat still, his jaw slack, his gaze vacant.

Obadiah helped many of the people move toward the path, lifting an old man to his feet and setting a child in his mother's arms. Finally, when much of the crowd had cleared, he went over to his parents and brought them to their little group. "I think it is safe now for you to walk down," he said, bowing to his father and to Saba. "It is dark, but this torch will light your way." He handed the torch to Elon, who nodded and began walking down the hill.

"You will not come with us?" Keziah asked her brother, even as her father started to walk.

"Not yet. The prophet has asked me to stay with him and his servant for a while."

"He cannot find another? You must be exhausted," Keziah said. "You did not sleep last night."

"I cannot say no to the prophet," Obadiah said. "But I will join you as soon as I can." He looked at Abital and paused, and then smiled shyly. "Please be careful on the path. I will see you soon."

They began the slow descent down the path. Elon held the torch aloft, lighting the way, and watched out for animals and other dangers on the path. It was not a long walk, but it felt as though it took hours. When they made it back to the camp, they quickly made a meal of boiled oats and dried lamb. They gave thanks to God with a fresh appreciation, and then they ate, and, finally, climbed into their beds, exhausted.

The king's tent was quiet. There was no raucous laughter, no music. Though there were voices inside, as if people were eating and drinking, it was quiet.

But Abital could not sleep. Around her, the soft breathing of her saba and Keziah filled the tent, but as much as she longed for sleep, she could not make it come. Her mind kept replaying the scene from earlier, over and over and over. She saw the fire raining down from the sky, smelled the metallic scent as it lit the offering aflame, seeing, with disbelief, as it burned up the rocks and licked up the water. Truly none could say that there was any god but Yahweh. She knew this knowledge would change things. She prayed that Israel would turn back to the Lord, that God would bless His people once again.

Abital wondered, also, where Obadiah was. She wondered what was happening to the king, and the prophet Elijah. She wished she could see them.

Finally, late into the night, she fell into a deep sleep, and when she woke at dawn, she was stiff and sore but could immediately feel that something was different. The air was cooler, carrying with it the scent of the sea.

CHAPTER TWENTY-SEVEN

After everyone else had gone down the hill, Elijah had told Obadiah and his servant to follow him, and they climbed even higher, to the very top of the mountain. By this time Obadiah was hungry and thirsty and so tired he could barely stand, but he could not refuse the prophet after everything he had seen. He wanted to know what Elijah would do now. He followed the old man up the path in the darkness, their way lit only by the milky light of the moon. He feared that a wrong step could send them over the side, but Elijah was sure-footed and seemed to have no concern.

But when they got to the top of the mountain, all he did was bow down on the ground, his head between his knees, and begin praying. Without waiting for instructions, the servant did the same, and Obadiah followed suit. Elijah muttered his prayers to the Lord. Obadiah tried to ignore his muttering and focus on turning his heart to Yahweh.

They continued to pray quietly for a while, and then, at some signal known only to him, Elijah told his servant, "Go and look at the sea."

The young man rose to his feet, walked to the precipice, and gazed out, looking out toward the sea. The sky was black, dotted with stars and the bright moon.

"There is nothing there," the servant reported. "The sky remains clear."

"We must continue to pray." Elijah leaned forward again on his knees, placing his head on the ground, and began to pray once more. Obadiah did not know how long they stayed like this, but after some time had passed, Elijah turned to his servant again. "Go look at the sea again."

The servant rose again and gazed out at the sea, but his report was the same. "There is nothing there."

Elijah returned to praying, and Obadiah and the servant did as well. Elijah ordered the servant to look once more, and then again, and each time he reported that there was no change. Obadiah prayed for God's mercy and His peace. He prayed that rain would come, but more than that, he prayed that Israel would not forget what they had seen on Mount Carmel today. He prayed that the whole nation would turn its heart back to Yahweh, that the false gods would be abandoned in Israel, their temples destroyed, and that Yahweh would bless His nation once more.

A fifth time, Elijah ordered his servant to go look at the sea. A fifth time, the servant reported that there was still nothing there.

Obadiah prayed that the coming rain would bring food and water to the people who had lived so long in scarcity, and that their health would be restored. He prayed for prosperity for the nation. He prayed for the king, that Ahab would have the courage to lead according to what he now knew to be true. He prayed that Jezebel would know the truth and willingly give up her idols. He prayed for Keziah, who would no doubt face the anger of the queen.

A sixth time, when the sky was starting to lighten with the pink glow of dawn, the servant reported that there was still nothing.

Obadiah prayed again for Israel, but he also found his thoughts turning, as they always did, to Abital. He asked the Lord to bless her and her saba. He asked God to protect her. When he had returned to the palace and found her gone, he had panicked. He had seen what a future without Abital in it would be like, and he could not face it. Beyond that, when he learned why she had been dismissed, he had known that she had given her heart, fully and truly, to Yahweh. She had risked everything to stand up for the One True God, and he knew that she was not only beautiful but also had a character and devotion to the Lord that he found more beautiful still.

He knew that it would defy all expectations and all logic for him to marry the queen's seamstress, and yet he could not see how he could do anything else. He loved her and would be thinking about her until his dying day. He would be miserable without her. There was no choice but to make her his wife, if she would have him. He prayed that his father would forgive him for what he intended to do.

The seventh time Elijah directed his servant to look out over the sea, the sky was the palest blue, just edged with a fiery gold on the horizon. The servant replied, "A cloud as small as a man's hand is rising from the sea."

Hearing this, Elijah rose and walked over to the edge of the mountain to see for himself. Obadiah followed and saw that indeed there was one puffy white cloud sitting over the horizon. Surely this could not be the sign Elijah had been waiting for. This one tiny cloud could not portend rain.

But Elijah turned to his servant and said, "Go and tell Ahab to hitch up his chariot. The storm is coming."

CHAPTER TWENTY-EIGHT

When daylight finally reached the tents, Abital slipped out and gazed up at the sky. It had dawned a brilliant blue, but the air was heavy, and it carried a moisture in it that she had not felt in a long time. Off in the distance, Abital could see a tiny cloud sailing its way across the sky, but as she stretched and walked around, she saw that a few more small white clouds followed behind.

Soon, the people of Israel began to stir and quickly packed their tents and loaded their bags onto donkeys and into carts. They would return, each to their own homes, and tell of what the Lord had done. The story would spread throughout the land, and surely those who had missed it would soon hear that the Lord was God.

Keziah said that they would wait until she heard news from her brother. The tent where her parents stayed also remained. The flat plain cleared out slowly, and as the hours passed, clouds began to build. These clouds were darker and gathered in thick clumps in the sky.

When she had finished packing, Aaliyah left the mountain, along with her household. She came to Abital and said goodbye, asking Abital to let her know if she would be returning to the palace. Abital promised to do so, though she knew she would never go back.

"What is rain?" Ayla asked.

Abital realized with a start that it had not rained in so long the child had never seen it.

"Water will fall from the sky in big fat drops," Abital told her.

"Or sometimes in little drops that seem to just spit," Keziah added.

"Will it hurt?" Ayla asked.

Keziah laughed. "No, it does not hurt. You will get wet, though."

"It will make the plants grow?" Ayla said.

"That is right. It will make the plants grow, and the trees turn green and lush, and there will be plenty of food for the animals to eat. We will have good things to eat too. Cheese, and fresh meat, and wine. So many fruits—apricots and pomegranates and berries."

"It sounds wonderful," Ayla said, sighing.

Keziah laughed. "It will be wonderful."

It was several more hours before Elijah's servant came down the mountain. The sky was now covered with a thick layer of gray clouds, but there had been no other sign of rain. The servant, when he arrived, walked directly to the king's tent. Abital could not hear what he told the king, but after a short conversation, the young man turned and began to walk toward the path that led to the bottom of the hill. The king's guards and servants began hurriedly loading the wagons with the king's things. The king emerged from the tent a few moments later, and, taking several of his men with him, he started across the clearing toward Keziah's tent. Keziah stood before him while he spoke to her.

"I must go quickly," King Ahab said. "I will see you soon at the palace."

"Yes, my lord." Keziah bowed her head.

The king's men were still loading the wagons when, sometime later, Elijah came running down the hill. Obadiah followed behind him, racing to keep up.

Everyone who was left in their tents came out to see what was happening. Elijah was running along the path, his bare feet striking hard against the dirt, his long hair blowing back behind him. His robe lifted with each step, revealing his thighs, but he did not seem to care.

He looked completely mad, but Abital suspected that did not mean that there was anything wrong. Elijah seemed to care little for appearances, or for the way things were normally done. He cared only about delivering the message that the Lord had given him to deliver. He did not know or care that others found him odd. He was faithful to the only One whose opinion mattered. As she watched him race down the hill, his long legs kicking up ahead of him, Abital wondered whether they had seen the last of the prophet, or if he had a further role to play in the story of Israel.

Obadiah followed not far behind the prophet, and he stopped before the king and spoke quietly with him and with his guards. The king and his guards nodded and soon started down the path.

After the king had left, Obadiah made his way to his sister's tent and explained what had happened over the course of the night and the morning. Saba rested on a mat, worn out from the excitement of the night, a sleeping Ayla beside him.

"How far do you think he will run?" Keziah asked, shaking her head.

"There is no telling," Obadiah said. "It would not surprise me if he ran all the way back to Jezreel."

They were all quiet for a moment, thinking.

"He is an odd one, isn't he?" Keziah said. "Elijah?"

"He is indeed," Obadiah said. "I have never met anyone like him. I wonder if anyone like him has ever existed in Israel, or if Israel will ever see anyone like him again."

"I suspect Israel has not seen the last of Elijah," Abital said.

"We should probably get these things packed up," Keziah said after a moment's pause. "It does look as though it truly will rain." The gathering clouds were dark, and the tops were tall and round.

"I barely remember what it looks like when rain is on the way," Abital said.

Reluctantly, they woke Saba and Ayla, and while the guards packed up Keziah's tent, Abital packed her own things. Obadiah crossed the clearing and spoke to his parents, who were also packing up their tent, and then he came back and insisted that he would accompany Abital and Saba back to their home, while the guards took Keziah, Ayla, and Channah to the palace. While they worked, packing up the bags of food and sleeping mats, more thick clouds gathered, turning the whole sky dark. Somewhere off in the distance, thunder rumbled, and a flash of lightning split the sky.

"Mama?" Ayla cried. Keziah held her close, trying to comfort her child, but she was laughing at the same time.

"Is it—" Keziah started, and Abital nodded, but before she could speak, a drop of water splashed onto the dirt at their feet.

"It is," Obadiah said as a drop landed on his arm. "Praise God, it is really raining!"

Another drop fell, and another, and in an instant, the sky had opened up, and water was pouring down. Sheets of water fell, one drop after another coming so quickly that Abital could not tell one from the next. In moments, all of them were soaked through, but none of them cared. Keziah had thrown her arms around her brother, and he tossed his head back and laughed. Saba held his hands out to catch a pool of water like a bowl, and he drank thirstily. Around them, people were coming out of the few tents that remained in the clearing, and they were shrieking and shouting and dancing as they also took in what was happening.

After three and a half years, the Lord had finally sent the rain.

"Praise the Lord, who has answered our prayers!" Abital said. She laughed, letting the rain pour down over her, feeling it wash away her fears, her worries, her doubts.

God delivered His people once again.

CHAPTER TWENTY-NINE

When they finally made it back to Saba's land the next day, everything they had brought with them on the trip was soaked. After the initial cloudburst, they had walked through a spitting, misty drizzle for much of the day. Their clothes clung to their skin, their feet were caked in mud, and none of them cared one bit. The rain, after so much time, felt delicious. Like new life. Already, the earth looked healthier, the bushes less parched. The thirsty ground soaked the water in as fast as it could, and the small creek beds were quickly filling with splashing streams.

As wearying as traveling was, Abital dreaded reaching home, because she knew that Obadiah would need to return to the palace, and she would be left behind. She would likely not see him again after he left. She would never forget the memory of these days together, of how he had come to get her, and she wanted to cling to every moment.

The house finally came into view, draped in a misty rain. The silvery-green leaves of the eucalyptus trees shivered in the breeze, and a line of smoke from the chimney made the home look warm and cozy. Still, she did not want to go inside, dreading the moment she would need to say goodbye. She could not imagine what her life would be like without Obadiah in it. She would live here with Saba, clean out sheep stalls, sew simple clothing for the women in town. Saba would probably arrange a marriage, now that the rain had come back. It would not be long before he would be able to afford a dowry once again. It would not be long before Obadiah would be forced to take a wife, and no doubt raise many beautiful children with her.

"You will stay the night," Saba said to Obadiah, and Obadiah nodded.

"I would like that. I must return to the palace shortly, but I would appreciate one more night of your hospitality."

"You are always welcome in this home. You do us a great honor, being here."

"It is I who feel honored."

Saba led them inside, where Elkanah had lit a fire in the hearth and Ofir was cooking grains and lentils over the flames. Seeing the fire spin and dance now, Abital was reminded of the flames that had consumed the offering to Yahweh, and she was stunned all over again by what had happened, what they had witnessed on that mountain.

They all changed into dry clothes, and when Saba said he needed to attend to the animals before they ate, Obadiah asked to help. The two men walked out to the covered sheep pen together, and Abital helped Ofir finish cooking the meal. Abital told her all that they had seen and witnessed, and Ofir cried, praising Yahweh.

"As soon as the rain began to fall, I knew that Yahweh had proven His power, but I did not know how," Ofir said, tears streaming down her cheeks. "Praise the Lord."

Saba and Obadiah were gone for quite some time, far longer than Saba usually spent on caring for the animals. Abital tried to be patient, but she grew frustrated. This was probably the last night she would ever see Obadiah, and he was spending it all with Saba. When they finally came back inside the house, her stomach growling and both men grinning, she wondered what they had been up to in the barn.

"Let us eat before it grows cold," Abital said.

But Saba shook his head. "Not yet. Supper will wait."

"Will you please take a walk with me, Abital?" Obadiah asked.

She gazed at Obadiah, then at Saba, and back again. What was happening?

Saba was smiling and nodding, and she did not know what else to do, so she said yes.

She followed Obadiah out of the house. A soft mist was still falling, and the light was starting to fade from the sky. It felt strange to look up and not see stars, but the water on her face made her feel more alive than she had in a long while. When they stood in the yard, he took her hand.

"Let us go see the vineyard again." He led her up the hill, walking the land as if he owned it. She followed just behind him, relishing the feeling of her hand clutched in his, until they stood on the hill that overlooked the valley. Dead grapevines clung to the lines that held them up, but drops of silvery rain caught the evening light, holding the promise that what was once dead would soon be brought back to life.

"It is beautiful here," Obadiah said, gazing out over the valley. "I will be sorry to take you away from here. Will you miss it terribly?"

"What are you talking about?" Abital's heart thudded in her chest. What could he mean? She did not understand, but somewhere within her, a flame of hope was lit.

"I mean that I spoke with my father while we were on Mount Carmel, after I came down from the mountain. I told him that I could not live without you in my life. That I would not marry anyone but you, and that if he wanted to see his son and meet his grandchildren someday, he would agree."

"You—what?" He could not mean it. This was a cruel trick. He could not really mean—

"My father was not pleased, of course, but after meeting you this week and seeing what I love about you, he has come around."

"But my saba cannot afford—"

"I know this." He waved the concern away with his hand. "My father is rich enough. He does not need more sheep and goats or ornaments in gold. What he wants is grandchildren, many of them, and I told him he would only get them from me if he gave his consent for me to marry you."

Abital found she could not speak. This was not how things were done. She had never heard of a son speaking to his abba this way. She had never heard of an abba allowing a son to choose his own bride. "You cannot be serious."

"I am, Abital."

"This is a cruel trick to play on someone," she said. "Do not tell me this is a trick."

"It is no trick. My father saw that you are a kind woman, loyal to Yahweh, and he knows that I am only alive because of your quick thinking. He has given his consent for us to marry. Tonight I spoke with Saba, who shared the same incredulity that you are showing me now."

"I have never heard of such a thing happening this way," Abital said.

"And yet, it is. We have seen many strange things these past few days. If that is not reason enough to do what no one expects, I do not know what is. We will be married. If you agree, that is. Saba approves and has promised to talk with my father about the arrangements, but he said that you must also agree before it is decided."

"He did?" Surely that could not be right. He had never before suggested that she would be allowed to make such a decision.

Obadiah grinned. "Nothing about this is happening the way things usually happen in Israel, Abital. But nothing about what we have been through these past few years is normal. So, it comes down to you. Will you agree? Will you marry me and serve Yahweh beside me all of your days?"

"I—" She still could not believe what was happening. But when she looked at him now, he did not appear to be joking. He seemed, instead, to be entirely serious.

"Do not torture me, Abital." He pulled her hand, clasped in his, to his lips. "Please say you will."

In the day's dying light, she thought he had never been more handsome. The rain that fell softly all around felt fresh and new like a promise that things would grow and blossom once again.

"Of course," she said. She did not know what it would look like. Would she return to the palace? Would she be welcome there? Would Obadiah leave the palace altogether and work for his father in Samaria? There were no answers yet. But she trusted this man. She knew that he loved her and that she wanted nothing more than to be with him and serve the Lord beside him as long as they lived. "Did you doubt? Of course I will."

A smile broke out across his face. "I am not easy to live with, you know. I have a tendency to slip out in the middle of the night to hide in caves, or to flee for my life in the darkness."

Abital laughed. "Let us hope those days are behind you. All know now that Yahweh alone is God. And we will serve and worship Him all of our days."

Obadiah smiled, pulling her closer. Through their damp cloaks, she could feel his heart beating and the strength of the muscles in his chest. "I cannot wait," he said, just before he kissed her.

Suddenly, she was not worried about the rain or the plants or the drought. A flame of hope sparked, lit, caught inside of her. She did not know what would happen. She did not know whether Jezebel would have her killed if she saw her in the palace once again. She did not know whether King Ahab would ban the idols and lead Israel back to true repentance.

In that moment, all she knew was that Yahweh was the Lord and that she wanted to be with this man, whatever the future held.

FROM THE AUTHOR

Dear Reader,

Before I started working on this story, I had read enough Scripture and heard enough sermons that I vaguely knew the broad strokes of the story—Jezebel is evil, Elijah is good, God sends down fire to burn up the bull, God wins—but it wasn't until I dug deeply into it that I realized how fascinating and complicated this period in the history of God's people truly was.

I hadn't really understood the implications of the fact that this incident occurred in the period after the people rebelled against the excesses of King Solomon and the kingdom was divided into the two parts, with ten of Israel's tribes in the North and two in the South. The nation God had established was struggling to survive, and His people were fighting to hold on to the land He had given them.

I also didn't understand that Baal and Asherah—both are mentioned in the text as false gods King Ahab worships, though only Baal is challenged on Mount Carmel—were very common and popular gods worshiped throughout the region at this time, and so they posed a direct threat to the covenant Yahweh made with His people.

I had never noticed the character called Obadiah—one of many Obadiahs in the Bible and not the same one the book is named after—who, we're told in a parenthetical statement, almost as an aside, saved one hundred of Yahweh's prophets when Jezebel tried to have them all killed. (If you read 1 Kings 18, you'll see that it's almost like the writer of the text forgot to mention this major event and then is like, *Oh, and by the way, Jezebel slaughtered hundreds of Hebrew prophets and tried to wipe out Israel entirely, and this Obadiah character is the one who saved the faith from being wiped out altogether, but anyway...*

And I had heard of the widow of Zarephath and knew her oil and flour never ran out, but I had never truly considered why that mattered, and had somehow overlooked the whole part where Elijah brings her dead son back to life. Wait, what? This incredible miracle doesn't get enough attention because it's overshadowed by the main event that Elijah does on Mount Carmel, but I bet it changed the life and the faith of that widow forever.

In short, in writing this book, I learned so much about not only the history of God's people but also the unchanging, persistent message that is threaded throughout Scripture: God is after our hearts. He doesn't need our sacrifices or our outward devotion but only wants His people to love and pursue Him first. That's a message I always need to be reminded of, and one that I hope encourages you today, no matter what drought or insurmountable mountain you're facing.

I hope you enjoyed reading this book as much as I enjoyed writing it.

Signed,
Beth Adams

KEEPING THE FAITH

These questions can be used in a Bible study or book club discussion:

1. In 1 Kings 16:30, we're told that "Ahab son of Omri did more evil in the eyes of the LORD than any of those before him." Based on this book and the text of 1 Kings 16–18, where the story of Ahab and Jezebel and Elijah is told, what evidence do you see of this?

2. At the beginning of this story, Abital is not sure which, if any, god she believes in, but the influence of Saba and his faithfulness, as well as Keziah and Obadiah, eventually help her understand the truth. Are there people in your life who have acted as examples of faithfulness and drawn you to the Lord?

3. Toward the end of the book, Abital defies Jezebel's orders and refuses to worship Baal, and it costs her her position (and, Abital assumes, her life). Have you ever had a situation where you chose to stand up for your faith at great cost? Why did you decide to do what you did in that situation?

4. At various points in this book, different characters wonder why Yahweh would not just allow but cause a terrible drought that brings so much suffering. How does this make you feel,

and how does it change your understanding of the character of God?

5. Why do you think God does not do a dramatic miracle today, like He did on Mount Carmel, to prove to all that He is the One True God? What do you think might happen if He did?

DIVINE MESSENGERS

By Reverend Jane Willan, MS, MDiv

From stormy confrontations on mountaintops to valiant challenges against corrupt royalty, the prophets of ancient Israel
were nothing less than heroic. These dynamic individuals shaped
the social, religious, and political landscape of their world. The
prophets who were dedicated to Yahweh left a distinct and powerful
mark on history. Their stories are not simply ancient tales, but vivid
accounts of divine battles and unwavering faith that still inspire and
captivate people of faith today.

Yahweh's prophets were unique individuals, chosen by God to be
messengers of the divine. These prophets acted as liaisons between
God and the people of Israel. Their primary role was to guide the
Israelites to obey God's will. They were also called upon to help their
people repent from their sins and return to faithful worship.

Yahweh's prophets were both spiritual leaders and champions
of social justice. Vocal advocates for the poor, widows, orphans, and
marginalized members of society, they condemned systemic wrong-
doing and urged societal reforms. They pushed for a more equitable
and compassionate community. In addition to their moral and

ethical guidance, these prophets predicted future events, including impending disasters, exiles, and the coming of the Messiah.

One dramatic example of a prophet's influence is found in the story of Elijah. In 1 Kings 18, Elijah challenges the prophets of Baal on Mount Carmel. He calls the people of Israel to decide between Yahweh and Baal, stating, "How long will you waver between two opinions? If the LORD is God, follow him; but if Baal is God, follow him" (1 Kings 18:21). In a dramatic display of divine power, Elijah calls down fire from heaven to consume his offering, proving Yahweh's supremacy and leading the people to proclaim, "The LORD—he is God! The LORD—he is God!" (1 Kings 18:39).

The activities of Yahweh's prophets often included public proclamations, sermons, and prophecies delivered in public spaces, temples, and royal courts. For example, Isaiah prophesied in the courts of kings, advising them according to God's will and warning them of impending consequences if they strayed. To make their messages more impactful, these prophets performed symbolic acts, such as Jeremiah's wearing of a yoke to symbolize the coming bondage of Israel (Jeremiah 27:2). Ezekiel's dramatic portrayals of Jerusalem's siege (Ezekiel 4:1–3) served as vivid, visual reminders of the consequences of disobedience.

These prophets frequently found themselves in conflict with kings and religious leaders who promoted idolatry and social injustice. Jeremiah's life was marked by such conflicts. He was thrown into a cistern and left to die because of his prophecies against the ruling authorities (Jeremiah 38:6). Despite the dangers, Yahweh's prophets remained steadfast, driven by their divine mission to call Israel back to faithfulness.

Unlike the pragmatic prophets of Yahweh, the prophets of Baal—the Canaanite god of fertility, rain, and agriculture—were much showier. Their influence surged during the tumultuous reign of King Ahab, mainly due to the fervent support of Queen Jezebel, Ahab's formidable wife, who was a passionate advocate for Baal worship. This dramatic shift set the stage for one of biblical history's most intense religious showdowns.

The prophets of Baal were deeply involved in cult activities, conducting rituals, sacrifices, and ceremonies to invoke Baal's favor, especially for agricultural prosperity. Supported by the monarchy, they held significant sway in the royal court. Their public rituals were elaborate, involving sacrifices designed to appeal for rain and fertility. On Mount Carmel, Baal's prophets called on him from morning till noon, slashing themselves with weapons until their blood flowed, but there was no response (1 Kings 18:26–29).

Despite their efforts, the prophets of Baal were powerless against the true God. The dramatic showdown on Mount Carmel demonstrated Yahweh's power and marked a turning point in Israel's religious history. Elijah's challenge to the prophets of Baal exposed the futility of their worship and reaffirmed Yahweh's sovereignty.

Other prophets and priestesses served the goddess Asherah, who was associated with fertility, motherhood, and the sea. Although specific figures are less documented, their presence was significant in the religious practices of Israel and surrounding regions. Their worship often blended with other local deities, creating a mix that sometimes merged with worship of Yahweh. This frequently brought them into conflict with Yahweh's prophets, who vehemently opposed idolatry.

Asherah's prophets performed rituals meant to ensure fertility and prosperity. Intricately carved wooden poles were erected in sacred groves, high places, and near altars. They symbolized the goddess's presence and were central to worship and fertility rites, enjoying royal and popular support when rulers promoted multiple gods and goddesses or idolatry. For example, during the reign of King Manasseh, the worship of Asherah was incorporated into the temple of Yahweh itself (2 Kings 21:7), which led to severe condemnation from prophets like Jeremiah (Jeremiah 17:1–4).

Yahweh's prophets often spearheaded religious reforms, striving to eradicate idolatry and leading to significant societal and political upheaval. King Josiah's reforms in 2 Kings 23 involved the destruction of Asherah poles and the removal of idolatrous priests, reflecting the profound impact of prophetic influence on national policy.

These prophets' advocacy for monotheism—belief in only the One True God—sharply contrasted with the polytheistic practices that were common at the time. Yahweh's prophets influenced the ethical and spiritual direction of the Israelite community, promoting a vision of justice, mercy, and faithfulness. The moral authority they held is exemplified in Micah 6:8, which sums up the prophetic call to action: "He has shown you, O mortal, what is good. And what does the LORD require of you? To act justly and to love mercy and to walk humbly with your God."

In contrast, the prophets of Baal and Asherah often enjoyed royal backing, making their roles politically significant. This support ensured that polytheistic worship remained prevalent despite the efforts of Yahweh's prophets to promote monotheism. Their influence was not just religious but also cultural and political, intertwining the fate of their worship with the nation's leadership.

The prophets of Yahweh, Baal, and Asherah were not merely religious figures but critical players in ancient Israel's vibrant and often turbulent spiritual life. Yahweh's prophets, with their relentless focus on God's supremacy, ethical conduct, and social justice, stood in stark contrast to the prophets of Baal and Asherah, whose practices sought to secure fertility and prosperity through elaborate and often controversial rituals.

The fierce clashes between these prophetic factions underscore the intense religious and ideological struggles that shaped the history and faith of the Israelite people. These epic battles of belief, marked by dramatic showdowns and divine interventions, continue to captivate and challenge us today. They are a testament to the enduring power of faith and the relentless quest for spiritual integrity in a world fraught with competing ideologies. The legacy of the prophets lives on, inspiring us to navigate authentic journeys of faith with courage and conviction.

Fiction Author

BETH ADAMS

B eth Adams lives in Brooklyn, New York, with her husband and two daughters. When she's not writing, she's trying to find time to read good books.

Nonfiction Author

REVEREND JANE WILLAN, MS, MDiv

R everend Jane Willan writes contemporary women's fiction, mystery novels, church newsletters, and a weekly sermon.

Jane loves to set her novels amid church life. She believes that ecclesiology, liturgy, and church lady drama make for twisty plots and quirky characters. When not working at the church or creating new adventures for her characters, Jane relaxes at her favorite local bookstore, enjoying coffee and a variety of carbohydrates with frosting. Otherwise, you might catch her binge-watching a streaming series or hiking through the Connecticut woods with her husband and rescue dog, Ollie.

Jane earned a Bachelor of Arts degree from Hiram College, majoring in Religion and History, a Master of Science degree from Boston University, and a Master of Divinity from Vanderbilt University.

Read on for a sneak peek of another exciting story in the Mysteries & Wonders of the Bible series!

COVENANT OF THE HEART:
Odelia's Story

BY HEIDI CHIAVAROLI

The Ninth Year of King Zedekiah's Reign

Odelia gasped and sat up in bed, her breaths cinching tight in her chest. She clasped at the linen fabric of her night tunic, waiting for her heart to steady.

The dream. Again. Would the vision of the shattered clay jar and the words that accompanied them ever cease to haunt her?

She threw aside the quilt that twisted around her legs and pushed herself off the straw mattress. Air. She needed air.

Not bothering to slip on her sandals, she allowed her bare feet to slide along the smooth stone of their home. Her *abba's* snores echoed outside her parents' bedchamber. Not until she entered the cobbled courtyard with its palm tree and limestone bench and climbed the stairs to the roof did she allow herself a full, satisfying breath.

She tilted her face to the twinkling stars above. As always, she remembered the story of Adonai instructing Abram to look to the heavens and count the stars, of the Lord's promise that his off-spring would be as bountiful as the shimmering lights, that He would give them the land of Canaan.

This land. Odelia's homeland, now threatened by famine. Now threatened by King Nebuchadnezzar's army.

She inhaled a quivering breath. It was more comforting to meditate on the ancient promise rather than the promise in her dream that accompanied the shattered jar. Even now, the prophet Jeremiah's words sliced through the clear night and pierced her mind. Though she hadn't been older than four, Odelia would never forget them.

"I am going to bring on this city and all the villages around it every disaster I pronounced against them, because they were stiff-necked and would not listen to my words."

She shivered. What was wrong with her that she could not forget the words as easily as her abba? As her aunts and uncles and friends? Was it the sight that followed the words? The fact that her abba, Pashhur, the priest in charge of the temple, had ordered Jeremiah whipped and put in the stocks for his emboldened claim? Or perhaps it was the name the prophet bequeathed to her abba: *Terror on Every Side.*

Would the Lord enact His justice on Odelia simply for who her abba was? Would Adonai break her and her people beyond repair, as Jeremiah had broken that clay jar?

She rubbed her bare arms against the chill of the night air. Abba had cast off Jeremiah's words as ludicrous treason. But now, sixteen years since Jeremiah smashed the jar before the leaders and priests in the valley of Ben Hinnom, it appeared his words would finally come to pass.

The pungent, familiar scent of incense met her nostrils, and Odelia looked behind her to the rooftop adjacent to their *bet*. In the moonlight, a shadowy female figure in filmy garments and copper bangles on her ankles danced seductively around a small altar, waving the incense toward her as she moved. Odelia's face burned.

Avigail.

Perhaps Odelia could slip back into the walled courtyard below without her cousin's notice. She ducked down and with poise akin to that of a water buffalo, attempted to shimmy across the stone roof.

"Odelia!" A loud whisper came from the direction of the incense.

Odelia squeezed her eyes shut. She supposed it neither neighborly nor familial to ignore her cousin.

"Shalom, Avigail." She stifled a yawn, hoping her kinswoman would allow her to pass without conversation. But her cousin had never been one to be dissuaded, pressing Odelia into adventures outside the area of her comfort since they were small children. She gestured Odelia over. Sighing, Odelia made the short jump to the adjacent rooftop.

Avigail greeted her with a kiss on the cheek. "Shalom, cousin. It has been too long. How do we live so close and yet never see each other?"

Even in the dim light of the moon, Avigail's face glowed. Without the covering of a veil, her beautiful brown curls cascaded over her shoulders, framing high cheekbones and wide kohl-lined eyes. If Odelia were half as pretty as her younger cousin, she would be married by now, starting her own family.

"*Imma* has suffered aches in her head of late. I have stayed close to help her." Though what Imma truly needed—water—was something all lacked the past few months. A drought had wilted the plants and leeched the soil of moisture. Their city was blocked by Nebuchadnezzar's army from receiving imports. People wailed at King Zedekiah's gates, begging him to do something. Others turned to their gods.

"Has she burned incense to the queen of heaven for healing? I am sure she will answer her. Join me now, Odelia, on behalf of your imma."

Odelia's gaze fell on the smoking incense, the rich scent of myrrh strong in the air. Beside it lay a small cake marked with the queen's image, and beside that, something wet. Odelia's stomach churned. She prayed to Adonai that her cousin did not waste precious water on the queen of heaven. "I am tired. I think I will return to bed."

Avigail squeezed Odelia's hands. "Come now, Odelia. You are far too serious for your own good. I am beseeching her for love and fertility, both of which I will soon find. You would do well to join me. You are not getting any younger, you know."

Odelia wrinkled her nose. "Thank you for that reminder, sweet cousin." And what good were love and fertility if they were to be taken away by the Babylonians?

Avigail smiled. "I do not mean harm. Remember our adventures as children? How we followed the tunnels until our lamps threatened to burn out? You used to be so exciting, Odelia. What happened to that girl I once knew?"

What happened? Their land had been pillaged by the Babylonians, many of Odelia's friends taken captive in her tenth year. And now, the Babylonians returned, building siege ramps outside Jerusalem's walls. It would happen all over again. Perhaps even worse this time.

"I am going to bring on this city and all the villages around it every disaster I pronounced against them."

Odelia blinked and the image of Jeremiah's broken jar was replaced by Avigail's cake offering to the queen of heaven.

Avigail ignored Odelia's silence, wrapping fingers with hennaed nails around Odelia's wrist and pulling her closer to the small altar. "I had a prophecy from the Lord at the Asherah pole today."

"A prophecy from the Lord at an Asherah pole? Avigail—"

Odelia's cousin shook her head. "The Lord will bless me, I am certain of it."

Odelia sighed. She could hardly keep up with Avigail's many gods. That she threw in the One True God with all the others made Odelia's head spin. And yet, it was not uncommon to worship all the gods. On any given night, Odelia could look out upon the rooftops of Jerusalem and see the people burning incense to Baal or the queen of heaven. Her own imma, wife to a temple priest, had been known to participate in such activities.

Avigail tugged Odelia toward the burning incense. Something warm and wet dropped onto Odelia's hand. She turned Avigail's forearm over. "Cousin, what—" But the dark crimson stripes of blood on Avigail's flawless skin stopped her words. That wasn't a liquid offering of wine or water on Avigail's stone rooftop, but one of…blood.

Avigail avoided Odelia's gaze. "Sometimes the gods fall asleep. We must spill blood to wake them."

Odelia shook her head, the sight of her cousin's slashed and bloodied arm spinning in her mind alongside that of Jeremiah's shattered jar. Fury welled inside her. "Avigail, listen to yourself. What kind of god needs you—a mere mortal—to wake them up? What kind of power can they hold if they are so apt to fall asleep?"

Avigail snatched her arm from Odelia. "Do not judge me, cousin. All the gods—even Adonai—require sacrifice, do they not? The greater the sacrifice, the greater the reward."

She was right, of course. Gooseflesh broke out on Odelia's skin. Her next words came forth carefully and measured. "Please tell me you have never been involved in the sacrifices of children at Topheth." Sacrifices in the very valley where Jeremiah had thrown his clay jar before her abba and the other priests and elders.

Avigail crossed her arms in front of her chest. "Fine. I will not tell you."

A muted groan of agony passed Odelia's lips. "Avigail, it is abominable. Jeremiah warned—"

"Who is to say Jeremiah is a true prophet?"

"Even if he were not… The killing of innocent youth, cousin?" She had heard stories of children being made to gather the very wood from which their abbas built sacrificial fires to offer their offspring.

"I did not invite you onto my rooftop to judge my beliefs. You have always thought yourself better than me, have you not, Odelia? But now, let us see who is to marry first and bear sons."

"What will any of it matter if our sons are dead at Nebuchadnezzar's hand?"

"We have the temple with us. We are protected."

Odelia bit her lip. According to Jeremiah, Adonai grew impatient with His people—people who put their faith in His temple instead of Yahweh Himself.

Tentatively, she reached out a hand to her cousin. "I care for you, Avigail. That is why I show concern. Not because I think myself better than you. I know I am not." Had not Odelia's own abba been responsible for the whipping and discipline of a man of God? How many times had Odelia seen the pagan worship of those around her and kept quiet, even wondered if it would prove effective? How many times, in her silence, had it been as if she participated in the rituals herself?

If only she wasn't so weak.

Avigail took a step away from Odelia. "You need not worry over me. Worry over yourself and how any man will want you if you keep up your prudish ways."

The words stung. But Odelia forced a small smile. "If the Lord does not intend for me to marry, I will accept that fate." She did not know of any worthy man to marry anyway. "Good night, Avigail."

Her cousin did not answer, and Odelia returned to her rooftop, the heady scent of incense still lingering in the air.

Odelia passed through the market, its stalls filled with useless wares. For who needed a wooden spoon without food to stir or a hyssop broom without crumbs to sweep?

She entered the Great Court of the Lord's house, passing the temple guards, seeking out the chest in which to drop her meager offering. The weaver had paid her for the work of three wicker baskets the day before and since she'd finished her monthly course two days ago and purified herself in the *mikveh*, she'd been eager to make a trip to the temple.

She deposited her coins and sought a space off to the left where she could just glimpse the entrance to the Court of the Israelites and the stairs leading up to the Bronze Altar, the place where the high priest made sacrifices for the people. She tightened her prayer shawl about her shoulders, glancing beyond the Bronze Altar to the huge pillars on either side of the Holy Place. As a woman—even as the daughter of a temple priest—she would never get closer to the Holy of Holies than this. Never get closer to the *Shekinah*, the divine radiance of *El Shaddai's* spirit. Her abba told of the Holy Place decorated with beautiful etchings of flowers, trees, and fruits—priceless symbols of Eden. Of the thick blue curtain, embroidered in gold thread with cherubim representing the heavens and the Holy of Holies beyond. What would it be like to be in the presence of God?

She knelt, bowing her head to the smooth mosaic tile. She breathed deeply, attempting to push aside her empty belly and muscle aches to center her thoughts on Adonai. But even then, instead of prayer, Odelia's encounter with Avigail came to mind.

Her cousin believed she could enter the presence of the queen of heaven by burning incense, making cakes, and spilling blood. Would Odelia willingly spill her own blood if it meant being able to enter the Holy of Holies—or even the Holy Place, with its golden lampstand and table of showbread... Anything that would put her just a bit closer to knowing Yahweh's presence?

She blinked, chastising herself. What was wrong with her that she became obsessed with such thoughts? Had not Adonai heard the cries of Hannah when she prayed in the temple at Shiloh? And yet a priest had interceded for her. A priest. One like her abba? If so, she would take her chances that Adonai's ears could discern her pleas through the sturdy walls of the Holy Place and past the thick curtain of the Holy of Holies.

And what would she ask of Him?

For a husband? Perhaps. More so, she'd ask for a friend. Someone who understood the struggles of her heart, someone who would not judge her for the weakness of her faith, someone who could see how badly she *wanted* to place her trust in Adonai but how she often struggled to do so.

Or better yet, she could pray for a strong faith—a faith as sturdy and bold as Jeremiah's.

Adonai, God of my salvation, even my prayers are aimless. Lead me.

After a long while, she lifted her head, meeting friendly gray eyes. A smile softened her lips, and her heart shifted into place.

Shaphan.

The older priest who served as a secretary in the temple was like a *saba* to her. When Odelia's abba would take her to the Lord's house as a girl, Shaphan would slip her honey cakes and raisin pastries. He engaged her with stories of Abraham and Moses and Joshua while her abba attended his duties inside the temple.

Shaphan had been old then. Now he appeared ancient with his thick gray beard, his violet robe seeming to dwarf his shrunken frame. Best known for bringing the recovered scroll of the law to Josiah, he had become a legend in her mind until she became comforted not by his notoriety but by his simple yet gracious spirit.

He shuffled closer, placed a hand on her head, and spoke a blessing over her. When he removed his hand, he lowered his voice. "Child, may we speak?"

She rose, her knees sore from kneeling on the polished marble. "Of course."

With his cane tapping gently on the marble floors of the Great Court, he led her past the music gate and the chamber of lepers to a room just off the upper courtyard, near the New Gate entrance. He opened the ornate oak door and entered.

Odelia hesitated, looking around, half expecting her abba to jump out from behind a column and demand to know what she was doing.

"Do not fear, child. This is the temple room of my son, Gemariah. Come."

She swallowed and slipped into a room with tall marble pillars, several clay lamps, a couch with fine cushions, and a wooden bench. She stopped short at the sight of the high priest in his elegant priestly garb. His ephod surpassed even the king's in beauty—gorgeously crafted colors of blue, scarlet, purple, and gold. The *miter* he wore upon his head, with the gold plate inscribed with the words *Holiness unto the Lord*, caused her throat to dry.

Three other priests, one captain of the guard with a leather breastplate and captain's robe, and a young man with probing eyes, his simple vestments and turban indicating him to be a priest in training, completed the circle. Odelia's skin prickled and she shifted where she stood, drawing her prayer shawl more tightly around her shoulders.

She glanced at Shaphan. What was the meaning of such an invitation? Were they not fearful she would defile them in this space?

Shaphan shut the door before turning to his guests. "You may sit."

The men did so, and Odelia looked around for a water basin to wash their feet. Nothing.

"Odelia, please sit." Shaphan gestured to a striped red-and-blue cushion.

She did not obey.

"Do not fear, child."

The repeated words did little to calm her. She lowered herself to the cushion. Shaphan remained standing. "We have invited you here, Odelia, to ask for your help."

Odelia swallowed. What need could they have of her—a small maiden who should have been married long ago?

Shaphan lowered himself to the wooden bench with rigid movements. "The Babylonians will attack soon, there is no mistaking that. We need to transport an item of value beneath the city before they break our walls. Several items, in fact."

So Shaphan did not write off the danger of the Babylonians as her abba and Avigail did.

And yet, what did any of this have to do with her?

"I understand you are familiar with the tunnels and waterways beneath the city." Shaphan raised a bushy gray brow in her direction, his words a statement rather than a question. Odelia's face heated and sweat gathered beneath her tunic, the need for air consuming her constricted lungs.

How could he know such information? Odelia, Avigail, and Joash—Avigail's brother—had never told anyone about their adventures. "My lord?"

"Would you be willing to help us on this most important task?"

They did not chastise her. They wanted her *help*.

She dared a glance at the young man close to her own age. He was strangely familiar, and though a warmth filled her belly at his intense stare, she couldn't place him. One corner of his mouth lifted almost imperceptibly, as if to encourage her.

She wet her lips. "My lord, I am your servant, of course, but I am not sure my abba—"

"Your abba must not know of what we discuss." This from the high priest, a tremble in his voice. "We need your word that what we speak of in this room will not leave it."

Odelia's gaze flew to Shaphan. She'd trust him with her life, but this secrecy? What had driven him to such desperate measures? What was he so anxious to save from the Babylonian army?

More importantly, how could she, an insignificant maiden whose abba would be furious should he learn of her involvement, be the one to lead such a holy group out of Jerusalem?

A NOTE FROM THE EDITORS

We hope you enjoyed another exciting volume in the Mysteries & Wonders of the Bible series, published by Guideposts. For over seventy-five years, Guideposts, a nonprofit organization, has been driven by a vision of a world filled with hope. We aspire to be the voice of a trusted friend, a friend who makes you feel more hopeful and connected.

By making a purchase from Guideposts, you join our community in touching millions of lives, inspiring them to believe that all things are possible through faith, hope, and prayer. Your continued support allows us to provide uplifting resources to those in need. Whether through our communities, websites, apps, or publications, we inspire our audiences, bring them together, and comfort, uplift, entertain, and guide them. Visit us at guideposts.org to learn more.

We would love to hear from you. Write us at Guideposts, P.O. Box 5815, Harlan, Iowa 51593 or call us at (800) 932-2145. Did you love *A Flame of Hope: Abital's Story*? Leave a review for this product on guideposts.org/shop. Your feedback helps others in our community find relevant products.

Find inspiration, find faith, find Guideposts.
Shop our best sellers and favorites at
guideposts.org/shop
Or scan the QR code to go directly to our Shop

If you enjoyed Mysteries & Wonders of the Bible, check out
our other Guideposts biblical fiction series!
Visit https://www.shopguideposts.org/fiction-books/
biblical-fiction.html for more information.

EXTRAORDINARY
WOMEN OF THE BIBLE

There are many women in Scripture who do extraordinary things.
Women whose lives and actions were pivotal in shaping their world
as well as the world we know today. In each volume of Guideposts'
Extraordinary Women of the Bible series, you'll meet these well-
known women and learn their deepest thoughts, fears, joys, and
secrets. Read their stories and discover the unexplored truths in
their journeys of faith as they follow the paths God laid out for them.

Highly Favored: Mary's Story
Sins as Scarlet: Rahab's Story
A Harvest of Grace: Ruth and Naomi's Story
At His Feet: Mary Magdalene's Story
Tender Mercies: Elizabeth's Story
Woman of Redemption: Bathsheba's Story
Jewel of Persia: Esther's Story
A Heart Restored: Michal's Story

Beauty's Surrender: Sarah's Story

The Woman Warrior: Deborah's Story

The God Who Sees: Hagar's Story

The First Daughter: Eve's Story

The Ones Jesus Loved: Mary and Martha's Story

The Beginning of Wisdom: Bilqis's Story

The Shadow's Song: Mahlah and No'ah's Story

Days of Awe: Euodia and Syntyche's Story

Beloved Bride: Rachel's Story

A Promise Fulfilled: Hannah's Story

ORDINARY WOMEN OF THE BIBLE

From generation to generation and every walk of life, God seeks out women to do His will. Scripture offers us but fleeting, tantalizing glimpses into the lives of a number of everyday women in Bible times—many of whom are not even named in its pages. In each volume of Guideposts' Ordinary Women of the Bible series, you'll meet one of these unsung, ordinary women face-to-face, and see how God used her to change the course of history.

A Mother's Sacrifice: Jochebed's Story
The Healer's Touch: Tikva's Story
The Ark Builder's Wife: Zarah's Story
An Unlikely Witness: Joanna's Story
The Last Drop of Oil: Adaliah's Story
A Perilous Journey: Phoebe's Story
Pursued by a King: Abigail's Story
An Eternal Love: Tabitha's Story
Rich Beyond Measure: Zlata's Story
The Life Giver: Shiphrah's Story
No Stone Cast: Eliyanah's Story
Her Source of Strength: Raya's Story
Missionary of Hope: Priscilla's Story

Befitting Royalty: Lydia's Story
The Prophet's Songbird: Atarah's Story
Daughter of Light: Charilene's Story
The Reluctant Rival: Leah's Story
The Elder Sister: Miriam's Story
Where He Leads Me: Zipporah's Story
The Dream Weaver's Bride: Asenath's Story
Alone at the Well: Photine's Story
Raised for a Purpose: Talia's Story
Mother of Kings: Zemirah's Story
The Dearly Beloved: Apphia's Story

Interested in other series by Guideposts?
Check out one of our mystery series!
Visit https://www.shopguideposts.org/fiction-books/
mystery-fiction.html for more information.

SECRETS FROM GRANDMA'S ATTIC

Life is recorded not only in decades or years, but in events and memories that form the fabric of our being. Follow Tracy Doyle, Amy Allen, and Robin Davisson, the granddaughters of the recently deceased centenarian, Pearl Allen, as they explore the treasures found in the attic of Grandma Pearl's Victorian home, nestled near the banks of the Mississippi in Canton, Missouri. Not only do Pearl's descendants uncover a long-buried mystery at every attic exploration, they also discover their grandmother's legacy of deep, abiding faith, which has shaped and guided their family through the years. These uncovered Secrets from Grandma's Attic reveal stories of faith, redemption, and second chances that capture your heart long after you turn the last page.

History Lost and Found
The Art of Deception
Testament to a Patriot
Buttoned Up

Pearl of Great Price
Hidden Riches
Movers and Shakers
The Eye of the Cat
Refined by Fire
The Prince and the Popper
Something Shady
Duel Threat
A Royal Tea
The Heart of a Hero
Fractured Beauty
A Shadowy Past
In Its Time
Nothing Gold Can Stay
The Cameo Clue
Veiled Intentions
Turn Back the Dial
A Marathon of Kindness
A Thief in the Night
Coming Home

SAVANNAH SECRETS

Welcome to Savannah, Georgia, a picture-perfect Southern city known for its manicured parks, moss-covered oaks, and antebellum architecture. Walk down one of the cobblestone streets, and you'll come upon Magnolia Investigations. It is here where two friends have joined forces to unravel some of Savannah's deepest secrets. Tag along as clues are exposed, red herrings discarded, and thrilling surprises revealed. Find inspiration in the special bond between Meredith Bellefontaine and Julia Foley. Cheer the friends on as they listen to their hearts and rely on their faith to solve each new case that comes their way.

The Hidden Gate
A Fallen Petal
Double Trouble
Whispering Bells
Where Time Stood Still
The Weight of Years
Willful Transgressions
Season's Meetings
Southern Fried Secrets
The Greatest of These

Patterns of Deception
The Waving Girl
Beneath a Dragon Moon
Garden Variety Crimes
Meant for Good
A Bone to Pick
Honeybees & Legacies
True Grits
Sapphire Secret
Jingle Bell Heist
Buried Secrets
A Puzzle of Pearls
Facing the Facts
Resurrecting Trouble
Forever and a Day

MYSTERIES OF MARTHA'S VINEYARD

Priscilla Latham Grant has inherited a lighthouse! So with not much more than a strong will and a sore heart, the recent widow says goodbye to her lifelong Kansas home and heads to the quaint and historic island of Martha's Vineyard, Massachusetts. There, she comes face-to-face with adventures, which include her trusty canine friend, Jake, three delightful cousins she didn't know she had, and Gerald O'Bannon, a handsome Coast Guard captain—plus head-scratching mysteries that crop up with surprising regularity.

A Light in the Darkness
Like a Fish Out of Water
Adrift
Maiden of the Mist
Making Waves
Don't Rock the Boat
A Port in the Storm
Thicker Than Water
Swept Away
Bridge Over Troubled Waters
Smoke on the Water

Shifting Sands

Shark Bait

Seascape in Shadows

Storm Tide

Water Flows Uphill

Catch of the Day

Beyond the Sea

Wider Than an Ocean

Sheeps Passing in the Night

Sail Away Home

Waves of Doubt

Lifeline

Flotsam & Jetsam

Just Over the Horizon

Find more inspiring stories in these best-loved Guideposts fiction series!

Mysteries of Lancaster County

Follow the Classen sisters as they unravel clues and uncover hidden secrets in Mysteries of Lancaster County. As you get to know these women and their friends, you'll see how God brings each of them together for a fresh start in life.

Secrets of Wayfarers Inn

Retired schoolteachers find themselves owners of an old warehouse-turned-inn that is filled with hidden passages, buried secrets, and stunning surprises that will set them on a course to puzzling mysteries from the Underground Railroad.

Tearoom Mysteries Series

Mix one stately Victorian home, a charming lakeside town in Maine, and two adventurous cousins with a passion for tea and hospitality. Add a large scoop of intriguing mystery, and sprinkle generously with faith, family, and friends, and you have the recipe for *Tearoom Mysteries*.

Ordinary Women of the Bible

Richly imagined stories—based on facts from the Bible—have all the plot twists and suspense of a great mystery, while bringing you fascinating insights on what it was like to be a woman living in the ancient world.

To learn more about these books, visit Guideposts.org/Shop

Printed in the United States
by Baker & Taylor Publisher Services